THE BODINE AGENCY

THE BODINE AGENCY

Richard M Beloin MD

Rev. date: 09/11/2020

To order additional copies of this book, contact:
Xlibris
844-714-8691
www.Xlibris.com
Orders@Xlibris.com
818945

Contents

Dedication

This book is dedicated to the volunteer tourist guides of The Old Hundred Gold Mine in Silverton Colorado. As knowledge is passed down thru generations, they certainly made the tourists, and me, understand what it was like working deep in mines before electricity. Their stories were a direct inspiration for this book.

CHAPTER 1

Leaving Texas

Palmer was left at the Amarillo City Orphanage at two years of age by unknown parents. The only note said, "this is Palmer whose birthday is February 18, 1860. I cannot feed or care for him with his mother gone off with another man, so I am leaving him forever in your capable hands. Please be kind to him, he's a good boy and deserves more than I can give him."

Ever since the age of recollection, somewhere around age four, Palmer only recalled living at the orphanage. Since the age of six, he worked every day, some four morning hours, in the garden that fed the children with basic vegetables; and received formal schooling four afternoon hours a day. At Christmas time when he was 12 years old, a man with white hair and a shiny badge on his shirt came to see him.

1

Meeting with the headmaster, Palmer was offered a private home with the childless lawman, Sheriff Bodine and his wife. Palmer was at a loss to provide an opinion when the headmaster said, "I know this is new to you, but very few 12-year-old boys ever have this opportunity, so, I want you to try it for one month. If you don't like it, you can come back till you're 18 years old like the other boys. Starting at age 14 you will be entering the trade's program to prepare you for the outside world."

***

Life in town was very different and he quickly fell in love with his new adopted parents. Palmer ended up with all new clothes, didn't have to pull weeds in the garden, went to school five days a week, could walk the streets of Amarillo, made friends easily and got to learn how to shoot a 22 pistol/rifle and a 410 shotgun. By the age of 15 he graduated from the 10th grade, and his graduation gift was a Smith and Wesson Model 3 pistol in 44-40 and a double barrel 12-gauge coach shotgun. Shortly thereafter, he started doing walk-around rounds with his dad.

By age 18 he became very proficient with these two firearms. He learned to fast draw and point and shoot with one hand. The coach shotgun, also called coach-gun, was slow in reloading but deadly once fired with OO Buckshot at +-30 yards, and totally devastating with #3 Buck at +-5 yards. A shell of OO Buckshot had nine .33-inch pellets and the #3 Buck had twenty .25-inch pellets.

The drawback to the coach shotgun was the slow time to eject two spent shells and reload with two fresh ones, close the action, manually cock the hammers back, and fire the two separate triggers. Palmer went to see a local gunsmith who had a lathe and could build parts. He had designed a way to convert a double trigger to a single trigger and to avoid the manual cocking by making the cocking automatic upon opening the double barrels. Palmer got his hands on this speed shotgun but had to work two months, four hours a day, to pay for it and all the ammo he needed to practice.

He practiced shooting this shotgun for days on end. He would fire two rounds, drop the double barrel open, shuck the two spent shells by jerking the shotgun backwards while holding it with his right hand as his left hand slipped two new shells from the double shell holder on his belt. Closing the double barrels would make the shotgun ready to fire, and pulling the single trigger twice would sound like an automatic Gatling gun. After long months of practice, he could make four or six shotgun shots sound like a revolver without the audible reloading dead time.

After two years of working for a gunsmith and as a deputy sheriff for his dad, Palmer was ready for something new. On his 20th birthday his dad asked him, "well son, you work equal time as a deputy sheriff and as a gunsmith apprentice. Is this what you want to do with your life?"

"Yes and no. I know that my life will be spent using the gun and my head to help people. It won't be as a lawman but as a private individual. Right now I'm too young to open a security business. So, since we live in a cattle ranching part of Texas, I'd like to work on a ranch for a while." His dad added, "that's fine experience, but under the condition that when I need help to make a difficult arrest or handle a tough situation, that you'll help me out."

For the next three years Palmer worked with the other cow punchers to take care of the herd. He learned to ride, rope and work the spring roundup. Nights he would spend in the bunkhouse and help out with the care of the horses. Weekends, when most of the cowboys spent their spare time in the town saloons, Palmer would move back to his home and spend Saturdays working as a part-time lawman for his dad.

Amarillo was getting to be a rowdy town with the railroad yards becoming a cattle buying and shipping area. Palmer was getting a reputation as a speed shotgun shooter with the modified shotgun he carried. Unfortunately some arrests turned into a gunfight and Palmer was known to put down gunfighters who were trying to kill him. It was at this time that he learned from his dad, "once a man goes for his gun, it's time to kill or be killed."

At age 23, Palmer knew it was time to find his destiny. Cattle ranching was not for him, he didn't want to work in a gun shop, and was not keen on becoming a fulltime lawman. He then had a long discussion with his parents and decided it was time to head out on his own. Since he was sick of the cold winters and looked forward to exploring new lands, he decided to head to southeast New Mexico looking for the warm desert weather and a new life amongst the mining towns north of the Mexican border. His goal was Las Cruces some 425 miles cross-country, where he could then take the train west to Deming which had rail spurs north to Silver City and Lake Valley as well as stagecoach service to many other communities.

Gearing up for the long journey, Palmer went to the local mercantile and bought a map of west Texas and south/central New Mexico. Then he bought two extra-large saddle bags and filled them with vittles, an extra pistol, cooking grate, coffee pot, one frying pan, two tin cups, spoon/fork, and 2 tin plates. Other items included: field glasses, compass, hand ax, bedroll, rain slicker, canvas tarp, winter coat, extra pants, socks and shirts, one scabbard for his shotgun and spare ammo for both his pistol and shotgun. With all this gear, he went light on vittles since he would stop every two days, and restock on food while riding thru towns on his way.

It was a sad day when he left home. His last words to his parents were to remind them there would soon be complete rail service to Albuquerque and points south to Las Cruces. The Bodine's had a different idea, once retired, there was nothing keeping them in north Texas with its cold winters—they too could look for warmer weather.

***

Palmer's horse was a 17 hand 4-year-old chestnut gelding by the name of 'Nutcase.' The horse got that moniker when he refused to let anyone ride him except for Palmer. Over the years, he seemed to understand Palmer's voice and could respond to his verbal commands. The best feature was that Nutcase would come running at the sound of Palmer's unique whistle.

When Palmer got on the trail, he was carrying almost five years of income from ranching, gun shop work, deputy sheriff wages, and receiving several reward monies from arresting outlaws, wanted dead or alive, with a bounty on their heads. He placed $1,000 in his money belt, $500 in a backup pair of socks, and $500 in a homemade ankle wallet. That way, if he was waylaid or robbed, the odds would be that he wouldn't be broke.

Getting on the trail felt surreal since he had not done much trail riding looking for outlaws. He had 40 miles to travel the first day. That would put him in Hereford Texas where he could get a hot meal and a real hotel bed. Being their maiden day on the trail, with Nutcase loaded down, Palmer rested his horse every 15 miles or when water was found. After two stops, they were approaching Hereford when the cross-country trail turned into a well beaten path. Suddenly, Palmer saw a dust trail two miles ahead. He stopped and kept watching till he finally saw three riders at a fast trot. When he saw the top quality of all three horses with fancy saddles, he suspected he would be meeting some highwaymen since outlaws always had the best of horses, saddles, and firearms.

Sitting in the saddle, he waited to greet the on-comers with his shotgun laying on his saddle horn. "Good day, where are you boys going at that fast pace?" "We're on our way to Amarillo on business." "And where are you going?" "I'm going to Deming New Mexico." "Wow, that's near 400 miles. I see your large saddlebags are over loaded, what are you carrying in there? Gold dust, maybe?" "Naw, just vittles and cooking gear, nothing of value." "Well, maybe we want to check out those bags ourselves, heh boys!"

Palmer knew things were about to degenerate. "Now, that's enough. My belongings are none of your business. This is your only warning, ride by and keep going."

"Mighty big talk for one holding a double barrel with the external hammers not yet cocked."

"This is a specifically modified shotgun; the external hammers are only left on for show. If you go for your guns, I'll have to put you down since my shotgun is already cocked."

"Yeah right"—laughter and guffaws. "Let's find out boys"—as all three went for their Colts.

Palmer let two quick shots off as the outlaws were pointing their pistols at him. The two outlaws were hit in mid chest and were both blown backwards in a summersault over their horses' rump. The third man's horse reared up in response to the shotgun blasts. As the horse's front hooves hit the ground, the last outlaw never realized that his face had turned into a bloody stump.

Palmer could not believe how stupid these outlaws could be. All they had to do when facing a shotgun was to ride thru, but no, they had to rob an innocent rider. Looking at the bloody mess, Palmer decided that it was too late in the day to ride into Hereford where dusk would find most businesses closed. So, he decided to load the three bodies onto their horses and ride to the nearest water supply and make camp.

Making camp was a big ordeal. He had to unload the three bodies, unsaddle all four horses, bring the horses to water, start a fire and set up camp. While the coffee was boiling, he went thru the outlaws' pockets and found $89 in cash which he pocketed. In the saddlebags he found $5,000 which he figured belonged to a bank in Hereford or Clovis New Mexico. He also found several boxes of 44-40 which he confiscated. The three Colt Peacemakers were new and well cleaned. There were also three Win 1873 rifles in 44-40 with their own scabbards.

After preparing a meal of bacon, biscuits, cheese and beans, he retired with his winter jacket inside his bedroll to ward off the cold. The next morning, after a breakfast of oatmeal, biscuits and coffee, he saddled the horses, loaded the dead bodies again, and closed up camp. He then arrived in Hereford at noon and went straight to the sheriff's office. After informing Sheriff Howard Duff of the highwaymen's activities the sheriff went outside to check on the dead men.

"Young man, these are the outlaws that robbed our Community Bank yesterday. They're a small gang lead by Shorty Burkoff and all three have a $500 bounty reward, dead or alive. Also the bank is offering a reward of $500 for the return of some $5,000."

"Well, here is that $5,000. How long will it take to get the bounty reward money? "The poster reward money has already been paid to the telegraph office and the bank reward is readily available. I can have all three bounties by tonight thru telegraph vouchers."

That night, he stabled his horse at the local livery, took a room at a small hotel, had a bath and shave, and a hot meal at a local diner. The next morning he went to the livery. A man by the name of Buster Hawkins greeted him. Palmer asked, "what would you give me for the three horses with the fancy saddles that I left here yesterday?"

"I know they are worth more, but I can't offer you more than $60 per horse and $30 per saddle/saddlebags/scabbards."

"I'll take $270, but minus one scabbard which I'm keeping. Now what do you have for a packhorse/packsaddle?"

"The only one I have is the gelding called 'chicken-shit.'"

"Why is he called that?"

"Because, he's scared of being alone and left behind. So, he'll follow your horse within five steps, and you won't need to hold a lead rope to keep him following."

"That is hard to believe, can I take him out with my horse to see if he'll follow my very finicky horse?"

"Sure, take him out, if you want him, I'll let him go for $70 and include the pack saddle and two paniers."

"That's a fair deal. Let's see if Nutcase will tolerate him."

Out on a ride, Palmer could not believe his eyes. Whether at a walk, trot, or full gallop, Chicken-shit was on Nutcase's heels. To make it more believable, the two horses would neigh and nicker at each other in some type of communication. Returning at the livery, Buster was smiling as he said, "by the smile on your face, it looks like you're buying, I guess I should have asked for more money, but a deal is a deal. So enjoy him and I know you'll laugh every time you try to leave him behind, heh?"

The next items to dispose of were the guns. He had two 73 rifles and three Colt Peacemakers to sell. The only place in town that sold guns was the mercantile. The storeowner was very happy to get these fine guns and offered Palmer $25 each for the Colts and $35 each for the 73 rifles. Palmer had decided to keep one of the rifles for himself.

The next day, Sheriff Duff appeared with the three telegraph vouchers totaling $1,500. Palmer handed the sheriff a $100 bill to pay for his assistance in securing the vouchers. His next stop was the only bank in town, the Community

Bank. He opened an account to include $1,500 from the vouchers, $500 from the bank reward, and even added $1,000 of his earned wages. He then informed the bank president that he would eventually send for his money by bank transfer sometime in the future—when in New Mexico. Palmer also found out that branches of this bank were well established in the border towns of New Mexico.

After filling both paniers with vittles and all the other gear, including the newly acquired Win 73 rifle, Palmer was off to Clovis New Mexico, some 60 miles southwest. That first day, he covered 30 miles despite the three rest periods he took to let the horses graze. Palmer could not believe that Chicken-shit was usually within five yards of Nutcase, and Nutcase would even nicker at Chicken-shit when he happened to be out of reasonable range. Palmer even found himself talking to both horses saying, "now don't you two look silly playing the 'I'm OK, you're OK game.'"

That night, Palmer set up a full camp with a large fire to ward off the cold nights while still in west Texas. As he sat there eating his supper, he decided to heed his father's warning.

"The only private safe camp is a cold camp without a fire. When you decide to have a regular camp with a fire, you are inviting all sorts of nighttime visitors, of which most have nefarious activity in mind. So, take precautions, bring your horse close to camp where he can warn you, lay a cord six inches off the ground attached to some tin cans to trip any incoming visitor. Finally, put your winter coat on and sit 10 yards off the fire and sit behind a tree—and don't forget to put your spare pistol or the rifle hidden in the bushes. If you were to be overcome, you would still have the money on your ankle wallet and a firearm in the bushes. With your whistle, Nutcase would find his way back to you.

There were no visitors that night and, in the morning, after a full breakfast of coffee, ham and beans, and a full bait of oats for each of his horses, they were back on the trail. They expected to reach Clovis New Mexico by nightfall.

Arriving in Clovis, Palmer headed to the livery where he asked that his horses be watered, fed hay and a half bait of oats after a complete rub down. In the morning, he asked that the horses be reshod after traveling 100 miles on old shoes, and needing good shoes for the next 300+ miles. After a full night's sleep on a real bed, he headed to the nearest diner for breakfast. Sitting there with a pot of coffee, while waiting for his meal, a tall man with white hair sat down at his table, poured himself a cup of coffee and said, "are you Mister Bodine from Texas who returned $5,000 instead of high-tailing it out of Texas?" "Yes sir, that is me." "Why would you do that?" "Well sheriff, it's a matter of value of wealth. Would you rather legally collect $2,000 and leave a lot of good will, versus, illegally collecting $5,000 and be on the run for years to come?"

"Nice to meet you, I'm Sheriff Craven Harper." "The pleasure is mine, Palmer Bodine at your service."

"Ironically, at your service is why I'm sitting here. It appears that there is a gang of thugs wanted for kidnapping and murder who have commandeered one of our saloons with working girls and cribs. The town council expects me to gather these miscreants. Do I look like I can accomplish this task while avoiding a casket?"

"Probably not, but you could with some help"

"Yep, like a kid who put down the Burkoff gang with a shotgun"

"That could be arranged. Have some breakfast on me, and we'll make a plan as we eat." "Don't mind if I do!"

The plan was simple, wait till the entire gang was up and awake, preferably partially drunk and ripe for an intervention. The sheriff walked thru the batwing doors at 11PM and found all four animals sitting at a table playing poker. Sheriff Harper walked right up to the outlaws and said, "I don't know your names, but you're under arrest for murder." "Well sheriff, before you die, I'm Abe Wallace and these are my men, Boris Webb, Buford Freeman and Dusty Wagner. Now be a smart fella and go back to your office."

Sheriff Harper, drew his pistol and said, "not going to happen, now get up so my assistant can put manacles on you." "You and this boy, heck his shotgun is not even cocked. Before you can pull back your hammer, you'll be dead............Now, boys!"......................

Palmer's brain went into slow motion mode and he acted quickly as other participants could only act slowly. Palmer's shotgun went bang-bang--- bang-bang. Sheriff Harper was wiping his face of blood and brain gore while holstering his yet un-cocked hammer.

Sheriff Harper simply said, "jumping je-Josephat, how could you shoot that smooth bore, the hammers are still up and un-cocked." "It's a long story, let's just say for now that it's a feature that just saved our lives." "Yes, it certainly did, but don't forget that laying these four well known outlaws down with a shotgun will quickly get you a name of recognition such as 'the shotgun kid.'" "It is what it is!"

Two days later, Palmer sold four horses/saddles for $360. Four pistols for $100 and four rifles for $140, and collected $514 in petty cash. Sheriff arrived with telegraph vouchers for $2,000. Palmer went to the Community Bank of Clovis and started an account with a deposit of $3,000. Again, planning a bank transfer in the future.

Like other western towns, Clovis and Hereford were small towns less than 500 people. The towns were there to support farming and ranching enterprises and were not expected to expand until the railroad came to town or gold/silver was found. The communities had stagecoach service for travel, mail service, and freighting of goods was done by wagons in and out of town. The center of each town was the mercantile, which housed the post office, and the hardware/feed/seed store.

***

Palmer eventually stocked up with supplies to cover the next 110 miles to Roswell New Mexico. With talk of rain, Palmer added a large tent to hold him, his saddle and paniers. The tarp would be used to make a temporary roof for the horses. A small bag of oats was added for his horses.

The first day showed a change in terrain. The Texas plains were gone, and pine trees of central

New Mexico appeared. Palmer passed many small farming homesteads and ranches for the first 20 miles out of Clovis, but the remaining 60 miles were in the middle of nowhere. For two days and nights, Palmer saw no humans in a wild country. By the third day, now withing 20 miles of Roswell a traveling trail finally appeared, and homesteads and ranches again appeared by the roadside.

As nightfall was approaching, Palmer decided to make camp. Without even thinking, he built a fire and started cooking his supper of canned beef stew, boiled fresh potatoes/carrots, and the usual pot of coffee. After supper, he took out his leather bag containing the "fixings." Opening a paper, he added tobacco and hand rolled his own cigarette called a "quirly." Ever since he went to work as a cowhand, he started the habit which was common amongst the cowboys.

Sitting there in the night's quietude, Nutcase came running into camp with the frantic Chicken-shit at its side. "I heard them boys, it's Ok to go back to grazing. A few minutes later, Palmer heard the clop-clop of several hooves. With his shotgun at port-arms, he waited for the four riders to appear at the edge of the camp. Once in full view he thought—*Oh great, good looking horses, fancy saddles, pearl handle pistols, gunfighter holsters, fancy leather vests and new hats. I hate to imagine how this meeting is going to go?"*

"Hello the camp, can we light down and visit, your coffee smells good." "Sure, step down and stretch a bit, but stay where you are so I can see you. I don't want you in my camp."

"Why not, we're only travelers in the night just like you. We were hoping to share a cup of coffee and chat a bit."

"Bull-ticky, you saw my fire miles away. Most travelers would have made camp before coming to check out the campfire. Now if you were highwaymen who worked this road, you'd know that I was no highwayman and would be an easy target for a robbery, being in the middle of nowhere. So, GET ON YOUR HORSES AND GET THE HELL OUT OF HERE BEFORE I SHOOT THE LOT OF YOU—THIS IS YOUR ONLY WARNING."

"Them are big words for someone holding a double barrel shotgun with two shots against our four guns."

"True, but the first shot will take your head off, after that it don't matter does it."

The gang leader said, "Ok, you win, we're leaving."

"Good, in response," Palmer let his shotgun drop to his side.

As the four men turned, instead of putting their boot in the saddle's stirrup, they all drew their pistols. Palmer had anticipated the move. In slow motion, the shotgun went bang-bang---bang-bang. Waiting for the smoke to clear, Nutcase arrived with his appendage to see what the shooting was all about. Palmer said, "looks like we'll have dead company to trail to Roswell tomorrow."

That night, Palmer went thru the outlaws' pockets and saddlebags. He collected $81 in cash. In the saddlebags he collected $2,731 in paper currency and a beautiful gold watch with an alarm. Again, four premier Colt 45 pistols with action jobs and four new 1873 rifles.

The next day at noon, the strange caravan of Nutcase trailing two horses with a dead man flopped over the saddle and Chicken-shit also trailing two similar horses but on his own following Nutcase.

Stepping to the sheriff's office, the sheriff stepped outside and said, "well, who are you son and what have we got here?"

"My name is Palmer Bodine and these four men tried to rob and kill me, so they met the wrath of my shotgun. I'm sorry for the inconvenience but it was unavoidable self-defense."

"My name is Sheriff Harland Butler and I know who you are. Sheriff Harper sent me a heads-up that you were coming here and expressed his gratitude for your help. Now, these four birds match the description of many of their highway victims. I've already found their wanted posters and they all have a wanted bounty on their heads. The leader here has a $1,000 reward and the other three have $500 each. If you're willing to spend a few days, I'll get you some telegraph vouchers to cover these rewards."

"Sounds great. All I'll need is a livery, a hotel, a diner, a gun shop, a tonsorial shop, a bank, and a mercantile to restock my vittles."

"Heck, except for the saloons, that's 70% of the businesses in town. Well, make yourself at home, and I'll start the process at the telegraph office today."

For two days he took care of selling the horses. At the livery, the hostler saw some fine horseflesh and top of the line saddles. During the negotiations, the hostler said, "I'd be very happy to take all three saddles, but I think you ought to replace your old worn out saddle for this one fancy dark red saddle that matches your chestnut. Here, let's try it on your horse and step up." Palmer was skeptical but once his butt sat in the saddle, he realized the comfort he had missed. So, they finally settled for $360 to cover three fancy saddles, one plain saddle, four horses with saddlebags, tack, and scabbards.

His next stop was the gun shop. Walking in with four beautiful Colts and four nearly new Win 73's, the gunsmith was drooling over this windfall of modern firearms. Palmer happened to notice something in the gun display, and finally said, "Sir, what is that?"

"That was a special order. An old timer had problems with coyotes and wanted to carry a shotgun like a pistol. So I sent for a 12- gauge self cocking model, without external hammers (what are called mule ears), and a single trigger. I cut the barrels off at the tip of the fore-end grip and added a ¼ inch brass bead on the barrel's tip. I also took the shoulder stock off and added a pistol grip. I then built a holster for it that fit on his right sided belt. I call it a masterpiece, but then the old timer died of old age three months ago and it hasn't sold yet."

Palmer handled and inspected every detail and finally said, "would you sand down the hinge, so the barrels open with greater ease and how much do you want for it?" "I can sand them down, so the barrels almost fall open by gravity; just remember that the opening of the barrels cocks the mechanism and always keep the tang safety on with the shotgun in its holster. Now, tell me what you want for all eight guns and I'll tell you what I want for 'Shorty' here!"

"Fair enough, just remember that my eight guns won't be sitting in your display for three months like Shorty did. I normally get $25 for the pistols and $35 for the rifles, but these eight firearms have had an action job and the pearl handles are an expensive accessory. Normally $240—how about

$180, plus two boxes of OO Buckshot, 2 boxes of #3 Buck, 'Shorty' and the holster."

"Son, those eight firearms are worth a lot more than $180." "I know, but you need to make a profit, and I really want 'Shorty.'"

"Well, it's a deal, and I'll give you six boxes of each buckshot so you can get use to drawing and shooting 'Shorty.'"

With one more day to spend waiting for telegraph vouchers, Palmer wanted to pay some restitution for locals who had been robbed by the highwaymen. First, he went to the Community Bank of Roswell and opened an account. Then he went to two mercantiles, the hardware/feed store, the blacksmith, and Sheriff Butler. At all five places, he asked the same question— "do you know if the people who were robbed had been coming to town to pay their credit bills with their hard-earned money."

The answers were surprising. A total of 20 victims had been shorted of hard-earned funds. Palmer made a list of victims and planned to cover their credit balances which amounted to $979.

The next day, Sheriff Butler showed up with four telegraph vouchers totaling $2,500. Palmer gave the sheriff $100 for his assistance in securing the bounty vouchers. Afterwards, he deposited the $2,500 in the bank, along with $1,500 of other monies. Before leaving town, he paid off all of the victim's credit balances.

He then loaded up with vittles and embarked on the second half of his journey. Some +-200 miles to Las Cruces—broken down it was 75 miles to Ruidoso, 40 miles to Tularosa, 15 miles to Alamogordo, and 70 miles to Las Cruces.

Palmer thought, *"it certainly would be nice if I could finish my journey without any more confrontations or interruptions but, with such a violent land, that is probably wishful thinking."*

***

That first day on the trail/road to Ruidoso, while resting his horses, Palmer did some regular practicing with Shorty. First, he had to modify the right hand draw out of the holster because of the longer barrel. Then he had to learn to slip off the tang safety with his right thumb. The last new maneuver was to handle recoil which required that his left hand had to grab the fore-end stock. The reload was then the same as his standard coach-gun. It was after several stops that Palmer finally mastered the one hand draw and the two-hand point—ready to shoot.

That night, he made camp early because he wanted to continue practicing with Shorty. Tonight he would start actually shooting the monster handgun.

After ground hitching the horses, so they wouldn't spook with the shotgun blasts, Palmer fired Shorty for the first time. Not accustomed with the upward recoil of the cut off front barrels, Shorty ended up pointing 45 degrees upwards—too high to get a second shot on the target. That correction would take a long time to sink in. Knowing that practice makes perfect, he stayed with it to study the dynamics of recoil.

The next day, he continued his shooting exercise with Shorty during the horses' breaks. Arriving in Ruidoso in midafternoon, he heard some gunshots and, instead of stepping down and take cover, Palmer rode down the street at full trot with his coach-gun out of the scabbard. To his surprise, the sheriff and his deputy were both down on the boardwalk, obviously ambushed when they came out of the office. Palmer quickly noticed that both lawmen had been hit and were no match for the two riflemen on the roof across the street.

Palmer, automatically pulled his horse to a stop, jumped on the ground and aimed his coach-gun. He quickly estimated the 50-yard shot and decided to shoot both rounds directly between the two rifle shooters who were stupid enough to be elbow to elbow in proximity. The sheriff later recalled hearing two shots that almost sounded like one shot with an echo. Looking at the rooftops, he then saw the shooters' rifles fall out of their hands onto the ground below and then saw both men fall off the roofs with a loud thump as both hit the boardwalk.

"Sheriff, how bad are you hit?" "it's my shooting arm below the elbow, the bone is broke. Never mind me, my deputy was hit bad and needs help." Palmer took one look at the deputy and knew that the chap had left this life. After the sheriff was brought to the doc, Palmer walked towards the gathering at the Community Bank. The president was speaking, "folks, we've been robbed of all our funds—over $20,000. Unless the money is returned, we're going to have to close our doors and file for bankruptcy. This means that your deposits will be worth 10-25% of their value. I'm sorry. Someone needs to organize a posse and get after this gang—unfortunately we recognized them as the McCleod gang who ravaged many Colorado banks. They killed old man Brewster out of evilness. They are a dangerous bunch, so if you're joining the posse, be careful."

In the crowd, Palmer heard a man ask, "what's the bank offering in reward?" "$2,000." Before long, men were all sitting in the saddle ready to roll. Palmer noticed that each man had a rifle but no bedroll, canteen, saddlebags or any coat. A ragtag town's men that were ill prepared and probably not very proficient with those rifles. He sadly knew that several of those men would be coming back straddled over the saddle and secured with their wrists tied, under the horse, to their ankles.

After the nine-member posse rode by, Palmer thought, *"it's not that I need the money, but $2,000 is not a bad day's pay. If I could find their camp tonight, I'd arrest them, and could be back by late* *tomorrow. Besides, it's not just about money, what about the two lives lost, and how will this bank's loss affect all the state customers of the Community Bank organization? Let's go Nutcase."*

Palmer had been following the tracks for three hours when an all-out shootout was heard down the road—either a directed posse attack or an ambush. Palmer stepped down and waited by the road in case a runaway outlaw came his way. The shooting abruptly came to an end. Either the outlaws were dead or had all surrendered, or the other side had been slaughtered or retreated to safety. Palmer waited when the remnants of the posse finally appeared. Four men were belly down on their horses. Three were wounded but able to ride, the posse spokesman was barely holding his head up. When asked what happened, he said, "we were right on their tail when we took a sharp bend at full trot only to find the seven outlaws leaning behind boulders and shooting rifles at us. We shot it out and managed to kill one of them, but we had no defense in the open road, and after losing four good boys, we had to pull back and save our hides.

The money is gone, and those killers got away with it and with murder."

Palmer waited for the posse to move along and then decided to continue on the trail. A dead outlaw was left by the roadside. Palmer stepped down, picked up his pistol, gun-belt, and rifle. Checking his pockets, he found $87 in cash. He then proceeded down the road following the tracks of six men on horseback and a rider-less horse. It was getting dark and Palmer was thinking of finding water to set up camp when suddenly Chicken-shit stopped, turn sideways and was smelling something that neither Nutcase nor I could appreciate. Palmer could see that this was worth investigating.

Turning to the right, 90 degrees, Palmer walked the horses slowly for 10 minutes till he smelled camp smoke. Palmer stepped down with his coach shotgun (now calling it Longy), his canteen, Shorty and two sticks of dynamite he had purchased in Roswell. He secured both horses to trees to guarantee they couldn't walk in the outlaw camp— out of curiosity.

Crawling on hand and knees with his Longy in one hand, he made it to within 50 yards of camp.

He hid under a large pine branch and watched the camp. The men were pouring the whiskey straight out of the bottle into their gullet. Within an hour, every man in the camp was drunk as a skunk. It was prime time to strike while the iron was hot.

Moving behind the pine tree's trunk, Palmer lit the two fuses, stood up, pulled his arm backwards and heaved the two sticks of dynamite at the camp. Hurriedly, with hands on his ears, he sneaked behind the massive pine tree trunk. KABOOOOM-BOOOOOOMB. Palmer quickly looked at the camp. The blast had turned the camp into a burning inferno. The firewood was strewed all over, one saddle was in a tree, all the outlaws were laid out flat, one man's body had been torn to pieces by being too close to the explosion, most men were vomiting from perforated ear drums. It was simply unbelievable to see so much devastation from such small sticks that appeared so innocuous.

Coming out of the shocking reverie, Palmer rushed to the camp site. Palmer yelled out, stand up and put your hands up, if you go for a gun, you're dead. The outlaws were all barely standing and kept looking at the unrecognizable torn apart corpse that had been their partner. Palmer asked, "who killed old man Brewster in the bank?" When no one would answer, Palmer shot the nearest outlaw in the face and decapitated him. While reloading he added, "well, I'm sure it was him, heh. Now, who is McCleod?" No one answered and Palmer then shot the furthest outlaw in the gut and nearly tore him up in two. When he asked the same question again, several men pointed to a furious dude. Stepping up to him, the dude said, "I will kill you and your loved ones, even from the grave." Palmer stepped up to him, face to face, and wacked him in the forehead with the butt of his shotgun.

"Now according to my ciphering, two outlaws killed in town, one killed along the road, one in pieces from the dynamite, one decapitated, one with a belly full of lead and that makes six down, three to go. McCleod here is sleeping and that leaves you two birds, are you going to give me any trouble?" "No sir, we'll go with you peaceably." "Ok, then drag McCleod to that tree and manacle him to it, then you do the same to yourselves on your own tree."

That evening, after bringing in all the horses that had scattered from the dynamite, Palmer did the usual, gather the cash, guns and even found the saddlebag with the stolen loot. After a full supper of canned potatoes, a nice beefsteak, canned peaches for dessert, and a full pot of coffee; Palmer thought how this kind of work had to be done when the odds were six to one, as was the case tonight. He thought, *"A solo operator has to get control and impress his strong will to keep control. That would be the beginning of justice for the victims. In this case, the dynamite gave him control, shooting two outlaws impressed the living that he meant business, and three living would be all he could bring back alive, to the nearest lawman, without getting killed on the way by the living outlaws."*

At sunup, the caravan took off and even picked up the dead outlaw by the roadside. By mid-afternoon, he rode the impressive caravan consisting of three living outlaws, four dead outlaws tied to their saddles, and one packhorse with the two paniers full of guns. Stopping at the bank, the sheriff was there talking with the bank president. Stepping outside the sheriff said, "Welcome back, I'm Sheriff

McBaine. When I saw you bring those two roof shooters down with a coach shotgun, I knew you were the 'Shotgun Kid' from Roswell."

"Huuumm, that's not good, the telegraph can make that kind of gossip spread like wildfire." "Hey, people need heroes. Besides, you just brought in the McCleod gang and the stolen loot by yourself. I've already notified the authorities who have posted rewards on this gang. I have a current poster on McCleod and he's worth $1,000 dead or alive. I'll get back to you tomorrow on the eight others. Meanwhile, you have rights to their guns, personal property and their horses. Palmer thought, *"I guess personal property includes the $7,600 I found in the outlaws' pockets and saddlebags."*

The next day Palmer sold the nine horses, saddles and tack for $810 and the nine pistols and rifles for $540. The bank reward was $2,000 and each of the other gang members had a bounty of $500 which equaled $4,000 plus the $1,000 reward on McCleod. Total came up to $8,350. On settling day, Palmer gave the sheriff $500 for medical care, $1,000 towards the deputy's elderly mother and $1,000 for old man Brewster's elderly brother. Before leaving town, he opened an account in the Community Bank for $13,000 ($5,500 plus $7,500 from the so- called personal property) and kept several hundred dollars for operating cash. Restocking his vittles, he added two sticks of dynamite, two beartraps, and six boxes of 12-gauge buckshot for practice.

Leaving town before dawn, Palmer was intent on traveling the 40 miles to Tularosa and beyond if the weather and road conditions allowed it. Stopping only to water the horses, feed them some oats, and do some shotgun practice, Palmer was finally wiping out the miles. Arriving in Tularosa by 3PM, he decided to ride thru and gain on Alamogordo before nightfall. Along the road, he came up to a wagon-train that was circling the wagons to prepare for night camp. Palmer decided it would be nice to visit with humans for a change, and basically, he needed to find out what a wagon-train was doing out here.

***

Riding in the center of the wagons, he asked who the wagon boss was and was directed to a man wearing the typical miner's garb—denim overalls, blue jean shirt, and a leather flat top head cap. Sitting on his horse wearing a Colt on his side, he was still directing wagons to circle for the night. As the horses and mules were freed of their harnesses and released to the center of the wagons, they immediately started grazing.

Palmer rode up to the wagon master and after introductions were made, asked if he could bed down amongst the train for the night. The wagon master, Emmett McGivern, instructed him to set his gear under his own wagon, the white wagon with red wheels. After things got settled and the ladies were gathering food to make a communal dinner, Emmett started, "you are welcome to join us for supper but it will be a light meal since we are running out of supplies till we get to Alamogordo tomorrow." "Heck, I've got a pannier full of vittles, have the ladies take it all and let's have a full meal for everyone. I can resupply myself tomorrow as well."

After a satisfying supper, Palmer and Emmett were sitting by the fire enjoying a final cup of coffee with a quirly. Finally, Palmer asked, "what is a wagon-train of miners doing here in the middle of nowhere?"

"Well, it's like this, I have 18 families in 17 wagons and three wagons bringing another 12 single men. We are miners from Trinidad Colorado. When the silver mine ran out, some miners went to other mines for less pay. The people on this train wanted more and we decided to travel over 400 miles to the mines of south New Mexico. The terrain has been good, especially since we entered New Mexico. Our goal is Silver City, but you can't get there from here, so we are headed for Deming and then will travel north to Silver City. We've run out of money, so we plan to live in our wagons until we become solvent once we find work."

"Have you had any run-ins with Indians?" "No, should we be aware of that possibility?"

"Well, I was told by Sheriff McBaine in Ruidoso that the Mescalero Apaches have been terrorizing settlers around Tularosa, so until you get to Las Cruces, I would post some guards at night. These Indians today don't attack by circling your wagons and shooting arrows. They will attack with a group raising havoc to 2-3 wagons by silently killing people with their knives, then disappear in the night after killing everyone they encountered. They've also been known to shoot at people with rifles from the bushes. You never know with these renegades."

"How many guards do you suggest?"

"By the size of your protective circle, I would suggest at least four between 10-2AM and four more between 2-6AM. I'm well rested and I'll take two shifts to encourage the men."

Palmer had an extra cup of coffee and by 10PM he was on duty. Things were quiet and by Midnight, the guards to his right and left were seen sleeping on the job. Palmer was about to shoot off a shotgun blast, pretending to be shooting at an intruder, but to scare the wits out of the sleeping guards, when he heard the snap of a twig. Going into slow motion he saw four Indians approaching with knives in their hands as they were backed up by several rifle toting Indians. With Longy resting against a wagon wheel, Palmer pulled Shorty and fired, BANG-BANG---BANG-BANG. All the four Indians were blown backwards from the devastating #3 Buck. Palmer then grabbed Longy and let go four rounds at the men holding rifles out in the distance. The four shots yielded some groans followed by the sound of escaping Indian ponies.

Emmett, and most of the men, came running in their union suits. Emmett could not believe that Palmer had been the only one shooting. "Holy sassafras, what are you sir, some kind of gunfighter?" "No sir, just an AWAKE GUARD who has a lot of practice shooting shotguns. The remainder of the night was otherwise quiet, and Palmer stayed wound-up till 6AM arrived.

After coffee, beans and biscuits Palmer mentioned that with men tired of being on the road all day, it would be wiser to change the guard times to two hours, with coffee to help. After wishing the wagon-train some good luck in relocating, Palmer took off for Alamogordo and covered the five miles at a medium trot.

Arriving in town, there was only one mercantile for goods. Palmer refilled his paniers to cover the next 70 miles to Las Cruces. When it was time to pay for his vittles, the store owner said it was $7.25. Palmer pulled a wad of US currency and peeled off seven one hundred-dollar bills. He handed the seven bills to the store owner who said, "sir, it's only $7.25, not $700, and I can't make change for $100."

"Sir, are you an honest man?" From the back of the counter came a female voice, "yes sir, my husband is a good honest man who would not rob you of a penny."

"Ok, then these two $20 double eagles are your fee for services rendered. Shortly, a wagon train will arrive, and they need everything, clothing, dresses for the ladies, work clothes for the men, kids need new clothes, plenty of food, ammunition, firearms, axle grease, coffee, tea and candy for the kids. A few toys would be nice. Everyone needs new shoes or boots and a lot of material to make clothes and WHATEVER THEY NEED. Food is the most important. Spend every penny and make sure you make your standard profit plus the double eagles.

The store owner seemed to be in a suspended state of shock. So his wife said, "I promise on my parent's grave, we will take care of your people. And thank you for your generosity. If there is any left-over money, we will give it to the wagon master to distribute to the needy."

"Huum, that's a great idea. Pulling out his wad, he collected all the bills $20 or less. "Would you ask the wagon master to distribute this to the needy." "Can we have your name?" Palmer was already gone.

***

It was 70 miles to Las Cruces. The first 15 miles showed ranchers and homesteaders heading back to Alamogordo. The next 40 miles was again "middle of nowhere" country. Then within 15 miles of Las Cruces traffic picked up again. This time there were no highwaymen to interfere with his journey. The one night of camping outside turned out to be a mild evening that Palmer welcomed, and had a long practice with Shorty. The next day at 4PM, he arrived in Las Cruces.

Compared to the small towns he had encountered; this was the beginning of a sizable city. There was a strong Hispanic culture present, especially with its proximity to Mexico. The population approached 2,500 people and the railroad access came from El Paso and San Antonio. Las Cruces had a strong trading and farming community, in contrast, Palmer was moving west and northwest to mining country.

Palmer bought a ticket to Deming, some 60 miles west. With his two horses in the stock car, Palmer finally experienced what it was like to cover a two-day trip in two hours. Normally at 2 cents a mile on long trips, this short trip cost 3 cents a mile, or $1.80. Seeing the desert scenery with few ranches, Palmer found himself dozing off. When the engineer sounded the whistle, he woke up and found himself in Deming.

Palmer had finally reached his destination. What he didn't realize was whether he wanted to open his security business in Deming or closer in mining country such as Silver City. Palmer finally decided to spend some time in Deming to see if this was a good base of operations. He stabled his horses in a local livery, registered in a hotel and walked the boardwalks during the day.

There were several mercantiles and hardware stores to support 1,100 people. The only employee-based business was the railroad. This was a terminus that connected the Texas southern route to the Arizona southern route and onward to

California. This was more than a railroad town, it was a cattle rail head, a freight transferring station, and an access point to a northern spur to Silver City. All gold and silver bars ended up in Deming before taking their final trip to processing centers.

The biggest employer was the railroad's southern route repair shed with a round house. To be certain that there was not more, he rode his horses in surrounding areas and all he saw was the occasional ranch. So after spending a week in town, visiting all the saloons and hearing all the local stories, Palmer was certain that Deming was not what he wanted. Since he had always wanted to be on a railroad line or even a spur, he decided to take a trip to Silver City—considered one the many mining hubs in the area, and could possibly become the Bodine Agency's base of operations for his security/investigation/protection enterprise.

*****

CHAPTER 2

Building a Reputation

Palmer arrived in Silver City with his two horses, two saddlebags and two paniers full of stuff. Once with feet on the ground, he rode his horses to a livery located in the center of town. The sign said, "Foster's Livery, Hector Foster prop." There he made arrangements to stable the horses and lockup his paniers in the secured room which also served as the hostler's living quarters.

Walking along Main Street's boardwalk, he noticed the three mercantiles, the one feed store, the two hardware stores, a post office, a small hospital with two doctors, four diners, two blacksmiths, several fancy hotels and a basic one called the RR-General Hotel. The telegraph office was next to the sheriff's office and the courthouse. There was a claim office and several attorneys. The assay office was next to the entrance to a hammer mill and smelter located about 200 yards from the center of town. There were three separate freight companies with the magnificent draft horses--Percherons and Belgians. There were three tonsorial shops with access to hot baths and laundry. There was one haberdashery, two construction companies and one stagecoach line.

All in all, this town had the basics and so much more. Plus it was the end of the railroad spur and served at the hub of activity and resource for all surrounding small towns and mines. Palmer decided that he needed to meet the sheriff and explain who he was and what he would propose as a new business in town.

At the sheriff's office, Palmer walked in as the front door was open. A deputy asked, "how may I help you, young man?" "I'd like to meet and talk to the sheriff, if I may!" "Certainly, go on in."

The sheriff stood up and said, I'm Sheriff Branch Belknap and who might you be?" "My name is Palmer Bodine and," "Hold it right there, son, I just got a telegram about you from Sheriff McBaine in Ruidoso—oh my, you're the Shotgun Kid who brought in the McCleod gang. Well, I mighty proud to give you my hand." "Thank you, you're very kind. Now, I'd like to explain to you what I'm planning to start in your city." "Go ahead, I'm all ears."

"I am starting a detective agency that will provide private security to businesses, investigations to private individuals with personal issues and act as bodyguards to private individuals who have been threatened. Note that the key word is 'private.' I will not be competing with you or your deputy, and I'll make you one promise, If you or your deputy ever have the need to use my services with my shotgun, I will do so anytime, at no charge, and no questions asked."

"Well that sounds like a business that will have plenty of customers in a mining town with the robberies, payroll shipments, gold and silver shipments, kidnappings and the like. Your offer to give us a hand is very noble, and I appreciate it. So good luck and we'll talk again."

As Palmer was leaving, Sheriff Belknap said, "say hold up a bit Mister Bodine. I have a common situation that is out of the law's control. A man beating his wife. We can put him in jail for 48 hours but have to release him after that. Then the man goes home and beats his wife again for reporting him to the law."

"Yes, that's the proverbial catch 22 situation."

"Yeah, well unlike medieval times, when according to the 'rule of thumb,' a man could beat his wife as long as he used a stick no bigger than the width of his thumb, today men use their fists, bull whips and firewood. Today, Doc Sims has in his hospital, a 50-year-old lady fighting for her life. She's been beaten repeatedly for months because her husband wants her to leave town so he can live with another gal. He won't grant her a divorce because he won't give her a financial settlement. He's well off with a small mine but he's a cheap bastard. Do you think you can handle something like this?"

"I understand your dilemma and I'll take care of this for you."

"Ok, his name is Ambrose Barkeley and he lives at 15 Maple Lane. Watch out, he's a mean and dirty brawler and has a devastating right round house punch."

Palmer went to Grady's Diner for the noon dinner. Over a bowl of beef stew, homemade bread and coffee he laid out his plans. After lunch, he went to see and attorney and for a $20 double eagle, he left with a standard divorce application already prepared and ready for his notarized signature. Afterwards, he stopped at Craymore's Mercantile and purchased an eleven-inch sap.

Then he went to 15 Maple Lane, hid in the bushes and waited for Barkeley to come out of his house. At dusk, he came out and walked two blocks and stopped at 72 Pond Street. When he saw a young blonde with extra endowment, he knew he hit jackpot. Palmer walked to the neighbor and knocked on the front door. When an old man came to the door, Palmer held a $20 double eagle and said, "for you, if you give me the name of your neighbor." "Why you must mean that young cow, Hildegarde Stanley." As the man grabs the coin with a big smile.

The next morning at dawn, when smoke was coming out of the chimney, Palmer knocked on Barkeley's door. The door opened and Barkeley said, "who are you and what do you want this early in the morning?" Palmer was carrying a box in his hands and said, "I am delivering a gift from Miss Stanley." "Oh really, well let me have it."

Palmer dropped the box containing a fifty-pound rock on Barkeley's foot. The delayed reaction was somewhat humorous since Barkeley's eyes squinted as his mouth exploded with curse words. Palmer tried to help him as he was hopping on one leg by grabbing his right hand. Instead of simply holding his hand, Palmer grabbed the index and middle fingers and pushed them back till they touched the back of his hand with several loud snaps. Barkeley again started screaming as he caressed his two broken fingers.

Palmer looked in his face and said, "now you're going to know what it's like to be beaten. Palmer took his sap and smacked it on the man's mouth while breaking several teeth. Then after four punches to the nose and cheek areas, Blakely collapsed to the floor. Palmer didn't quit but delivered several kicks to the man's chest snapping several ribs. Finally, with the man standing, Palmer pulled Shorty out and fired at the man's crotch. Palmer had removed the Buckshot pellets and half the powder, but the remaining powder still produced a foot-long flash out of Shorty's muzzle. Hearing the bang, Blakeley's mouth opened in total terror. The result was a burning union suit over his privates except that the tip of his tally-wacker got a flash burn.

Standing there staring at his red burning tool, Palmer said, "this is what needs to happen. Bring these divorce papers to the bank tomorrow to be notarized, leave a $200 deposit in Doc Sims account to cover for your wife's medical bills, and open an account in your wife's name with a $10,000 deposit. I'll be sitting outside by 9AM to be certain you come to do the deed. If you're not there by 10AM, I'm coming back to shoot your nuts off with live ammo—you see, that's the price you pay for putting your tally-wacker in your bank book! Oh, and by the way, you'd better put some salve on the tip, pending seeing the doc, if you ever want to use it again, heh?"

By 9AM, Palmer and Sheriff Belknap were sitting on the Community Bank's boardwalk. The sheriff said, "I'll believe that Ambrose will heed your demands when I see it. He's so cheap that putting out a $500 contract out on you will be the best investment. Mark my words, he won't show up today."

"Care to put a small wager on that?"

"Sure, how about a dollar." "Deal."

Palmer got up, walked to the next-door diner and returned with two mugs of coffee. They waited when Palmer put his hand out and said, "fork over that dollar sheriff." Ambrose slowly made his way to the bank on crutches, his left foot and right hand were in casts. His face was a mess, puffy toothless mouth, split upper lip, flattened nose and two black eyes.

As Ambrose made it up to the boardwalk. Sheriff Belknap said, "Gee Ambrose, looks like your horse dumped you, stepped on your foot and kicked you in the head. Better get rid of that wild horse."

Ambrose turned and spoke to the sheriff, "just keep that crazy fella away from me." Palmer interjected, "well that's going to be difficult since I'm moving to town and I'm setting up a protection agency. Remember, if you ever beat up on ANY woman again, I will blow your nuts off, and that's a promise as witnessed by Sheriff Belknap."

During the week, Palmer started looking for some office and living space. Walking the Main Street, he saw a sign on an apartment/office building adjacent to Elmer Craymore's Mercantile. Walking in he introduced himself and Elmer gave him a surprising big hug. "That hug is for bringing justice to Louisa Blakeley. She's out of the hospital and has taken the apartment next to the office space. She'll be starting work here in a week thanks to you. So, how can I help you?"

"I'm looking for living quarters and an office for a detective agency." "Well, I have the office for you, let's go over and show you."

The entrance had a standard half windowed door, and one window facing the street, but a 4-foot space between the windowed door and the front window—a perfect place for a business sign. The office had a small waiting room/chairs with a desk for a receptionist. The actual office had a desk, filing cabinet, gun cabinet, customer chairs and several drawered cabinets. There was a second door in the office that opened to a one room apartment with parlor chairs, kitchen table, cooking stove, sink, cabinets, and one double bed with a large chifferobe. There were two coal heating stoves, one in the office and one in the kitchen, plus a backdoor to the privy.

Palmer liked what he saw and asked, what is included in the rent?"

"It is furnished, if the roof leaks I'll repair it, the ceiling and upstairs floor are six inches apart and the space is insulated against footsteps above, you get cold running water from my windmill/well and the sink drain works. Otherwise, the extra expenses are yours."

"How much is the rent?" "The previous tenant, an attorney, paid $50 a month. I like the idea of having a security person next door, so I'll let you have it for $30 a month."

Mister Craymore, this combo office and apartment is worth $600 a year. $360 is not enough. Here is a bank draft for $500 for the year. I'll be moving in today. Thank you, a security agency next door is a plus for you, but I'm getting free traffic advertisement from your customers."

That day, he left the hotel, went to get all his property at Foster's Livery and moved into his apartment. Although furnished ne needed office supplies and more clothes, especially business clothes and work shirts with the business logo. Fortunately, being on the ground floor, he had an underground cold room, so he filled his cupboards with food and filled the cold room with items to keep cool. Then he went back to Craymore's store and bought several blue shirts, coats, and vests; and had a logo embroidered over the left upper chest that read "Bodine Agency." Along with this he bought dress and work pants.

After the shopping was done, Palmer went to see about a business sign at Weber's Construction Company. There he ordered an oval sign that was 18 in. wide and 30 in. high that said on the left edge—Security, and on top—Investigations, and on the right edge—Protection. With the words in the center that said "Bodine Agency" and his name in the bottom of the sign's edge—P. J. Bodine. He also had a smaller sign made for the door that said, "If door is locked, please leave a note under the door with name and address."

His last order of business was to open a bank account in the town's Community Bank. Entering the bank with a business appearance and a folder under his arm, Palmer got in line for service. While waiting, he noticed a tall, skinny female employee with jet black short hair working over a large bank ledger. Actually, he found himself staring at this beauty, when all of a sudden, the lady looked up and literally fixed her eyes on Palmer. Palmer knew he had been discovered, but instead of imitating a furtive look, he acted subconsciously and waved at her. To his surprise the lady smiled as the bank cashier spoke up and said, "next."

"Yes, I'd like to open an account and transfer funds from other banks." "Is the amount greater than $1,000?" "Yes." "Then follow me to the president's office."

The office was next to the one where the gorgeous skinny lady was working but was not visible at this time. Stepping in the President's office he came face to face with the skinny lady who had been talking to the bank's president. As the skinny lady walked by, he heard, "welcome Sir, I'm Ellsworth Myers, how may I help you?"

"My name is Palmer Bodine, I'm new in town, I'm opening a security business and would like to open an account and transfer my savings from your other Community Banks. I wish to transfer $3,000 from Hereford Tx, $3,000 from Clovis, $3,000 from Roswell, and $13,000 from Ruidoso for a total of $22,000.'

"Yes Sir, be glad to assist you. The transfer fee is 1% or $220, and the funds will be available in your account in 48 hours via the telegraph service. This book of bank drafts will go in effect in 48 hours as well."

After the paperwork was completed, Palmer mentioned to President Myers, "if you ever need extra security, feel free to ask, my fee is $50 a day. Upon leaving, he slowed down at the cutie's door, but the lady was nowhere to be seen.

For the rest of the day, he organized his office. As thanks for helping out Sheriff Belknap, Palmer was given a copy of every wanted poster in the sheriff's office. He studied the facial reproductions and committed them to memory. The second thing he did was study in detail the town map. By the time he ran out of chores, the front doorbells and chimes were ringing as the first potential customer entered.

The man asked, "Sheriff Belknap tells me you're the Shotgun Kid and if so, I need your help." "I am he, but please call me Palmer, now what is the problem?"

I came to town from Pinos Altos to pick up my niece. My wife has been ill with pneumonia and needs help, so my niece has volunteered to come and help her aunt out for a week. While here, I made arrangements for the bank to prepare a payroll of $10,000 to pay my 25 men's six month back pay. I need someone to bring it by stage from Silver City to Pinos Altos some 10 miles by stagecoach, and then 5 miles to my mine by horseback. I just tried to hire some dozen men to do the job, but no one wants to deal with the robbers on the trail to my mine. On the trip back, you'll be responsible for two passengers. The first is my niece, Myra, returning to Silver City. You'll be her personal bodyguard. The second are fine crushed ore samples. There will be 200 pounds separated into eight leather bags each weighing 25 pounds each. These are samples from eight locations and their analysis will determine whether we mine that area or not. They are very important and should be entered in the railroad locked vault for transport to Silver City."

"Ok, what kind of pay are you offering for this kind of work?"

"Well what is your daily rate?"

"For routine work such as an extra bank guard, or investigating a divorce case, or providing intown personal bodyguard service, I charge $50 a day plus expenses. But this is combat work and requires combat pay because of the likelihood I'll be facing killer highwaymen, road agents, Mescalero Apaches, or kidnapping Comancheros. For that I charge a minimum of $1,000 plus expenses assuming I can complete the job in five days, otherwise if it goes over, it's an extra $150 a day."

"It's a deal, and here is my bank voucher for $1,000 as I'm sure you can accomplish this job in less than five days. The job starts one week from today." Palmer looked at the signature, *Cyril Myers*.

The next day, Palmer went to a local blacksmith and ordered a 3/8 steel plate measuring three feet wide and two feet high in a form of a T. This T shaped plate was fitted, to a nearby broken stagecoach, next to the box (top seat) where the

Jehu and the Shotgun guard sit—as a protective and deflective shield. This would allow the driver to scoot into the knee-well/floorboard, giving the Shotgun guard ample room to shoot, right and left, at attacking road agents.

Upon his return to the office, he found a note under the door that read; "the merchants have had it, we need help. Please see me, Elmer." Palmer relocked the office and walked next door to see his landlord. "Elmer, why the note, what's the problem?"

"The Merchants Association whose members include three mercantiles, two hardware stores, one feed store, four diners and two hotels have been paying weekly protection money from crooks. The three enforcers threaten us or our families with bodily harm, or threaten to burn down our businesses. This has been going on for two years. The first year it was 5% of our profit, the second year it was 7.5% and last week the enforcers told us the price was going up to 10%. Sheriff Belknap cannot help us since there are no witnesses and no one dares to file a complaint for fear of getting burnt out. Can you do something about this?"

"Sure, I'll put an end to this ramrodding, no one should exert control over other people. These three enforcers are just toadies for another man running this racket. Any idea who that may be?"

These three animals work for Fenton Brubaker who owns the 'Back Alley Bucket Saloon' on the west end of Main Street."

"When do you next expect the three goons?"

"Tomorrow morning, the first of the month, on opening time before customers arrive."

"Fine, my fee is $50 a day and I'll be here before opening. I should be able to resolve this issue in one day. One last thing, how much have you given this extortionist over the past two years?"

"I'm ashamed to admit it, but I've lost $500 to that slime ball!"

***

The next morning, Elmer arrived an hour early, only to find Palmer and the deputy sheriff waiting. "Before you ask, Deputy Burke is here for the sole purpose of witnessing what I do to those enforcers and hearing the conversations especially about names."

Deputy Burke went hiding behind a garment section but could easily see and hear what would be said at the cash register. On cue, the three enforcers entered, and the lead man said, "Well the price for protection goes up to $8 a week for you."

"I'm not paying you a damn cent. This is extortion."

"Now Elmer, you know that Mister Brubaker can't have a renegade for fear the other eleven customers will rebel like you do. Simply said, pay or I break your arm this week. If you don't pay next week, we'll burn your store down."

"That's enough, Elmer is done paying. Now get out and don't ever come back. In addition, the other eleven victims won't be paying you today as well." As Palmer was within touching distance of the three enforcers, one went for his gun as Palmer did a quick draw for Shorty, and slammed the barrels under the man's chin, busting his jaw.

The leader then realized that Palmer was going to be a problem and said, "Ok for now, but Mister Brubaker will retaliate." As the three men showed signs of leaving, Palmer turned his back but kept Shorty pointing level. As he heard the click of a

Colt hammer being pulled back, he turned 180 degrees only to see the other two enforcers pointing their pistol at Palmer. Without thinking, Palmer pulled Shorty's trigger twice and both crooks were blown thru the spring-loaded front door. Missing the boardwalk, they ended up on their backs, in the street's horse manure.

Hearing the two shotgun blasts, Sheriff Belknap came running to the scene, "what happened here, Elmer?" After the story was told, Sheriff Belknap looked at the man with a busted jaw and asked if the story was true as told. As expected, the enforcer shook his head sideways. Sheriff Belknap then said, "in a case of he said, you said without a witness, I have to bring this to the prosecutor and judge."

A voice from the back of the store came out loud and clear, "that won't be necessary boss, I heard and saw everything, and Elmer's version was correct. Plus Palmer shot in self-defense."

"In that case, this dude is going to jail, and we need to pay a visit to Brubaker who needs to make restitution. Walking toward the Back Alley Saloon, Sheriff Belknap said, "I'm going to let you take the lead here since you can get restitution for the

12 victims. Afterwards, I'll take over to make the arrest for extortion and racketeering."

Walking in the saloon, the bartender sent them towards the office. Palmer busted thru the door as splinters flew everywhere. Brubaker went to open the top drawer to pull out a pistol, but Palmer was quick to shove the drawer shut and crush his hand. With Brubaker still standing with his other hand palm down on the desk, Palmer took out a Marlin nail and shoved it full force thru the top of his left hand. Brubaker was shouting so loud that all the patrons were trying to see what the goings on were, but Sheriff Belknap pushed them all back and shut the door.

"Well Fenton, this is the situation. We know you have been coercing twelve local merchants to paying you protection money and the sheriff is here to arrest you. You will be going to prison, two of your enforcers are dead, and the third will be singing to save his hide. Before we take you to jail, it's time for you to pay back all the money you stole. So open up the safe before I give you the trouncing you deserve."

"Go to hell, that combination will go to my grave!"

"Suit yourself. Say sheriff, didn't you say your prostate was acting up today?" "Oh yeah, gotta go to the privy." "Take your time sheriff!"

Once the door was closed, the Marlin nail came out and the drawer opened. Brubaker was thrown in his chair and Palmer went to work with his leather gloved fists. Three punches to the belly and one to the groin made Brubaker vomit all over his desk. "What's the safe's combination?" "Never."

"I guess that today will be the day you go to your grave, and getting beaten to death can't be the best way to go. Looks like I start working on that ugly face of yours. Seems a shame to bust you all up when, once you're dead, I'll get the blacksmith to bust the lock and hinges off and we'll all be able to enjoy your hard-earned money." "Ok, you win. Get the sheriff back here and I'll give him the combination."

Upon the sheriff's return, Fenton said '68-14-7 and only take out what is owed. This dude doesn't get a penny more."

Opening up the safe, Sheriff Belknap whistled, "holy moly, there are piles of $100 bills. Saloon business has been good. So, how much does Fenton owe in restitution?" "According to Elmer it's $500 times twelve or $6,000." "Ok, that's sixty $100 bills. Now how much does he owe in mental anguish?" "Normally, an amount equal to the payback restitution." "Ok, so that's another sixty $100 bills. Now, what is your fee for exposing this criminal?" "Normally $50 a day, but when there is gunplay or torture, my fee is $1,000." "Ok, well that's another ten $100 bills." "Anything else?" "No, that just about does it, heh!"

***

During the next three days, he packed and arranged for the two deflective plates to be installed on the stagecoach to be used on the trek to Pinos Altos. The day before departure, a man by the name of Gideon Ackerman came to see Palmer. Gideon started, "for the past year a wagon maker has been hounding me to sell my wheelwright business. I make light duty wooden wheels, heavy duty wooden wheels with a steel rim and steel axles. This wagon maker wants my business which consists of three fine woodworkers and two very talented blacksmiths. The wagon maker is not a very nice man and I would never abandon my five workers to the likes of him. Lately, the pressure is increasing by upping his offer. I'm not selling but I suspect things will get to violence and that is when I'll need your protection."

"Of course, I have a five-day job in Pinos Altos, but as soon as I get back, you can count on me. My day rate is $50 a day plus expenses, and that includes 24 hours a day when needed." "Fair enough, here is a bank draft for $100 as a retainer, and see you upon your return."

The next morning, Palmer went to the bank and signed for a $10,000 cash payroll of mixed bills that filled a large saddlebag. He made his way to the stagecoach office. The deflective plates were installed, and Palmer met the stagecoach driver. "I've been told that a driver has many names depending how he drives the coach. Are you a Reinsman, a Whip, a Charlie or a Jehu." "My name is Cletus and I'm a Jehu because I like to drive fast and furious, especially when chased by road agents or Indians." "Ok, but if we are attacked, scoot down in the knee-well so I can slide right or left in the box and get a shot at the attackers."

The Jehu said that it was 10 miles to Pinos Altos and five miles to the Myers mine. "At 5 mph, we'll make it to the mine in three hours. We have a full coach, six passengers to Pinos Altos and three to the Myers mine. We'll take a 15-minute rest brake in Pinos Altos to change passengers, use the privy and drink some cold well water. If we get waylaid, it will likely be between Pinos Altos and the mine."

The ride to Pinos Altos was fairly comfortable with the well maintained road. Palmer had the saddlebag full of money at his feet and kept his coach gun at the ready. He quickly learned from the Jehu what to look for as potential situations that could yield an attack on the runan open area for road agents to chase a coach and shoot the driver, an area with many sharp curves in the road making slowing down a necessity, and an area with a high spot that would allow a rifle attack on both the driver and shotgun guard.

The Jehu then explained the two most dreaded attacks on a stagecoach. "When you find a tree in the road with no place to go on either side, or the attackers shoot a horse, there is no choice but to stop and prepare for a fight. That's why there's a shotgun at my side."

Rolling along to Pinos Altos' way station remained uneventful. At the station, one extra passenger was added. Getting back on the road, Palmer asked what passengers were paying to ride. "It's like this, a train ride costs 2 to 3 cents a mile, but when there is no railroad, the stage lines take over and they charge anywhere from 10 to 15 cents a mile. A short trip like this one is 15 cents a mile."

As the Jehu finished talking, Palmer noticed four riders each side of the coach, frantically trying to catch up with the coach. "Get down, Cletus, we have company on both sides." Palmer was waiting till the road agents were at least 50 yards before his coach gun would have any significant effect. While waiting for the outlaws to approach, they were shooting off their pistols at the coach but most of the bullets hit the steel deflective plates. Eventually, the outlaws came in range and Palmer let out two quick shots knocking two riders to the ground and a third caught some pellets because he faltered in the saddle. Palmer turned to his right and after reloading, changed the coach gun to his left shoulder and knocked two more riders off their horses. The result was devastating to the remaining road agents and they gradually rode away out of range.

Cletus yelled out, "that was nice shooting, did you see the look on the idiots' faces when they realized they were shooting at an armored coach?"

"Yeah, I did. However, they will be ready for us on our return trip tomorrow, and likely shoot one of our horses. To prepare for such an attack, I need to know how many passengers will be at risk in an all-out shootout."

Arriving at the mine, Cyril came to the stage depot to greet Palmer. Being handed the saddle bag loaded with paper money, Cyril showed a big smile and said, "I was told you could get this money here and the sheriff was right. Thanks, tonight at 7PM, come to dinner at my house next door and meet my wife and niece. Myra will be your only living passenger and we'll get the ore samples ready for travel."

With several hours to spend, Palmer decided to go bathe in the nearby pond that mine workers used. Afterwards, he shaved and changed into his clean back up shirt and britches. He polished his boots and his leather vest, dusted his hat off and found himself ready to go take tea with the ladies.

Arriving at the Myers residence, a maid answered the door and said, "please come in, honored to meet you Mister Bodine, please follow me to the parlor where the family is waiting. Entering the parlor, Cyril introduced his wife Delfina and then pointed to his niece Myra, who was almost behind Palmer. As he turned to say hello, he nearly dropped his jaw. There in front of him was that skinny, tall, dark haired beauty he had seen at the Community Bank. Palmer turned tongue-tied as Myra decided to break the silence by doing a "silly wave" as he had done in the bank when he was caught staring at her.

Palmer finally recovered and said, "fair enough, Miss. Pleased to meet you." Speaking to the hosts, he added, "It appears we have seen each other at the lady's place of work." After some small talk to put everyone at ease, the maid invited all to the dining room.

As a surprise, Cyril said grace and the wine glasses were filled. The maid presented each dish to Cyril who then passed it to his wife, then to Myra and finally to Palmer. The first dish was potatoes and as Myra handed the plate of potatoes, she held on to the plate, enough to surprise Palmer who almost turned over the plate. Seeing a smile on her face, Palmer thought, *"Huum, this gal appears to be a jokester, well what is good for the goose, will be good for the gander."*

The supper was delicious, lemon tasting fresh trout, mashed potatoes, fresh pickles, a string bean casserole and rolls. Dessert was an apple pie with cheese. Plenty of coffee and tea. The talk during the meal centered on the guest's life history. Palmer gave a quick review of his formative years in Amarillo to include his adoptive parents and his years of work as a gunsmith assistant, deputy sheriff and a ranch cowboy.

Myra was more interested in his 400-mile journey to New Mexico. She was intrigued by the violent encounters and the change in scenery. The one story that brought some "Oh, my's" was the story about the wagon-train of miners—but omitting the donation in Alamogordo. Finally Cyril asked why he decided to start a detective agency, specializing in security, investigations and protection.

Palmer could only tell the truth, "I always felt that my destiny was helping people and living by the gun. Since I had no trouble handling those highwaymen and outlaws, I knew that I could rely on my shotgun skills to save my hide."

The lady responded, "and isn't it why they call you the Shotgun Kid and why you wear a modified shotgun at your side?"

"Yes, I guess so Miss. Unfortunately, people like to gossip and create heroes. I assure you, I'm not after fame. I just want to do the job I was hired to do and to remain safe in this violent land."

"Here, Here," said Cyril. Shall we retire to my office for a smoke and make plans for tomorrow. Thereafter, we'll visit with the ladies over a brandy and wine." The ladies were waiting in the parlor as Cyril was pouring the brandy and Palmer was preparing the wine. Handling the stem glasses, Delfina accepted hers graciously, handing Myra's glass by the stem, Myra grabbed the body of the glass as Palmer held the glass in place and lipped-talked the words, "say please"..........."Touché," as Palmer smiled and released the glass.

The evening was a pleasant gathering with plenty of laughter. When Palmer announced his departure, Myra said that she would walk him to the front door. "Well Miss, I never expected to find you here, when we get back to the city, would you consider having supper with me?

"I would love that under one condition." "And that would be?" "That we call each other by our given names and not Miss Meyers or Mister Bodine." "But I didn't know your family name was Myers, I thought you were of your aunt's family." "Really? Why do you think I work at the bank?" "I assumed you went to college and earned the right to work in a bank." "True, I'm a college graduate, but it also helps when your father is owner and president of the bank, heh!" As the door quietly closed in his face—with a smiling Good Night.

***

The next morning, the stage was ready to roll when Cyril arrived at the station with a buckboard loaded with eight bags already packed in a large set of heavy-duty saddlebags. With only Myra as passenger, the ore samples were left in the coach itself. Climbing onto the box, Cletus asked how this ride would be handled with the Miss Myers on board.

Palmer said, "the ore samples mean nothing since they can be replaced, but guaranteeing the safe delivery of Miss Myers is obligatory if we want to live in New Mexico. Now I know we will be waylaid, and not fighting back is the only way we'll all stay alive. Trust me on this, I have a plan."

Just two miles out of town, a powerful rifle shot from afar was heard as Cletus was pulling on the reins to stop the other horses. The right rear horse was being dragged by the other five horses. Once the stagecoach came to a stop, four mean looking road agents popped up behind large boulders. Palmer pulled his coach-gun and aimed at the outlaw nearest the coach. "Mister Shotgun man, put it down, there are four of us to you and you will die." "True, but so will you—I guarantee you." "Well, in that case, let me take the gold dust

and the passenger woman, and we'll let you live."
"Fine, go ahead, but I'll keep this shotgun on you
till you're gone."

One of the robbers opens the carriage door,
pulls Myra out and the other two pulled out the
heavy saddlebags. Myra was trying to get away by
kicking her assailant, but was finally tied up and
forcibly sat in the saddle. As Myra was taken away,
she managed to turn and give Palmer the eye of a
desperate victim.

Cletus finally said, "great, the one thing we
had to do was protect the lady and we failed. And
what was that about the gold dust, I thought we
were carrying ore samples." "So did I, but that's
irrelevant, what's of utmost importance is to get the
lady back. Let's cut out the dead horse, and I'll take
the fastest one and go after those road agents. You
need to bring in the stage on four horses and report
to Sheriff Belknap of the robbery and kidnapping."

"Watch out Palmer, you need to rescue the lady
no later than tonight, because by morning she will
have been sold to the Apaches or Comancheros and
will end up in the Mexican whore houses."

*****

CHAPTER 3

The Long Way Home

Palmer knew time was of the essence. It had taken an hour to move the dead horse out of the harness entanglement. Finally, Palmer took off bareback on the big gelding with a make-shift head gear and bridle. His coach-gun was in its scabbard and tied over his shoulder onto his back. In a backpack he had his ammo, long-range binoculars and several personal items.

Palmer tracked the four outlaws with Myra doubling on one horse. When darkness came, Palmer was on his feet to follow the tracks visible by moonlight. It was an estimated 2AM when Palmer smelled camp smoke. Ground hitching his horse near some good grass, he continued without the noisy hoofs of a harnessed work horse.

An hour later, half crawling on his hands and knees, he was close enough to the outlaw camp to see Myra tied to a tree, and completely nude. Standing over her, he was totally amazed how naïve he was, even at age 23. Yet, he knew what beauty was, and he was now seeing it. Kneeling next to her face, he put a hand on her mouth and stirred her awake. Myra naturally tried to cover herself as Palmer said, "don't bother trying to cover yourself, I've already seen your female attributes and trying to be modest is now a waste of energy—besides, it was just a peccadillo anyways. After I cut your ropes, please follow me—quietly."

They hadn't taken but a half dozen steps when an outlaw got up and started heading for the bushes. The duo froze in place, but the outlaw had spotted them and grabbed a rifle. When the hammer was pulled back, Palmer knew, it was time to kill or be killed. Palmer fired first and blew the outlaw backwards. The result was instantaneous as the head outlaw yelled, "get that dude or we'll hang."

What followed was a life's changing moment for Myra. Palmer was in a battle for both their lives. His coach-gun went bang—bang-bang, in what sounded like a triple tap. The smoke from four shotgun blasts filled the air to obscure all visibility. Myra had dropped to one knee when an outlaw bullet had creased the top of her left shoulder.

After the shooting, Palmer walked amongst the bodies to confirm that all four outlaws were dead. When he returned to Myra, he saw that her left shoulder was bleeding all over her chest and back. He immediately applied pressure to stop the bleeding. "Well Miss, you need stitches. Fortunately I have a sewing kit with carbolic acid and bandages in my backpack. Let's get started."

"Uh, could I get dressed first. They tore my dress, so maybe I could use some britches and a shirt from the outlaw's saddlebags." "Certainly, get some britches but hold off on the shirt till we take care of that bleeding wound, otherwise the shirt will be bloodied up."

While Palmer was getting his tools ready, Myra came back wearing britches that were too short for her long legs, and was holding a clean shirt in her hands. Myra never showed the least bit of shyness standing there with her breasts fully exposed. When Palmer started sewing after sterilizing the wound, Myra said, "are you sewing and looking at the shoulder or sewing and looking at my breasts?"

"Both, after all, I'm a man but I can multitask!"

After bandaging the area, Palmer said, "I'll wash your back of blood, while you wash the front of.......
your chest, heh." Once, Myra had put the shirt on, Palmer said, "I think we should now maintain some degree of modesty during our travels back home." Myra thought, *"yeah, right. Now that you've seen every part of me, well, what's good for the gander will also be true for the goose—in due time."*

It was then time to clean up the camp, make some breakfast, check the dead men's pockets for valuables, collect guns, look for some ID on the bodies and find the ore samples. Two of the bodies had letters identifying the gang's leader and another follower. The guns were gathered, and Palmer offered one to Myra. "Can you shoot?" "Of course I can, and I'm quite a shootist with a pistol." "Great, put this gun-belt on with a S&W model 3 in 44 caliber. Something tells me we're going to need our guns to get home."

Palmer then went to check out the ore samples. One quick look and he said to Myra, "we've got a real problem. This ore appears to be 80% gold. At $20 an ounce, these 200 pounds, minus 20%, are likely worth nearly $50,000. That is why the stage was robbed, and you were taken because you were available and a sellable commodity."

"How did the road agents know of the gold?" "Must be an inside job. Did you hear the outlaws say what they planned to do with you and the gold?"

"Yes, they were planning to stay in camp for a couple of days till a man by the name of Murietta and his men would join them and pay for the gold and me." "Are you sure they said a couple of days?" "Yes, I'm certain, because I realized that these animals would be gang raping me if they had to wait two days with me tied to a tree in my birthday suit."

After a full breakfast of ham, beans, biscuits and coffee, Palmer said, "we have a choice. If we head straight for Silver City by the main road, there's the likelihood we will run into Murietta and his boys. That means another shootout and the outcome is not guaranteed. The alternative is to change a 15-mile road trip for a 60-mile cross-country trip thru mountain terrain and prairie land—a circuitous western route that turns south back to Silver City."

"What makes you think that these Comancheros won't follow us cross-country?" "They will, but they'll be one or two days behind, and slower than us since they will need to do some difficult tracking."

Myra thought, *"seems like a no brainer, safety is paramount. Besides, two or three days on the road will give us plenty of time to get to really know each other."* "You make a good argument for safety; I vote we take the long way around."

Without wasting time Palmer chose the best two horses for riding, and the extra two horses were for sharing the gold ore, cooking supplies, vittles, extra guns, and other gear. The stagecoach horse was let loose, knowing he would find his way back to Pinos Altos or Silver City. At dawn, the duo was on their way west towards Gila, some 30 miles away as the crow flies. Palmer had both spare horses trailing on ropes while Myra was riding unencumbered.

The trail wasn't easy going, especially for Myra who wasn't used to riding in the saddle all day. When the trail was wide enough, they would ride side by side and talk. It would be quick and short questions with quick and short answers—but it was still better than silence. At one of the watering stops, Palmer commented, "Last night at supper, you all got my life's history, but I know nothing about you. Where do you come from, who are you, and what do you want with life?"

"Fair enough. I was born and raised in Silver City. All my life I was a late bloomer, late puberty, and late with social development. This was enabled because of our reserve way of life as a family under public scrutiny. After high school, I was sent to Albuquerque for two years in a business college. Again delayed in social development, I did not participate in the dances and other mixed gatherings. When I returned home, I went to work for my father as the head accountant. I guess I've had my head in the books for the past two years."

"Good background, now what do you want out of life?"

"I want out of the bank, I want a man in my life, I want adventure, I want a challenge, I want a goal, and I want a family of my own."

"Whoa, that would make you a superwoman, which will scare off 99% of the men out west."

"Heh, I'm no dummy. I have a sharp and determined mind, and I know there is that 1% of a man who can be my partner, friend, and lover—an equal soulmate."

Palmer thought, *"and this is the type of woman I can fall for, so maybe I'm that 1% of a man who can become her equal." Time will tell.*

Concurrently, Myra also thought, *"he asked, and I shared my inner most personal feelings. He either accepted me or he will soon run away. Time will tell."*

They continued their pattern of travel when the travelers noticed that the trees were beginning to thin out. So to avoid making camp in the open prairies, they decided to stop early and set up camp while still nestled away in the protective forest. Palmer noticed the cloud cover changing and decided to build a leaning roof with a canvas tarp. In case of rain, this would protect the saddles, tack and gear, as well as keeping the rain off their bed roll.

Myra had prepared the food, but before starting to cook, she decided to go to the bushes. Palmer had designated west of camp the bushes for Myra, and east of camp for him. Palmer was adding wood to the fire and also decided to head to the bushes before supper. Palmer in his rush, walked west instead of east as his designated area.

Arriving, he did not notice Myra pulling up her britches as he unbuttoned his fly and pulled his tool out. Suddenly he heard Myra say, "your name does not describe your anatomy, that's no 'palm size.' You should consider adding a middle initial to your name." "As he finished relieving himself and redressing, he said, "I have a middle initial, it's J. Should I change it?" "Yes, to B, for being hung like a bull!"

They both started laughing, but Palmer finally said, "I thought we agreed to follow a modicum of modesty." "Well then, stay away from my bushes—besides my sneaking a look-see was just a peccadillo, heh!" Palmer then realized, "oh my, I took a wrong turn, didn't I? Sorry and touché. I'd say we're even with our peccadilloes."

Supper was out of canned goods, beef stew enhanced with a can of potatoes and turnips. With a full pot of coffee, they started talking again. "Where do you think this security agency will take you?"

"Out west, there is no limit. But my long-term goals involve buying a silver mine and going into the mining business. Right now, I don't have enough money to outright buy even a small but productive mine. Working this profession, there is money to be made, but it's a dangerous profession. I can do the work and the gun play at my age, but as I get older, I'll use my savings and buy a mine before I die."

"I'm amazed that you have the vision for such a long-term goal. If more men could plan their life out like this, things would be a lot less violent wouldn't they."

"True, but there is a drawback to pursuing this plan. It keeps out the joy of sharing your life with a woman!" Myra couldn't help herself as she moved closer to Palmer and said, "can you be so blind as to not see that I want what you want." Palmer could see that the inevitable crossroad was in their sight. The Duo made the same choice as their bodies and lips came into contact. The kiss was prolonged and clearly had the intense meaning of acceptance. They held each other without a single word spoken and embraced several times.

Eventually, Myra said, "this is a wonderful revelation, but where do we go from here?" "I don't care what the people think, but I know you have a minimal standard to maintain as the bank president's daughter. What I would like is for you to come work for me as my receptionist, my partner in training, and see how things develop from there. Yet, I'm realistic enough to know that your parents will frown on this, even if you are of legal age. Trust me, we'll build our lives and not alienate your parents. Family is what life is about."

Myra wanted more, but for now would accept their present plan. As things were getting cooler, they decided to get in their bed rolls. Myra put two bedrolls together and used the other two as a top cover. They got inside the large modified bed roll and cuddled to warm up. Even in their clothes, Palmer could feel Myra's erect nipples as she could notice Palmer's distress. Despite the situation, nothing more happened except a very passionate kiss before sleep overtook them.

On awakening, Myra was laying on top of Palmer who found himself in extreme distress. Squirming about woke Myra up, as she said, "I'm glad to see that I'm the cause of your dilemma. I think I'd better get up though."

After ablutions were best completed in a camp's atmosphere, Myra shared with Palmer a morning kiss that only reaffirmed their sincere commitment. After a breakfast of beans, bacon and coffee, they saddled the horses and were on their way.

"Today, we have to watch for an attack from those Comancheros lead by Murietta. By the way, what business does he have in town?" "He owns the Silver Queen--Saloon and Gambling." "That's the second crooked saloon owner I come in contact with, in town. The other one was Fenton Brubaker, now in prison."

Hours later, over a long clearing on high ground, Palmer saw a dust cloud appear on his backtrail. "Myra, we have company about three miles back. Since we can't outrun them with the gold, let's push the horses and hold up as soon as we find a spot to put up a defense."

Finding an area full of boulders, they brought the horses to safety and set up for a fight. Myra had a rifle at the ready, along with her pistol at her side, as Palmer had both his shotguns and his S&W pistol. To gain control of the Comancheros, Palmer put four of the gold containing leather bags, some 10 yards out, on boulders. He then loaded his coach-gun with #3 Buck with 20 pellets per shell and waited. After discussing his plan with Myra, they both waited for the outlaws' arrival.

Eventually, four riders arrived at a full trot. With the tracks turning off the trail the Comancheros stepped down to check the change in direction. Palmer yelled out, "that's the end of the line Murietta."

The four outlaws quickly scurried behind some boulders and waited for their boss's move. "Señor, it is unfortunate that you know my name, for now I cannot let you live." "Well in that case, there is no reason why I should let you have the gold. See those four bags on the rocks between you and me, well take a good look," Bang-Bang, as two of the bags were totally atomized to powder. "STOP, STOP SHOOTING."

"Now there is no reason to be nasty and hasty, you want to live, and I want the gold. So, let's make a deal—an even trade, Si?"

"Naw, I'm keeping the gold, and you're going to jail just like Brubaker. This is a Mexican stand-off, and you know there's only two ways out of that. We both walk away, or we shoot it out. If we walk away, I have the gold and you have nada—hah, hah, hah." Whispering to Myra, "If that don't frost his freckles, nothing will!"

Well, Murietta was building steam. He was so close to a fortune, yet so far if he walked away. Suddenly, the bullets from four rifles peppered the boulders hiding the duo. When no one was shooting back, two of Murietta's men stood up to see what was happening as Palmer jumped up and his coach-gun went bang-bang. Both outlaws lost their recognizable facial features.

Murietta was heard speaking Spanish as the other man started darting sideways and out of sight. Myra knew he was trying to flank them, so she took off on her own to meet the outlaw face to face. With only her pistol she waited as she saw the outlaw hop from one boulder to another. As he was approaching her location, she pulled the hammer back on her pistol and waited gun in hand while still hiding behind a boulder. As the outlaw's footsteps were heard, Myra popped up behind her boulder and stunned the outlaw who still had his pistol holstered. As the pistol came out, Myra shot the man point blank in the neck, as the outlaw crumbled to the ground.

"Hey Murietta, that gunshot, was that your man or my woman doing the shooting?" "Woman, hah, hah. Pedro has eliminated her. Now watch your back, he's coming for you."

Myra snuck up to Palmer and suddenly jumped up and yelled, "Yooh-hooh" as she fired a round and knocked his sombrero off his head. Palmer chuckled and said, "that's going to irritate him, now let's piss him off. "Hey Murietta, look at your bags of gold." Palmer shot at the last two bags and pulverized them both.

Seeing an opening when Palmer was reloading, Murietta stood up ready to shoot but was surprised to already find Palmer aiming his coach-gun at him. Murietta never realized that his head had three OO pellets bouncing between one side of the skull to the other, turning his brain to mush.

Before leaving the site, Murietta was tied to his horse's saddle and brought to town to show people who was the crook in town. Arriving in town some five hours later was a large caravan of eight horses, one dead Murietta, several guns and $500 in petty cash from Murietta's pockets. Murietta's body was left at Sheriff Belknap's office along with the extra horses. At the bank, Myra's father was in tears at seeing his daughter again. He naturally started walking her into the bank, when he turned and looked at Palmer saying, "thank you and we'll settle later."

Palmer rode to his office with the two horses carrying the gold. He unloaded the gold and left it under his bed. He then brought all eight horses to Foster's Livery with a word that he'd be over tomorrow to agree on a sale price. The guns would stay in Hector's locked apartment overnight. With business taken cared of, he went to the tonsorial shop with a new set of clothes. After a bath, shave and haircut, he dressed and went to Bert's Diner for supper. Afterwards, he went home and crashed on his bed for a full night's sleep.

***

Meanwhile, in the Myers residence, Myra was sitting in the parlor with her parents. "Now that I've explained how Palmer Bodine saved me, I need to tell you that I've fallen in love with him and I'm going to marry him. You need to accept this for he will be the father of your grandchildren."

Mrs. Myers asked if she was pregnant. "No, we were not intimate, he's a real gentleman and it wasn't about lust. It was about accepting each other and making a commitment to each other. He wanted me to move in with him today, but I wanted to talk with you first."

Her dad spoke up, "Oh my, living with him out of wedlock is out of the question seeing we own the bank and everything."

Her mom spoke up. "Nonsense, if you two are in love, then you should move in together. Come with me, it's settled, let me help you pack. And dear, go have a brandy to settle your nerves. Our daughter is going to be happy, and that's what we always wanted, plus a few grand- children would be nice for us old folks."

The next morning, Myra with her luggage, appeared on the boardwalk facing Craymore's Mercantile. As Elmer arrived, she stepped in behind him. After explaining that she and Palmer had made a commitment, Elmer gave her a key to Palmer's office/home. Before leaving, Elmer said, "I don't know who is the luckiest, you or him, but I wish you both the greatest life." "Thank you."

Myra, entered the office waiting room, walked thru Palmer's office, and opened the connecting door to Palmer's apartment. Palmer was still sleeping and snoring loudly. She elected to let him sleep while she would busy herself with furnishing the receptionist's desk in the waiting room. Myra prepared a list of items she would need, and returned to Elmer's store next door. "Mister Craymore, I need: legal paper, ink well and fountain pen, standard paper, pencils, erasers, accounting ledger, filing folders, a filing cabinet, a manual calculator, town maps, and a typewriter." "Everything is in isle 4, including a new Remington typewriter."

The typewriter was $26, and the remainder of the items also totaled $14. Myra handed Elmer a $100 bill with the instruction to start an account with the remainder of the money. Elmer brought the typewriter to Myra's desk as she began to unpack her supplies. After setting up everything, she wanted to start typing a standard contract for services. She opened the apartment door again and saw that Palmer was gone to the privy with the back door open—so Myra went to work.

Palmer walked in and could hear a strange tapping noise with varying speed and spacing. He followed the tapping to his office where the sound was much louder and now coming from the waiting room. Pulling his pistol, he opened the door to the waiting room only to find a vibrant dark-haired gal pounding on a typewriter. "Myra, what are you doing here?"

"You said you wanted a friend, partner and lover, well I qualify on all three counts!" "Yes, but you said you needed to get your parent's blessing, so..........what did they say?"

"My father had a conniption fit, went into social shock, and this morning has a terrible brandy hangover, but dropped me off with my luggage and actually wished me happiness. My mom said that people in love should be together, over all other concerns. So I'm here".........but never finished her sentence as Palmer pulled her off her chair and took her in his arms into a full passionate embrace. Palmer only said, "I will always make you my primary concern and will do my best to make you happy." "Love me, that's all I need."

The duo brought in her luggage, Myra took ¾ of the closet, three of the four drawers, and both nightstands for beauty products. They then started kissing again and when hands started roaming, Palmer said, as much as I don't want to stop, we have a customer waiting and is actually overdue for our services. Let's have breakfast first. Palmer started the cooking stove as Myra put water to boil and started to prepare a pancake mix. Within a half hour, they had cleaned the dishes, put on their firearms and walked over to Ackerman's Wheel and Axle. The doors were still closed, so Palmer made a suggestion. Let's go over to that gun shop. We need a different firearm for everyday use in town. We'll keep our S&W Model 3, shotguns and rifles when on the trail. Let's see what is available for more concealed protection. A half hour later, the duo left with a Webley Bulldog 44 for Myra, a S&W Model 2 in 32 for Palmer, and two under arm shoulder holsters.

Now, with the wheelwright shop open, Palmer walked up to Gideon Ackerman and said, "we were a bit delayed because of road agents and Comancheros, but we are here to help out. This is Myra Myers my new associate. How are things with the wagon maker?"

"First, hello Miss Myers, I saw your father a while ago and heard the story, good for you and congratulations. Now to business, things are getting out of hand, yesterday one of my blacksmiths was offered twice his salary, and triple if he included my other blacksmith, also at double his salary. I countered that offer by offering them both the same salary plus 5% each of the profits. Knowing the wood artists would be offered the same, they also got a 5% perpetual bonus. I don't mind the loss of income, since I'm still making more money than I need. I thought that would end the strife, but this morning we found an empty can of coal oil in the back of the shop and the back wall was painted with coal oil. The workers are now cleaning up the fire hazard. In short, Ebenezer Brinkman is now a real threat to this business and possibly to my workers and their families. He now needs to be brought under control before it's too late."

"We will start tonight to protect your shop when you close up for the day. For today, are you all armed?" "No sir." "Then we'll be back with three rifles and three pistols, left over from the last caper. We'll then watch over your shop till you open up in the morning. Depending on what happens tonight will dictate our plans for tomorrow. See you at 5PM."

After delivering the firearms to the shop, the duo went back to the office only to find a note under the door saying, "need your help, daughter is missing." Signed Elma Anondale, 17 Waters Street. The duo checked the town map and, after changing their firearms to the concealed under arm shoulder harness, proceeded to the stated address.

Knocking at the front door, Myra introduced herself and Palmer as the Bodine agency. "Thank you for responding so promptly. Please sit down and I'll present the problem. My daughter and I operate the dress shop on Main Street. Rowena is 19 years old and a fine seamstress. At her age, she has been spending time with men, but there is an older man who has made advances beyond reason. This man is a wealthy rancher that doesn't accept rejection. Rowena has been trying to distance herself from him using age differences as the reason. He is 50 years old and his name is Franz Boswell. His ranch, the Double B, is five miles west of town." Myra interjected, "It's likely that your daughter left under one of three circumstances. One, she left voluntarily, two she was abducted against her will, or three, she went to talk with Boswell, but was not allowed to leave."

"Rowena and I are on good terms; she would never leave without confiding in me." Palmer then added, "then, that leaves the last two situations which are both illegal. We charge $50 a day plus expenses, and we will start immediately. We're on our way to the Double B."

Three miles out, the duo came upon a scene that would turn anyone's eyes in disgust. A man was buried in the ground up to his neck. It was clear he was an older Indian in dire need of excavation.

As they were pulling the loose sandy soil away with their hands. Palmer asked what happened to him.

"I am a Navajo Indian. My tribe is short of food and asked me to leave to hunt or work for white man's money to help feed the tribe. My tribe is constantly at war with the local Mescalero Apache, and when a party of six warriors captured me, this was their barbaric way of eliminating me."

Myra asked, "what's your name?" "Lightfoot, because I walk like a ghost." "What's your first name?" "I don't have one per Indian tradition. In the white's man world, I use the word Mistah and it seems to satisfy people when I spell it out. Palmer then said, "we're down to your belly button, you got anything on down there?" "No sir, the Apaches stole all my belongings including my buckskins." "Well, with your hands now free, you dig out the front, I'll dig out the back, and Myra will dig out the sides, heh!"

Once they freed the man, Palmer gave him his spare pair of britches and his one spare shirt. Then handed him a piece of paper and said, "give this paper to Elmer Craymore at his store. He will give you a pair of boots, some socks, a pair of moccasins, a hunting knife of choice, a heavy coat, and a hat. He will then let you into my office next door and you pick the rifle you want out of my gun case, then step into the back apartment and make yourself something to eat. Then wait for us, we'll be back soon." "Why are you doing this for me, you don't know me and I'm just an Indian."

Myra knew the answer, "we would like you to work for us for pay." "True, we need a tracker, someone who can walk like the wind and one who can use all local resources to accomplish a task. Your pay will easily support you, your tribe and your family." "But why, by saving my life, I would do all this without pay until I too would have the opportunity of saving your lives. I know that this is an old abandoned tradition, but it is the way I live."

"We'll talk again, just wait for us at my home. Ok?" "Yes, I will be there waiting."

Riding on to the Double B Ranch, the duo met a cowboy on the access road to the ranch house. "How can I help you folks?" "We're looking for Rowena Anondale, we have suspicions that she may be in Boswell's house against her will. Is this possible?"

"Anything is possible, but be careful, Mister Boswell can be a very dangerous man who doesn't respect laws—legal or moral." The cowboy simply rode away without another word.

At the ranch house, Palmer let Myra's gentle nature address the man. When the door opened, she said, "we are here on Elma Anondale's behalf, she believes her daughter Rowena is here against her will." "Go to hell, and get off my porch." Myra lifted her leg up and slammed the heel of her boot on the man's toes. Boswell screamed curses and was hopping on his good foot as Myra pulled out her Bulldog and smashed it on Boswell's forehead. With Boswell on all fours, barely holding on, Myra tells Palmer, "I think I heard a woman saying 'help.'" Palmer ran in the house, found no one in the parlor or office or kitchen, but a door to the last room was locked. Palmer put his shoulder in the door. As it flew open, it revealed a young woman tied to a chair with a mouth gag hanging around her neck. The girl started crying as Myra asked, "are you Rowena?" "Yes, and please get me out of here."

Palmer asked her a crucial question, "did Franz Boswell just bound you and keep you here against your will or did he also rape you?" "He asked for sexual favors, but when I refused is when he tied me up but never touched me sexually."

Boswell was still dizzy from Myra's pistol attack when told to get up. His hands were tied in his back, as he was thrown in the back of a buckboard. With the two ladies on horseback, Palmer rode the buckboard back to town. Sheriff Belknap was not pleased to receive the limping excuse for a man. Rowena, Palmer and Myra all wrote their report of the event and Rowena filed charges of abduction and restraint against her will. When Rowena walked into the house, Elma fell apart and lost all control. After the tears dried up, Rowena was able to tell her story of her abduction until it was aborted by the Bodine Agency.

As the Duo was leaving, Elma was writing a bank draft as she said, "I wish I could add two zeros to your $50 fee, but I can't. She finished the draft and handed it to Myra. Myra said, "we can't accept this, this is $500." "Well my dear, no one can refuse a wedding present, so you'd better get your wedding dress at my shop and invite me to the wedding,"

***

Arriving at the office, Mistah Lightfoot was enjoying a cup of coffee at the kitchen table. As the duo entered, Mistah said, "how come you trust me with all this stuff, plus a fortune in gold under your bed?" "It was a test of your character. Now I know you are an honorable man and I will never doubt your trustworthiness. Now instead of a weekly pay, why don't we share the assignment fees by giving you 10% of the payments." "Any amount is acceptable as long as I can contribute to the completion of the task."

As they were talking, the sheriff appeared in the office. "I was so disgusted with Boswell that I forgot to give you this." "This is a telegraph voucher for $4,500." "Why?" "It was the bounty rewards on the many road agents you put down while traveling to the mine and back." Palmer hands the sheriff $100 as a standard handling fee for certifying and obtaining the reward money. "Also, Cyril Myers is enquiring on his ore samples." "Oh really, would you tell him you know nothing about that?" "Why sure, I bet that's going to fire him up!"

After the sheriff left, Mistah asked, "I don't know what % means, how much would 10% of

$4,500 be?" "$450." "Pfeeeww....With that kind of money, I could feed my tribe for one year." "Now where do you live?" "I have a well-furnished canvas tepee a mile east of town, but nestled in a forested area. I don't have the traditional Navajo Hogan which was a square hut made of logs, mud and bark. They take too much time to maintain. I will show you the way for when you need me."

"We start tonight. Let's go to work." The Duo changed firearms to the "upgrade" as they labeled it. They brought several freshwater canteens and three large cold roast beef sandwiches. With the shop vacated, they put a fresh pot of coffee on the pot-bellied stove and discussed what could happen tonight. Palmer said, "since the coal oil did not yield results, I expect that Brinkman's hoodlums will break in tonight and start breaking equipment, tools and finished wheels. We need to be ready and neutralize them as we catch them in the act."

Mistah had an idea, "boss, I have an idea how we can catch them red handed without firing a shot or risking damage to the shop." While Palmer listened to Mistah's idea he started smiling, "Myra, follow Mistah's lead, I'm going to the hardware store to see Horace White."

"Mister White, I need four bear traps." "I have two with teeth and two without teeth." "I'll take all four." "That will be $19.59." "Here's $100 and start an account under the name of 'The Bodine Agency." By the time he arrived at the factory, Mistah and Myra had placed the inventory of finished wheels and axles within 20 feet of the back door. To make a target more appealing, they had moved boxes to form a false passageway from the rear door to the wheels. Palmer liked the set up and the two men set the traps from one end of the pile to the other. Their final preparation was to lock the rear door, thereby making them "break and enter" to do willful vandalism.

Guarding someone's property was a boring and stultifying task of "hurry up and wait" until something might happen. Around 2AM Palmer and Myra were asleep, leaning on each other on the office sofa, while Mistah was standing guard. He heard the back door break open and a steel bar drop to the floor. Without waiting, he woke up the Duo. "We have company", as everyone heard, "hey boys, looky-here. This is just what we wanted to find, come up with your sledgehammers and start swinging."

The first two men walked ahead as the third man kept looking at the back door. Instead of the thud noise from sledges hitting wooden wheel spokes, everyone heard SNAP------SNAP. The screams of terror that followed gave the third man the willies. He could see the two men squirming in pain as their blood covered the traps. Deciding to help his closest friend, he never saw the other trap and stepped on the paddle as he was running, causing him to fall flat on his face. Fortunately, this last man had stepped on a toothless trap, but not so for the first two.

Palmer stepped up to the moaning and crying threesome and said, "well don't you look like the vicious predators you thought you were. I suppose we have to free you, before you bleed to death. Myra, would you get the sheriff while we free them up and stop the bleeding."

By the time Sheriff Belknap showed up, still half asleep, the men were tied to posts. The sheriff said, "Harry, is that you, and Pete and Sam. What were you doing here in the middle of the night. Didn't you have a decent job with Brinkman, why this?" "Because, Brinkman said that if we didn't do his bidding, that we'd be out of a job since he could always get carpenters."

"Well boys, knowing this about Brinkman, you won't be needing to deal with him. He's going to jail, tonight and you boys need stitches at the doctors' hospital. Afterwards, you'll be joining him in jail."

After the three vandals were loaded in a wagon and brought to the hospital, the sheriff and the Bodine Trio went to Brinkman's house. The sheriff pounded on the front door till a lamp went on. As Ebenezer opened the door in his night shirt and long tailed head cap, Palmer recalled Ebenezer Scrooge in Dickens' "Christmas Carrol" and almost laughed at the similarity. The sheriff was not in a good mood and shocked Brinkman by kicking him in the rear as they walked back in the house for Brinkman to change into street clothes.

The next morning, Gideon was informed of the night's activities. Going to the jail to file a complaint, Sheriff Belknap explained the law as far as personal injury or vandalism. "Gideon, only you can file a complaint that I can take to prosecutor Craighead or Judge Hawkins. You have to file it before the 14th day of the event. I can keep these accused in jail for 14 days, but if you don't file a complaint in that time, I will have to release them."

Gideon responded, "In that case, let me think about it and discuss it with my Bodine agents."

"Perfectly Ok, but give me $20 to pay for meals twice a day for four men being held without a filed complaint, or file a complaint now and the town will pay for the meals." Gideon handed over the $20.

Back at Ackerman's shop, Gideon asked Palmer what he should do. Palmer answered, "I would let Brinkman and his toadies stew in jail for the entire two weeks. Then I would offer a settlement. For not filing an official complaint and avoiding them some prison time, you need to be certain that you or your men or your shop will never be threatened again. Ebenezer needs to sign a document, prepared by prosecutor Craighead, that if he resumes hostilities, he will immediately be arrested, and old charges will be reactivated. In return, you will give him a 10% discount for every axle or wheels that he buys from you."

THE BODINE AGENCY | 111

"Wow, that sounds like a King Solomon's ruling. I like it and will follow your plan to the 'T'. Now for your fee." "As agreed, it's $50 a day. So, I'll accept $75 to cover for four bear traps and a cold supper."

"Now that is ludicrous. Had I known you would take care of a problem, expected to take weeks, in one day; you could have set your price. So, in the future, don't say $50 a day plus expenses. Say that the fee will be negotiated after completion of the assignment and based on 'pay me what you think it was worth.'"

"I'll consider that fee schedule." "In this case, here is $500, as I feel this solution was worth the fee. Thank you. Be careful. Your reputation will make your business explode out of control."

After they got back to the office, Palmer handed Mistah $50 as his 10%. Mistah appeared mystified and added, "I've never had this much white man's money in my life. I can buy a beef and vittles to feed my entire tribe and myself for two weeks." Myra added, "it's your money to do with as you wish. See you tomorrow for morning coffee."

As Mistah left, Myra locked the door, pulled Palmer to the apartment, closed the door and shut the curtains. Before Palmer lost control, he took Myra in his arms and said, "you were very versatile and a real team player today. You were soft and kind with Missus Anondale when you suggested her daughter may have left home voluntarily. Then you were firm when you crushed his toes and popped him in the forehead. Last night you took my orders to move the wheels without asking, 'why the scutt work,' as I left to buy bear traps. Without an explanation, you attacked the task. I was really proud of you."

When I said that I could be your friend, partner and lover I meant it. When we're on a caper, you are the boss. If you have me take the lead as you did with Boswell, then I will plan to act independently unless I make a mistake. Now when we're in this apartment, we are equals, and this is where we can be lovers. Myra kicked her boots off, unbuttoned her dress and let it fall to the floor. Standing nude she said, take a good look, for this is the best you'll ever find me."

Palmer whispered, "this is the third time I see your female attributes, Mia. You are gorgeous and I'm falling in hopeless love with you." "What did you just call me?" "I called you Mia, Myra was the battleax floor mom at the orphanage, who would beat the kids with a whip she kept at her side. I cannot make love to a Myra, Mia is a soft and tender loving name." "But Mya still sounds like Myra." "No it is spelled Mia, but softly pronounced Mea."

"That's a small price for you to take me as your woman." The two met and kissed passionately as Palmer slipped out of his shirt, kicked off his boots as Mia was undoing his britches. The two went wild with passionate kissing and fondling. Between kisses for air, Palmer finally said, "if you keep using your hand, the inevitable will happen."

Mia responded, "I don't know man and I need to learn and see for myself." As she finished talking, Palmer felt uncontrollable contractions and Mia saw the result for herself. Palmer added, "and whose fault was that."

Mia was quick to add, "I've never been with a man, and I want you to pleasure me." "Well, I've never been with a woman, but I suspect with my fondling, that you can react as I did."

After Mia reached her first lover induced nirvana, they repeated their mutual pleasures again. Finally Mia asked, "why did you not have your ultimate way with me, you knew I would never refuse you." "I know that, but consummation should be reserved after our marriage. Right now, we are such greenhorns, that we need to learn how to live together, work together and love together."

***

In the morning, after another round at pleasuring themselves, they finally got up and made a well needed replenishing breakfast. Mistah arrived for coffee and Palmer planned their morning. The Trio was going to Craymore's Mercantile and White's Hardware to add Mistah to the business accounts. At White's, Palmer ordered a large safe to put in the office. At Craymore's, Palmer got a key to the office for Mistah. The Trio then went to the bank and Palmer counter signed for Mistah to open a bank account since an Indian could not open an account without a sponsor. With the errands completed, the Trio went to Nancy's Diner for the noon dinner. It was a feast of fried chicken, mashed potatoes, fresh bread with butter and coffee. After the meal, Mistah took out his money pouch to pay his 40 cents. Mia stopped him and said, "when we're working, your meals are included." "But we're not working."

Palmer smiled and added, "while we were walking about on our errands, I noticed a lot of activity at the sheriff's office. I bet we'll find a note at the office requesting some assistance."

Entering the office a note was found that read, "need assistance, wife kidnapped, waiting at sheriff's office. Signed, Archibald Longley. While walking over, Palmer asked Mia, "who in blazes is this man?" "The richest man in town, he owns four silver mines within a mile of town. Best be careful, rich men can be arrogant and demanding because they know they can. I don't know the condition we'll find him, but I suspect he'll act insulted towards outlaws trying to take his money, and not pay much attention to the victim—his wife."

As they entered the sheriff's office, Longley was seen sitting in the corner crying his heart out. Sheriff Belknap said, "let me tell you what's going on. A few months before you arrived, there was a kidnapping ring that succeeded in collecting three separate ransoms, despite the paid ransom, they still killed the victims. On the last kidnapping, a rancher and his cowhands chased these animals and got into an all-out gunfight. Four outlaws were killed and two cowboys. But one man got away to Mexico. We believe it was the gang's leader, Big Dick Blackburn."

"To continue, yesterday, Agnes Longley was abducted off the street and a ransom note, with a wedding ring, arrived last night demanding $50,000. If the money was not delivered by dusk tonight, the finger holding that ring would arrive by midnight tonight. This is the $50,000 ready to be delivered, but as expected, the law cannot be involved, or the lady would die a tortured death."

"I see, but what's wrong with Archibald?" "He knows I suspect Blackburn is back in town and that he doesn't leave any witnesses. Now, there is another side to the coin, if we let this new gang get away with kidnapping for ransom, we're going to get a rash of them since town is full of rich silver or gold mine owners. This kidnapping must be nipped in the bud."

Palmer added, "this kidnapping outcome can make us or break us. What do you think Mia?" "It is what we do, I vote yes." "What do you think Mistah?" "I'm a good tracker, I can track the pickup man to his hideout. Whether we can capture them and save the victim is up to you, boss."

Palmer turned to Archibald who was blubbering away. "I have all the money in the world, and the only thing that matters is Agnes. I'd pay them thrice the amount if they guaranteed her safe return."

"Mister Longley get a hold of yourself, we cannot help you if all you do is babble or blubber. Now, let me see the directions for delivering the ransom money." Palmer read the note, passed it to Mia who then read it to Mistah. Palmer got the nod from both Mia and Mistah.

"Mister Longley, the Bodine Agency will deliver your ransom money and we will come back with your wife alive and possibly your money as well."

Archibald Longley was so stunned that he didn't know what to say. It was Sheriff Belknap who said, "well Archie, this is the most you could hope for. If someone can bring Agnes back alive, it's this team."

*****

CHAPTER 4

Human Trafficking to Ore Thieves

"Mistah, in order to succeed with this caper, we need two things. We need to find a way to capture the pickup man and then we need to make him talk without physically torturing him and leave marks—since we don't work that way."

"Capturing the pickup man is no problem. I will go ahead of the pickup site, scout the area and when I find his tracks coming through the forest, I will wait and knock him off his horse after he picks up the money. For torture without physical marks, we need to pick up an order at Mister Craymore's store."

Elmer shows up at the counter and hands Palmer a book. The book had a bookmark labeled "read here." Palmer reads the two pages and starts to shake his head and shudder his shoulders. He hands the book to Mia who reads away as she squeezed her legs together and groaned with tight lips. She then looks at Mistah and was about to summarize the pages as Mistah politely says, "it's ok Missus Bodine, I can read and I'm the one who put in the bookmark." Mia looked at the book title and read, "Wayne's Calling, A Paladin." Elmer then hands Mia another book, "Paladin Duos," by the same author. "You'll both enjoy reading this one as well. I've read both and the capers apply to what you'll be encountering. I sure would like to know how Mistah knew about these two books." "Palmer then added, "no matter, I'll take the awl and both books. Put it on my tab."

Knowing they may not eat for a while; the Trio went to Bess' Diner for an early super. Afterwards, they loaded up with trail vittles, cooking equipment and a few sticks of dynamite of different sizes. The drop off spot was a triple pine tree by the road four miles east of town, or four miles west of Santa Clara. It was truly a mid-point from either Santa Clara or Silver City. The consensus was that the pickup man would be coming from the east closer to Santa

Clara—which would be where the kidnappers were along with Missus Longley.

Mistah took off first. When he rode by the triple pine tree, he just continued on as if he was oblivious to the triple pine tree's significance. A half mile past the triple tree he started scouting for a cross country trail used by the pickup man when he was choosing the drop off site. When he found the trail tracks, he followed them on moccasins till he ended up at the triple pine tree. Mistah then traced his steps back, hid his horse deep in the forest and waited for the pickup man to arrive.

The Duo made their way to the designated triple tree. Mia was stationed 50 yards away from Palmer in case someone started shooting. Palmer left the saddlebags as instructed and departed. They hid in the trees some 300 yards and watched the triple tree with 50X binoculars. When a rider walked to the tree from the forest, they knew the chase was on and everything depended on Mistah to capture the pickup man.

The Duo rode to the tree and followed the man's tracks as he had trampled some tall grasses. Suddenly, there was a loud scream of terror and the Duo knew the pickup man was now tied up. When they arrived at the scene, the pickup man was hanging from an oak tree by his feet. His hands were tied behind his back and Mistah was dancing circles around the upside down pickup man, while whooping up the classic Indian "Woo, Woo, Woo." Mia said to Palmer, "if that's not enough to make him talk, heck, you might have an awl failure." "Naw, that man is experiencing fear, now we add pain and he'll talk."

"Well Bubba, this is the end of the line for you. The question is whether you hang or get a prison sentence? Now, here is the deal, you tell us how to find your buddies and Missus Longley, and we'll speak on your behalf at your trial. Otherwise, you are about to experience the ultimate pain." "I ain't telling you nothin, but when the boss comes looking for ya, you'se a dead man!"

"Mistah, hold him from twisting away." Palmer opens his mouth and shoves the awl deep in a black molar. Palmer was somewhat taken back as pickup man stiffened up, wet himself and then started jerking his body as Palmer giggled the awl. Pickup man was squealing like a stuck hog. Mistah had to close his eyes and Mia had dropped to all fours and was emptying her stomach. When Palmer took the awl out, he added, "gee, that was fun, let's try another juicy black tooth, heh!"

Mia recovered and added, "it's too bad you'll still have to hang after feeling so much pain. Do it again Palmer"

"No stop. I can't go thru that again. I'll bring you to the hideout camp just this side of Santa Clara. Let me down and I'll explain why Missus Longley's life is in worse jeopardy than you ever imagined."

"Ok, talk or you go back up the tree and the awl comes back out." "The victim would not be killed as everyone seems to expect. Instead, she will be sold to an organization that deals with human trafficking. Every woman hostage is worth $2,000 and will spend the rest of her life in the Mexican whorehouses. The leader of the gang is not Big Dick Blackburn as everyone assumes, he's a human trafficker by the name of Rooster Courtright. Now if the ransom is paid the three gang members get 10% or $5,000 plus the $2,000 for the victim. The traffickers get the woman and $45,000."

"What does this Courtright do in the scheme of things?"

"Not much, we pick up the women, deliver the ransom note and pick up the ransom money. Courtright divides the money, escorts the woman to the privy since he doesn't trust us, delivers the woman to the next person in charge of the Mexican transfer, and orders the next kidnapping. We've been doing this in Arizona for six months but when the law got too close, we moved to Silver City because of the rich mine owners. And that's the whole story."

"We'll stick to the deal and help you out at trial. Now, bring us to their camp." Mia was some shocked to think that Agnes was doomed to a life of hell. She finally said, "Sheriff Belknap was right about one thing, not only do we need to free Agnes, but we need to close this ring of abductors in our town." Mistah had listened carefully to the outlaw's story and had picked up the one important tidbit that was crucial to the rescue—only Courtright escorted Agnes to the privy.

Riding to the outlaw shack, Palmer asked what this dude looked like. "He's a cocky one with an arrogant swagger. Has the facial hair of the famous Buffalo Bill Cody and has a huge eagle feather in his hat's band. He a sharp dresser with a well fitted frock coat, white shirt and dressy pants. Plus, he has a pearl handle Colt at his side. You'd have to be blind to miss him."

Eventually, the shack came into view. There was much laughter in the cabin as the gang was likely drinking. The dude was spotted on the porch thru the binoculars. Likely wondering why the pickup man had not yet arrived. Every half hour the laughter was cutting back as the dude's anger was likely building.

> Meanwhile, in the shack. "There's a problem, Vern should have been here two hours ago. Come daylight, you boys need to follow his trail to the pickup tree and find out what happened. If he took off with the money, then you need to go after him before he gets too far. So pack for a potential long trip. Just remember, anyone who steals from us is a dead man—sooner or later. For now, put the whiskey away and get

some sleep. It's going to be a long day tomorrow."

Around 2AM, the trio tied the pickup man to a tree and gagged him for good measure. They then put moccasins on and slowly made their way to the shack. Sneaking a peak in one window, Mia realized that Agnes was awake while everyone else was snoring away. Mia whispered, "I have an idea." She grabs a slab of wood and writes the word "Privy" with a piece of charcoal. She then reappeared in the window and showed the sign until Agnes nodded.

It apparently took some time for Agnes to waken Courtright. When they came out, Agnes went straight to the right side of a double- holer privy. Courtright decided to lock her in as he walked into the other separate hole on the left. Mia immediately unlocked Agnes' door and brought her to safety behind a huge oak tree 50 yards away as Mistah shoved a piece of firewood to Courtright's privy door, locking him in.

Next, Palmer came out with two sticks of dynamite, one was full length and the other was a half stick. Because, he wanted to just stun the sleeping outlaws, he decided to light the half stick. Once lit, he opened the door and threw the stick in as everyone ran to the protection of the oak tree.

KABOOM. The oak tree lost all its leaves. The Trio peaked over the tree trunk and saw that the cabin was gone. The bark roof had been blown skyward or pulverized, the four walls had been blown over and the real shocker was the privy. It had been blown over, but Courtright was standing up to his belly button in raw sewage. Courtright was furious beyond human control, but the Trio and Agnes couldn't stop laughing. Mistah said, "that is a mad man and I'm not giving him a hand to pull him out. Why, he's gonna smell like sheeeeet for weeks to come."

Palmer went to check on the remaining gang members. Both were unconscious and bleeding from the ears from blown out ear drums. It would be hours before they could ride. Meanwhile, Courtright had crawled out of the hole but was dripping with sewage. Palmer said, "Strip off those clothes and jump in the stream to wash up." "I'm not stripping with those two women watching." "Agnes has turned around and Mia has already seen the best, so your teeny-weeny one won't cause any undue thrills."

"No, I demand privacy." Mistah was not going to tolerate this predator's demands. He grabbed a bullwhacker's whip and cracked it as the tip hit one of Courtright's nipple. "The next one will contact your crotch, and it won't matter that it's only a teeny-weeny one. You'll still be upchucking and sucking air in."

It was dawn when Courtright was presentable and the two gang members were stable enough to sit in the saddle. Riding slowly, they made their way back to Silver City. Their first stop was the sheriff's office where A. Longley had refused to leave until the Bodine Agency returned with some news. He had even slept on a cot in one of the cells. Now drinking coffee, he saw Agnes thru the window. He rushed outside to jump in Agnes' arms.

"I can't believe it, you're here and alive." "Yes and we owe the Bodine Agency for that, you should have seen how they blew up the outlaws' shack with dynamite, and with them in the shack. Plus, the leader was................well I'll tell you later. For now you need to settle your account with them."

Mia walked up to Longley and said, "this is your ransom money, we think it's all there."

"What, that is ridiculous. You bring back the captive, the kidnappers and the money. Any man would have sent Agnes ahead, shot the kidnappers, and rode off with the $50,000. You people have a future in this town. Now how much do I owe you?"

Palmer answered, "you offer us what you're comfortable with. Customarily we charge a minimum of $1,000 if there is violence involved, but we'll accept whatever you give us." "You got to be joking!" "No Sir." Longley opens the saddle bags and takes out a huge handful of $100 bills. I think this is about half, and it's yours." Agnes steps up to Longley and whispers something. He nodded and Agnes stepped up to Mia and said, "this is my half." As they were leaving Longley said, "if I can ever do something for you, come and see me."

With the Longley's gone and the outlaws in jail, Palmer peeled off ten $100 bills and gave them to Sheriff Belknap. "What's this for, I can't accept money other than my salary and benefits." "Well you could call this a thank you, or a referral fee, or simply a donation to your retirement fund, or you could bury it like a dog bone, but I don't care."

Before leaving, he mentioned what the pickup man had said about human trafficking. "Courtright might be amenable to a plea deal. For a prison term, instead of hanging, and he might give us the name of the trafficking contact in town."

On their walk home, they stopped at the bank to make a deposit. Mia deposited $44,000 in their joint account, and Mistah deposited $5,000 in his. When he received his deposit slip showing his balance, he started twitching as if he was having a seizure. The Duo just walked away with a smile on their faces.

***

Getting home, there were two notes on the floor. Palmer suggested that they make supper before looking at them. The supper consisted of boiled potatoes, ham steak, boiled beets, coffee, and date pudding for dessert. The Duo enjoyed cooking together and talking about anything but the agency. Mia reminded Palmer, "my parents want to make Sunday dinner, after church, a regular get together.

They want to get to know you and be peripherally involved with our business." "That is great and I'm more than willing to participate. Does that mean that they intend for us to marry?" "I don't care what they intend to happen. I know lovers will marry, it's inevitable."

Palmer could not resist her and was all over her. When they landed on the bed, they had left a trail of clothes all over the apartment. After a private time sharing some intimacy, Palmer said, "will you marry me after we close the agency and go into mining." "Of course, but why wait?" "Because when we marry and consummate our marriage, you could become pregnant and I could never bring you out on capers for fear of hurting you or our baby."

Mia hugged him and softly said, "Ok, I love you. So what is our agenda for Saturday and Sunday?" "Well, let's look at the notes first." The first was from a lady in town requesting security for her husband to stop claim jumpers, and the other was a request from McMurphy Freighting for security to ship a special ore wagon-train.

"Tomorrow morning, we are buying you an engagement ring, then I am buying you and

Mistah your own modified single trigger coach-gun with automatic cocking to be used in a gunfight. Then we'll meet with both these potential clients. Afterwards, we're going to pick up Mistah, en route to the range, and start your speed shotgun training. Sunday we're going to church and have dinner with your folks. Then the three of us are resuming your shotgun training. Monday, we'll likely be starting one of these capers." "Ok, that's a nice plan, and I like the engagement ring the best as she passionately kisses him." Coming up for air, Palmer adds, "that kiss had the sincerest meaning that any person could ever express. And by the way, I love you too!"

The next morning, after a replenishing breakfast, the Duo got dressed and headed for a walk on the boardwalk. Mia had to slow Palmer down as she said, "last night, I used muscles that I've never used before and I can barely walk." "I can see you're in pain, but why do you have a smile on your face?" "That my husband to be, is the look of a well serviced and contented woman."

Palmer bought Mia a solitary clear diamond along with two wedding bands. Mia was ecstatic and in cloud nine as they walked to the gun shop. The owner already had several of the new models but had to modify the hinge to allow an easier opening of the box lock. The chambers would also be polished, for easy shell extraction, and the two coach-guns would be ready by tonight, with two scabbards, for $120.00.

Their first meeting was on Airdale Avenue with Muriel Bumstead. "Let me explain, my husband sent a note, via a freight wagon, that he had found a site along a river that yielded gold nuggets and fine gold in a sluice box. He could not leave the site to come to town to register his claim for fear of being ambushed along the way or claim jumpers taking over his site while he was gone. With Edgar dead, the unregistered claim would fall in the hands of the claim jumpers. Edgar needs a bodyguard and protection at the claim. Are you interested, and I assure you, that gun violence is a possibility."

"We'll take the case, and normally settle our fee after completion. However, if there is any gun violence, our minimum fee is $1,000."

"I accept that, and I'll be happy to sign a contract."

"Now, how do we let your husband know we are coming and to hold up until we get there on Monday." "I already sent that note yesterday when I heard about your services. There was no fee that I wouldn't pay to save my husband and our future in mining."

The second meeting was at the McMurphy Freight office. Ben McMurphy introduced himself and his problem. "There is a mine called Longley #4 that is a small ore producer, but very rich ore. It is 80% pure of either silver or gold. They only produce six freight wagon loads every two months. The last shipment cost me six men and six wagons. We were robbed of the entire six wagons and the teams of oxen. The wagon labels were changed to "Gem Star Freight" and the ore was accepted at the smelter in town. A new shipment is ready but none of my driving teamsters will work this route because of the massacre two months ago."

The teamsters finally agreed to a higher salary as long as I provided security with 'shotgun riders' on the wagons, and added a steel plate for shooting protection behind the rider's seat. We have been negotiating with potential shotgun riders, but no one in town would volunteer. Finally, one of the teamsters, who you once rode with, suggested your agency—actually, he suggested I hire the 'Shotgun Kid' and his agency. What say you."

"Palmer asked for some privacy to talk to Mia. "What do you say, there's going to be a lot of shooting with shotguns?" "Well, isn't that what we were planning to practice today and tomorrow. This caper may have a high fee for us."

"Ok, we'll take the job, schedule it for Wednesday since we have a job for Monday and Tuesday. Also, under two conditions, I want each driver armed with shotguns, not rifles. The second, we charge a minimum of"....................." "Don't say it yet, the last massacre involved an attack of some 20 riders and the wagon contents are worth thousands." "In that case, $3,000 and I'll have six men on the job."

Heading for the livery, Mia asked who he was planning to hire for the extra three men. "I have a plan, let's pick up your and Mistah's coach-guns, ammo and go see Mistah."

Palmer explained how he wanted Mistah to become competent with a speed shotgun. He also asked if there were three Indians from his tribe that would be willing to learn the art of speed shot-gunning and participate on a caper. Mistah simply said, "meet you at the range in one hour and I'll be there with three brave warriors."

Palmer had arranged for a bucket on a string as a swinging target. Palmer would hide behind a tree and release the bucket with a push. Mia had to learn to swing the gun, then lead the target and squeeze the trigger, and finally swing thru to prevent stopping the swing. It became an exercise of swing, lead, fire, and swing thru. All to simulate, a rider at full gallop some 50 yards away and broadside.

By the time Mia became proficient, Mistah arrived with his friends. Palmer demonstrated how to shoot at a bucket traveling at a horse's full gallop. The Indians paid attention at the mechanism of swing, lead, fire, and swing thru. Over the next three hours they practiced and laughed at their misses. By the end of the practice, they all agreed to meet again tomorrow afternoon.

On their way home, the Duo stopped to order three more modified coach-guns. The gunsmith said he had them in stock and could get them modified by 1PM tomorrow for an extra $20. Palmer handed him a bank draft for $200 and said they'd be back at 1PM for the three guns with scabbards.

That evening, the Duo sat on the sofa and for the first time could read their bounty hunting books. Mia broke the silence when she said, "those three Indians seem very capable and eager to perform. Tomorrow we get their names as we give them their own coach-guns."

The next day, they got up late and had to forgo their replenishing breakfast to get to church on time. Afterwards, dinner was a laid-back meal with pleasant discussions on the growth of Silver City. When the subject of the Agency came up, Mia said that they were as busy as possible and the income was very good. This progressed to many questions such as: how much do you make per caper, have you had shootouts, do you get into fistfights, and of course the big one, when are you getting married?"

It was Mia who finally said, Mom and Dad, security and protection is a very dangerous profession. We will need to kill men to protect our clients and we'll get married once we quit the profession."

Her mom added, "but dear, you are living together, what happens when you become pregnant?" "Mom, I am not going to get pregnant, yes we are intimate and have learned to pleasure ourselves without actual intercourse." "Oh my lord, TMI." "Oh dear, I know you're not that much of a prude. For me, I think it's great that a young couple can achieve that kind of intimacy, for we all know, according to the church, intimacy is only for procreation, ha, ha. ha!"

With the ice broken, future dinners would be even better. Making their way to the gun shop, the Duo picked up the three modified coach-guns with scabbards. Palmer bought a case of OO Buckshot for practice. Arriving at the range Mia asked the names of the Indians. Mistah did the honors: this is Redwood and is called Red, this is White Cloud and is called Whitey, and this is Blue Moon and is called Bluey. Mia added, "Red, White and Blue, heh!"

Palmer handed the Indians a heavy scabbard and said, "this is your personal coach-gun for you forever and your pay will be"............... "No, no, no boss. These men want to repay you for your generosity." "What generosity?" "The $1,000 I gave them to buy food, cattle, buckskin hides for clothing and things for the kids—you know toys and candy."

"Whoa there fellas, that money was Mistah's to give." "We know, but it came from you first. So we work for you free of charge and thank you for the coach-guns. Today, we practice, and we'll beat you. Chasing a buffalo or an outlaw on horseback is the same."

The practice went on for three hours, they went thru 25 buckets and 500 rounds. At the end, Whitey said, "generations ago, our galloping ancestors on horseback, shot arrows at wagon-trains. Now we will sit on a wagon-train and shoot Buckshot at galloping outlaws. Who would ever have thought of such a reversal?"

***

The next morning, the Duo stocked up on vittles and were off to find Edgar Bumstead's claim according to Muriel's directions. He was only 7 miles from Silver City, but because of major obstructions and necessary detours, they didn't get there till 10AM. "Hello the camp," as Edgar lifted his head out of the wooden sluice. "I'm Palmer Bodine, this is my fiancé Mia, and this is Mistah Lightfoot. I'm here to escort you to register your claim in town, while Mia and Mistah will watch and keep you from losing your claim to claim jumpers. "

"I don't know how Muriel got you to come to my assistance, but I'm glad you're here. Let me get my paperwork and I'll be ready to travel. Don't you think you should only leave one man here and two of you escort me. If I'm dead, then any one man can take over my claim."

"No, it only takes one guard to stop a bushwhacker from putting you down, but it will take several outlaws to take over your site—so it takes more guards to prevent claim jumpers from a violent takeover."

"I see and get your point. Well I'll get my horse, rifle, and canteen and be ready to ride." "Don't you have a pistol." "No." "Well, a firearm is only protection when it is on your person—a rifle in your tent is useless if accosted on the job. We'll correct that before leaving."

Mia and Mistah made themselves comfortable with fresh coffee on the campfire and hoe cakes cooking in the pan. Setting up a defense, Mistah was left to continue working the sluice box, while Mia had her shotgun in hand and was hiding behind a tree. It was six hours later when Mistah heard hoofbeats. Looking up, two scruffy and raunchy riders sat in the saddle holding pistols on him. "Hey Stinky, looky here, Bumstead got himself an injun to work the claim."

Stinky added, "well, what do we do with him?" "Shoot him and float him downriver, then we go to work pulling our nuggets."

Mistah spoke up, "if I was you 'idjits,' I'd put the guns down and get going before my lady partner blows you out of the saddle with her shotgun." "Ha, ha, did you hear that, a lady partner with a shotgun in the trees. Start your death song, cause you're joining your ancestors."

"Out of the tree-line came a BANG-BANG. Both outlaws bent over and fell off their horse. Mia walked over and both men had been hit in the belly causing a mortal but slowly fatal wound. Mistah walked over, picked up their pistols, checked for a belly gun and a derringer in their boots. Finally he spoke, "that was my lady partner, you 'idjits.'"

Meanwhile, Palmer and Edgar were slowly making their way thru a well-traveled trail. Palmer discussed the potential and management of an expected ambush. "Expect one or two bushwhackers. We need to travel side by side with our boots out of the stirrups, and use our four eyes to spot something moving or a flash reflecting the sun."

"Let's say I spot something, without even verifying what it is, I'll yell 'down.' Your reaction must not be a delay by saying 'where and why.' You are to immediately hop down and on one knee, look for a target. If none are visible, move to the nearest boulder or tree for protection. Remember, if I fail to warn you, you're a dead man and vice versa."

When the terrain was flat and open, Edgar's rifle was in the scabbard. When the terrain changed, he was carrying his rifle across the saddle behind the saddle horn. Palmer carried his coach-gun upwards and laying on his right shoulder—on the ready if needed. After two hours on the trail, it was Edgar who yelled 'down.' As Palmer hit the ground, a head popped up at +-50 yards and he let off one round.

At least one of nine pellets (a Hail Mary shot) must have hit the outlaw's face since the other outlaw kept saying, "are you alright, JB?"

Seeking the protection of boulders, a rifle gunfight started between the outlaw and Edgar. Palmer then told Edgar, "conserve ammo and only shoot over the outlaw's boulder, once every two minutes. I'll sneak around and flank him to end this stalemate. Just try not to shoot me, friendly fire is not the way I want to go out."

Twenty minutes later, Palmer was within 35 yards of the shooter. "Stop shooting, drop the rifle, put your hands up or get ready to meet your maker. This is your only warning." The outlaw was stunned but instead of surrendering turned his rifle on Palmer. Palmer let off one shot and nearly cut off his left arm as several pellets broke his arm and others entered his chest and heart.

Arriving in town, they stopped to see Sheriff Belknap. "Hello sheriff, I was escorting Edgar Bumstead to town when we were ambushed. These two lost the gunfight. They have some ID in their pockets, so maybe they have a bounty on their heads." "Speaking of bounty rewards, I have five telegraph vouchers for you when you have the time from the kidnapping gang. Four of them hanged, and the one called Vern got 10 years in prison. It was a shame that I never got a name from Courtright, so the human trafficking route may still be active." "I see, well only time will tell if the abductions resume."

Edgar registered his claim and then brought a bag of nuggets and gold flecks to the ingot maker. He then brought them to the bank, and entered $3,000 in their joint accounts. He then took a couple of hours to enjoy a conjugal visit with Muriel. Two hours before dusk, they made their way back to Edgar's claim. Arriving, Palmer checked the claim jumper's pockets to find some ID and whatever cash they had. Finding some ID, they then buried them.

During supper, Palmer asked, "how far apart are the claims on the river?" "100 yards either direction." "What security do the claim owners have." "Both my neighbors have partners, so one works the sluice box while the other just carries water to the sluice operator and is more available to watch for intruders."

"Well, there is no way you can work this claim alone. As soon as you travel to town, someone will take over your claim. You need a partner. Give him a percentage of the take and live to enjoy your money." "But I don't know who to trust!"

"It's simple, don't take any ne'r-do-well, find a hard worker who is working a bad claim and make him an offer he can't refuse. Now walk down the river and find this man while we are here for the night. And make sure he can use a gun. You now have two pistols and two rifles from the dead outlaws, and wear the pistols at all times."

The next morning, with a new man on the claim, Edgar handed Palmer a bag of gold nuggets. "Muriel said, you charge $1,000 when there is gun violence. Well, this bag has $2,000 to cover the shootouts at two locations. I hope we can do business again. Thank You."

***

The Trio made their way to Longley Mine #4. Greeting them at the mine entrance office were two men: the mine foreman, Harvey Elliot and the freighting foreman, Pappy Ruggles. Over fresh coffee, Harvey started the discussion. "We are a small operation with only 10 miners. We only get paid wages when we send ore samples to cover the payroll and generate the minimum profit quota. The last ore wagon-train of six wagons was expected to generate $3,000 of which $1,500 was for payroll. The rest, minus a small amount for tools and dynamite, was all profit for A. Longley."

"If the ore you ship is 80% pure as I've been told, what do you do with the ore in the 30-80% range?"

"It is stored in dead end tunnels that are boarded up with large rocks." "Why not ship it now?" "We're keeping to the minimum quota so the men will have work and the mine stays open. If we ever get a new owner, we could negotiate a percentage of the take instead of wages, and the stash would be the incentive to do some profit sharing." *Palmer looked at Mia and the unspoken word was understood.*

Pappy took over. "The six wagons are loaded, and four draft horses will be hauling them. I am told that last time, some 20 men attacked the bullwhackers and the oxen were unable to escape the men on fast horses. This time we have Percherons, Belgians, and Suffolks draft horses who can gallop for a short time. We are also carrying shotguns as you requested, and the wagons have had steel plates installed behind the driver's seat. So how do you want to play this out?"

"When the attack comes, slap the reins on the horses back and yell at them. Once at their max speed, throw the reins under the seat into the wagon and jump off the seat into the wagon next to the steel plate. Grab your shotgun and start shooting. The horses will slow down but don't stop them, since a rider on a moving horse is less than accurate with his pistol while shooting at a moving target. We are six strong, and don't be hesitant to rely on my fiancé and the Indians. They are well trained with shotguns and they will save your hides".

Later, the wagon-train was moving at a fast walk when all of a sudden, the hoof sounds of a military regiment was heard. It was a couple dozen riders, hooting and hollering with pistols drawn. The teamsters sped up the draft horses and jumped in the wagon next to the steel plate. The marauders were racing in the opposite direction of the train—but fortunately on the agent's side of the wagon.

The target zipping by was a challenge for even the trained agents, but each agent succeeded in knocking several off their horses.

After passing the train, the outlaws turned around to run after the escaping wagons—a fatal mistake. On the run, they compounded their fatal mistake. Half went left and half went right of the wagons. This time the teamsters had an easy shot of a slowly approaching target. The result was devastating as none of the outlaws made it past the lead wagon.

With the fight finished, the horses were rested. Pappy Ruggles looked at the Trio with the three Indian helpers and said, Now I know why Longley approved the shipment with you in charge. That was incredible shooting with that speed shotgun. Keep in mind, I'd work for you anytime. *Palmer and Mia looked at each other for the second time.* Every outlaw was searched for petty cash and the sum of $612 was distributed amongst the six teamsters. The pistols, gunbelts, ammo and rifles were collected and held in burlap bags. The 20 uninjured horses were sold in several liveries in

Silver City and a total of $1,800 was added to the Trio's pay of the agreed $3,000.

With the total of $4,800, Mistah got his $480, but the three Navaho Indians refused pay. However, they left with their modified shotguns and ammo in case Palmer ever needed them again. $4,000 was added to the Duo's bank account. The Duo then rented a buggy to carry two dozen pistols, gunbelts, ammo and rifles back to Mine #4.

Harvey Elliot again greeted the Trio. "I presume your presence is indicative that you succeeded in getting our shipment to the smelter." "Yes sir, and your back pay will be here soon. Now before we leave, I want you to know that we'll be putting in a bid to purchase this mine, and if we're successful, product sharing will eventually be an offer for everyone's pay. So keep those dead-end tunnels well hidden, heh! The pistols and rifles are for you and your miners. I want them to start practicing with the extra ammo I've included. When I purchase this mine, I want men who can defend their investment." "Yes sir, we'll start right away but won't say a word about the potential change of ownership."

***

Riding home, the Trio was quiet at best. Mistah knew that a lot was at stake if his bosses became mine owners. Mistah took the side trail to his teepee and the Duo continued home. Arriving at the office, they found a carriage waiting at the door. Elmer came out of his store and said, "this is a railroad man who insisted you would be coming home today since the ore had arrived at the smelter. He says, it's imperative that he talk with you today." "Ok, Elmer, thank you."

Addressing the carriage, "my name is Palmer Bodine, and this is my fiancé, Mia Myers. Please join us in the office over coffee and we can talk." "Thank you and my name is Miles Borland, Executive VP."

"Thank you for seeing me on such little notice. This is the situation. Seven mine owners wish to have their one-year accumulation of gold and silver ingots transferred to Deming and on to the mint for conversion to silver dollars and $20 gold double eagles. It is a dangerous transfer to be carrying a half million in bouillon on an ore spur line to Deming. Lloyds of London will not insure it until it gets to Deming. The railroad will only insure items up to $100,000."

"Whoa, sir. What makes you think we can get that amount of bouillon safely to Deming?" "Because, Archibald Longley says so!" Mia added, "oh really, well if we take this job, you can tell Mister Longley that he's going to owe us a big favor other than our ridiculous fee."

"Just for discussion, what would you charge us and under what conditions? Palmer was learning to be shrewd and said, "make us an offer."

"How about $5,000." "Way too low, how about $15,000."

"Way too high, how about $10.000?" "No, how about $20,000. Now let's stop playing games. The RR is collecting 10% and only offering $100,000 of insurance—that's $50,000 in shipping fees. We are risking our lives for $20,000 and you are still liable for the $100,000 of insurance and still making $30,000 off of us. So, it's $20,000 plus two conditions, and no guarantees from the Bodine Agency. Take it or leave it." "DEAL, what are your two conditions."

"The first, payment of services up front." "Accepted."

"The second, a passenger car of only rail workers with a flatbed car of tools to replace railroad ties and rails. This is the only way outlaws can confiscate this amount of gold and silver bars. They have to derail the train since there are no trestles between Silver City and Deming that can be blown up with dynamite." "Accepted." Mia added, "and don't forget to remind A. Longley of that favor, heh."

The transfer was scheduled for three days from now. The Trio met with Red, Whitey and Bluey and went over everyone's duties. The Indian Trio's job was to travel the rail. When a spot was found with missing spikes or rails pulled off the crossties, they were to start a fire on the tracks at least 400 yards ahead of the disrupted rails. When this was explained to the Indian Trio, Whitey suggested, "we need more warriors on the 50 mile stretch to Deming. My people will be honored to provide this assistance. With Red and Bluey, we will guard the derailed railings and warn the train to stop."

The Bodine Trio's plan was to ride the express car. It was expected that possibly two dozen outlaws would attack the train, board it and force the train to stop. The train setup would include the locomotive with its coal tinder, one passenger car of shotgun armed RR workers, and the express car. Palmer explained, "the outlaws will be waiting on both sides of the track, when the train passes by at 30mph, the outlaws would push their horses to catch up with the train. That means they would pass by the express car to get to the locomotive engineer. I will be standing in one open sliding door, and you and Mistah will be at the other door. We will be shooting down outlaws with our shotguns till they are all down or have abandoned the chase. When the Indian Trio stops the train for repairs, we will stand by to protect the workers in case of another attack from residual gang members."

The next day, six agents arrived at the railroad yard. Red, Whitey, and Bluey took off to go check the next five miles for altered tracks. The remainder of their tribe was checking ahead of the five miles. The Trio boarded the express cars. They were amazed at the piles of 10-pound bars of both gold and silver, locked behind the steel bars that could be used for prisoner transfers.

After opening the sliding doors, the Trio was ready for action. Palmer noted that Mia was kneeling on the floor and Mistah was standing over her—both by the edge of the door facing the back of the train where the outlaws would be coming from (swinging their shotguns left). Palmer was on the other door but facing forward (swinging his shotgun right).

Nothing happened for a while, but it didn't take long to spot a dozen men waiting on each side of the rails. Like clockwork, the outlaws took off riding hard to catch up to the train. As soon as riders were seen, the Trio started shooting.

Palmer let off four quick shots and dropped four lead outlaws out of their saddles. At the same time Mistah and Mia each shot both barrels off and four outlaws were blown out of the saddle. The remaining outlaws, in total surprise, automatically pulled their horses back and pulled out their pistols.

Palmer spoke up, "It's obvious that they didn't expect to be shot at. They all have to be pea brains, for why would the express side doors be fully open, to air out the boxcar? I bet they were just following the train because they knew the rails were off the crossties and the train would soon derail." All of a sudden, Palmer went quiet and then announced, "well, will you look at that, they're coming back, but this time they'll be shooting their pistols at us. Get ready for round two."

As they approached the express car, Palmer saw an alarming situation. The lead outlaw was carrying a stick of dynamite with a burning short fuse. Palmer yelled, "dynamite, shoot the man carrying it." Palmer followed his own order, but as the outlaw was 75 yards away, the shotgun's 9-pellets were spread too far, and the outlaw was only wounded. To Palmer's amazement, the outlaw tried to throw the stick away as the fuse was nearly burnt out, but he was too week and the explosion killed him, his horse and the two outlaws next to him.

On the other side, Mia yells out, "the lead man on this side is chickenshit, he didn't light it and they're out of shotgun range." Palmer runs over next to Mia, with a lit stick of dynamite, and says, "well, they're not out of range of this thing." Palmer heaves it way ahead of their riding paths, and it exploded as the outlaws were in very close proximity. The devastation was beyond belief.

Mia and Mistah were a bit taken back but never said a word. Palmer knew he needed to explain and justify his action. "I don't like to kill horses, you know that, but sometimes this collateral damage is necessary if it means saving innocent lives. These outlaws will now abandon the train and travel cross country. Their destination is the site of their nasty work. There are still a dozen outlaws remaining and seeing there is no derailment, they will attack the workers. The three of us would have been outnumbered to save the workers, train crew, and the gold/silver bars. Now, with the workers armed, the odds are in our favor."

A half hour later, the locomotive slowed down and the brakes were applied. Coming to a complete stop, the Indian Trio stood next to the bonfire they had started. Whitey spoke, "look Mister Iron Horse, no shoes for your horse. Better fix, heh?" The engineer pulled up his cap with a clear look of appreciation. The Trio came up and solidly thanked the Indian Trio for their work. Bluey shocked everyone by speaking in good English, "we stay till shoes put back up, we guard with our new fancy shotguns."

The workers had to replace the rails and several cross ties because the damage had been done with dynamite. To protect the workers, Mia was standing behind the front 'cow catcher' while Mistah was sitting behind the smokestack. Palmer and the three Indians were spread out between the workers—expecting a frontal attack by some pissed-off outlaws.

As expected, a dozen outlaws appeared at full trot, only to find an army of men waiting for them. It was an all-out gunfight. The outlaws never reached the track because every worker was now sending lead downrange instead of swinging a sledgehammer. After losing half their men, the remaining outlaws decided to retreat and abandon the cause. Running toward their horses, not a one was found where they had left them. Instead arrows were flying true, and every outlaw found his resting place on the ground before a single shot was fired.

Both Trios had heard the screaming, and decided to go investigate. They found six outlaws full of arrows with a Navajo War Lance planted in the ground. The guns and gunbelts were neatly stacked in one pile, money was placed in a leather bag, and the horses were secured to trees. This time it was Red who spoke. "Our people have repaid you, they have been honored by accomplishing this task and again walk proud with their heads held up high."

Once the tracks were repaired, the train made it safely to Deming. The outlaw bodies were secured to the 20 living horses and the caravan was brought back to Silver City. Eventually, on the next train, the Trio made their way back to Silver City. The next three days were spent sorting out guns, horses and outlaw identifications.

The guns were again sold for the usual price of $25 for pistols and $35 for rifles. The horses were distributed to several liveries for the usual price of $90 for horse, saddles, saddlebags, scabbards, and tack. Identifying the outlaws was a real problem. Most were unemployed saloon bums or "ner-do-wells." Some were identified by inscriptions on the inside of their gunbelts, some by letters in their pockets, and most were identified by local people and saloon patrons. Eighteen of the 24 outlaws were identified and 14 had bounty rewards totaling $4,000.

The Trio deposited the $20,000 fee, minus Mistah's $2,000 portion. The Indian Trio was given the value of the sold horses, the railroad workers were given the value of the guns, and the Indian Tribe was given the bounty rewards in the form of a nice cattle herd worth $3,000. Sheriff Belknap was given $1,000 for finding all the bounty rewards—another donation to his retirement fund.

The next morning after a very late replenishing breakfast, the Duo had a visitor. Cyril Myers showed up looking for his ore samples and said, "the assayer has not sent me my sample assays because he has not seen any ore to test. What happened, I heard that you had taken a long detour and had escaped with your lives and my ore."

"Mister Myers you are a hypocrite and a liar. Because you did not tell us that the ore was 95% pure gold, it put us in danger—you put your niece in danger for money! For that reason, it's going to cost you a generous fee to get the gold back."

"How much?" "The usual finder's fee of 10%."

"What, are you nuts? Those bags are worth $50,000."

"Yes, and $5,000 plus the agreed fee of $1,000 comes to $6,000."

"Alright, give me the bags and I'll bring you a voucher in a few days."

"No, I had this bag assayed, and was told it was worth $6,000. So we are now paid a proper fee. You can take your gold, get out and you're now 'persona-non-grata' with the Myers family—that includes your brother." "So be it. Where is the gold?" "Why under my bed, of course!"

"Under your bed! Damn, you are nuts!"

"No, not really, after all they were only ore samples, right?

"Besides, any man who puts his family in danger for money is below the pond scum variety. You must be suffering from the 'DF' disease." As Cyril finished pulling out the ore samples, he walked out of the Duo's lives forever, knowing full well what DF meant.

***

After Cyril left, Mia asks, "what is this DF disease?" "Oh, I just made it up. It means, D_ _ b

F _ _ k disease!" "I see, well I would have called him PM—for Pukous Maximus."

After some combined laughter, Palmer said, "I'm going to the private assayer and office smelter to reclaim pure gold and deposit it in the Community Bank. I will come back with our account balance so we can talk about our future." "Ok, well I have to do some housework, food preparation, and ledger entries. It will take you a couple of hours, so I can catch up on a woman's work."

Mia started her work by rushing to the privy. She never noticed the five horses tied to a railing behind the privy. Upon her return she decided to get the paperwork out of the way before other duties. She walked right thru the apartment and opened the door to the office. To her surprise, a man was sitting in front of her desk. She immediately recognized him as Mortimer Donahue, owner of the Silver King Saloon and Casino. "Well Mort, this is a surprise, what can I do for you?" "Id like you to meet my traveling boys," as three scruffy looking toadies came out of the waiting room. This is Pale Face, Stinky and Maggot." "My, my, Mort. These are not your usual saloon or casino employees. Why are you here with these miscreants?"

"Why Myra, or I hear its now Mia, we're here to escort you to Mexico and get some payback for hanging Courtright. My bosses are so irritated with your agency for thwarting their efforts to establish an outlying office to Mexico, that they decided to send you to the whore houses in Ciudad Juarez and for us to kill your partner/significant other when he tries to rescue you."

"Oh, soooooh, you're the local human trafficking guru that responds to the mob in Albuquerque. Well, I'm not going with you anywhere"………….. and the lights went out after feeling a sharp pain in the back of her head.

*****

CHAPTER 5

A Twist of Fate

Palmer finally got his ore smelted into a gold bar and then deposited it in their account, minus the bank's fee for conversion to US Currency. While walking back to the office, Elmer was seen knocking at the office door. "Go on in Elmer, the door is not locked with Mia working inside. Elmer took the door handle and said, "it's locked, do you have the key?" "What the heck, Mia doesn't lock up when she's inside." Palmer used his key and entered. "She's not in the office so she must be working in the apartment." He opened the door to the apartment and found no one, he then went to the privy and found five horse tracks. Palmer came rushing in the office, "Mia has been kidnapped by four outlaws, so please prepare vittles for a week for three people while I get my horses and Mistah."

To save time, Palmer paid the telegraph messenger a silver dollar to rush and get Mistah Lightfoot. Palmer had noticed the five horse tracks were heading south, and Mistah lived north of town. Palmer then helped Hector Foster saddle both Nutcase and Chickenshit. Running back to the office, Mistah was waiting outside. Palmer went inside to get his shotguns, Longy and Shorty, plenty of ammo, and two canteens. Coming outside Palmer stopped to tell Mistah what was going on. "Mistah, Mia has been kidnapped and I need your help tracking these bastards down. Now they are heading south. It's 80 miles to the Mexican border town of Puerto Palomas. Unless I'm mistaken, this is the work of the human trafficking mob, and it's probably revenge for foiling their lucrative kidnapping scheme and getting Courtright hung."

"After Puerto Palomas, it's another 80 miles to Ciudad Juarez, the likely place to put Mia in a whorehouse. We have to catch up before they transfer her to a relay team from Puerto Palomas to Ciudad Juarez."

Mistah said, "I'm ready. How much lead time do they have on us?" "Two and a half hours for sure."

"Even at a full trot, they're only 15 miles ahead of us. They'll need to stop tonight, and by tracking under moonlight, we'll meet up with them during the middle of the night."

Meanwhile, Mia had been tied belly down on the saddle with her hands tied under the horse to her ankles. After a half hour, Mia woke up and started yelling with a high pitch that spooked the horses. Mortimer told Maggot to cut her loose, sit her in the saddle, and tie her hands to the saddle horn. "Now listen to me really good, Missy. You're going to ride and keep up with us or we're going to stop, tie you to a tree and bullwhip you. As soon as we see Bodine, we'll gag and hog tie you so you can watch us bushwhack him." Mia interjected, "now you listen to me really good, asshole. The man coming after me is in love with me. Love can make a man do things that are not in his nature. He's going to kill all of you after he tortures you. You have no idea, but you'll be spending some painful time in hell while still alive on earth— and I'll be watching and cheering him on."

Mortimer thought, *"that bitch is probably right. But if I let her go, then the mob will send an assassin to kill us off. So, the only solution is to get her to Mexico and hand her off to the Juarez relay gang. Then we split up and I return to Silver City as a saloon/casino owner."*

The Duo was moving at a medium trot as Mistah had his eyes to the ground. Palmer couldn't believe how he could even see tracks when moving that fast. After two hours, they stopped to water their horses and let them blow. There was no time for cropping grass as they were back on the trail, now some two hours away from sundown.

Mistah would not let the horses' water two hours later because he knew that the time from sundown to moonrise over the horizon was absolute down time for tracking. Mistah said, "when it's pitch-dark, we'll stop, water the horses, feed them some oats and let them graze until the moon is up. We'll even have time to have one of Elmer's cold roast beef sandwich."

Meanwhile in Donahue's camp, the outlaws prepared a meal of bacon, beans and coffee. After their supper, Stinky suggested that everyone should have a turn with their captive. Mortimer then said, "It depends, has she been used, or does she still have her maidenhood." Stinky answered, "well she's been living with that detective, I can't imagine she's still intact!" "Well, I agree, but you never know. If she's intact, she's worth $5,000 and if she's used merchandise, she's worth only $500. Those female attributes are worth a lot of money and are marketable. Now, you three numbskulls won't be able to tell, so hold her down and I'll check her out." The four of them attacked Mia. She started yelling and threatened to cut off their oysters and sausage if they raped her. Once restrained, Mortimer took a good look and said, "you're out of luck boys, she's definitely intact, so she's a 'no go.'"

After darkness, Mistah started walking his horse. This was how he could see the tracks with moonlight and also avoided having the horses step in a gopher's or prairie dog's hole. Mistah persisted for five hours when both men smelled camp smoke. "We got em boss." The Duo was in moccasins and crawling on the ground. When they got to 25 yards off camp, Palmer saw Mia tied to a tree, on the left side of camp, and a guard was seen leaning on a large oak tree next to the campfire.

Palmer made a plan. "Mistah, that guard is an albino and is sleeping standing up. Can you sneak up on him, stick this awl in one of his eyes and make him scream to bloody hell. Then kill him anyway you can. I'll take care of the other three. No one is leaving this camp on their own two feet."

Mistah easily sneaked up to the big oak and then climbed it. He then lowered himself headfirst down the tree and dangled by his feet wrapped around a stout branch. Being face to face with the sleeping albino, he jabbed the awl in the eye's slit. The man jerked his head backwards, brought his hands to remove something in his eye and let out the scream that made the leaves rustle over the entire tree. Mistah then moved the awl in every direction, increasing the intensity of the screeching noise that pierced the night.

Meanwhile, Palmer had sneaked to Mia and softly awakened her with a kiss, then said, "I'm marrying you as soon as we get to town, and to hell with my previous reasons for not making you my wife." Just then, the albino's howl pierced the air. The three kidnappers jumped up from their bedrolls. Palmer shot Stinky and Maggot with shots to the edge of their bellies. Both fell to the ground moaning and holding their gut. Mortimer tried to shoot Palmer but missed. Instead of killing him, Palmer shot him in the foot. Mortimer collapsed to the ground while looking at a stump and dangling bones where his foot had been. Palmer then hog tied him and walked over to the other men, Stinky and Maggot. They were both thrashing, and Palmer stepped on their bellies to make the pain even worse.

Mia then asked Palmer, "you have every right to torture these men to their death. In reality, why would you. They are all doomed men who will hang for kidnapping, why summarily execute them, let the law hang them. Mistah showed up and Palmer asked him what he did with the albino. "After I punctured his eye and tortured him by moving the awl, I thought of shoving it into his brain to end his suffering. Instead, I pulled it out and tied him to the tree. If you want me to, I will shoot all four in the head and leave them to the coyotes, otherwise, we bring them back to town."

The decision was made, all four outlaws were to be brought back to town. After cooking a breakfast of ham, eggs, biscuits, fried potatoes and coffee, Donahue and the albino were loaded onto their horses with their hands and one ankle tied to the saddle horn or stirrup. Unfortunately, Stinky and Pale Face had died during the early morning. It took all day to get back to town. When they arrived, their first stop was Sheriff Belknap's office. To everyone's surprise, Mia's parents were there anxiously awaiting their arrival. Mia's first words were, "well mom, you're finally getting your wish, Palmer asked me to marry him and as soon as you can arrange a small wedding in our church, I'm getting the real man I've dreamt about all my life."

Sheriff Belknap sent for one of the doctors to care for Donahue's macerated foot. Albino would likely end up with laudanum for the pain and a trial would be set up within a few days. After agreeing on the basics for a church wedding and a reception in one of the local diners, the Duo headed back to their apartment.

As they entered the one room apartment, they came together in a heated embrace, clothes went flying and eventually they landed in bed. Mia asked, "are we going to pleasure ourselves like we've been doing or is it time to really make love."

"While we were riding back to town, I kept thinking how I had been wrong. We nearly lost each other today. You could have been raped or killed or sent to a whorehouse. I could have been shot dead trying to rescue you. Enough is enough, tonight we join our souls and consummate our love. Next week we can consummate our marriage to satisfy the rest of the world."

When two people are consenting, willing, and wanting, then things just fall into place. The participants had stimulated each other to a near frenzy when Palmer painlessly entered Mia. With little effort, they both reached their spasmodic nirvana. After the glowing period, Mia said, "I know you took my soul as I took yours. I love you so much." "And I promise to love you like this forever."

***

The next week was a busy time for Mia's mom who had accepted the responsibility of sending invitations and arranging a reception meal. The

Duo met with the Myers and Mister Myers presented twenty invitations to include his employees and several businessmen in town—plus all their wives or significant others. Palmer was new in town, so they elected to invite all their customers and agency businesses to include: Elmer and Missus Craymore, Horace and Missus White, Hector Foster, Sheriff and Missus Belknap, Deputy Liam and Missus Burke, Louisa Barkley Monroe and husband, Gideon and Missus Ackerman, Elma and Rowena Anondale, Archibald and Agnes Longley, Ben and Missus McMurphy, Pappy Ruggles, Edgar and Muriel Bumstead, Harvey and Missus Elliot, Reverend and Missus McMillen, and of course his mom and dad, Sheriff Ralph and Ella Bodine of Amarillo, Tx.

The Duo's responsibility included: making arrangement with Pastor McMillen, scheduling a carriage from church to the reception site, reserving the newlywed bridal suite at the Railroad General Hotel, buying their wedding dress and dress suit. Finding a best man for Palmer was an easy one. He had sent a telegram to his parents a week ago, inviting them to his wedding. They had responded in the affirmative and would actually arrive two days before the wedding—ample time to catch up and introduce their future daughter-in-law.

With arrangements under control, the Duo decided to take a ride to the Longley #4 mine and have a chat with the foreman, Harvey Elliot. After a pleasant five-mile ride, they arrived at the mine and went to the office outside the mine entrance.

"Well, hello again. I see we are having a wedding and my wife and I are thrilled to attend. So, what brings you here today?"

"After the wedding and honeymoon, we're going to speak to Longley about buying this mine. So, could you tell us what changes will be needed to modernize the equipment and improve safety."

"Certainly, this is an old mine worked by a small crew for years, Yet, we are now 400 yards deep, and air quality is beginning to impair our ability to put in an 8-hour productive day. The men try, but by the time the 8-hour shift is over, they can barely walk out of the mine. We need a 3X3 foot cribbed air shaft. That's a big investment, but with a coal burning exhaust system, we can pull fresh air down the shaft to the mine and escape noxious fumes thru a stove pipe. This will allow us to run a coal fired boiler that uses steam to power an air compressor. With compressed air, we can operate drills and use a slusher and mucker."

Mia stopped him and said, "whoa there, sir, but we are novices. So please explain how an air shaft pulls fresh air down the mine if there is a hot stove pipe in the air shaft." "It's all about the physics of air currents with hot and cool air passages. It's very complicated, but it works, and the detail mechanism is way above my pay grade."

Palmer added, "fair enough. Now I can see that compressed air can operate a drill, but what is a slusher and a mucker?"

"When we follow a rich vein, we form crosscut tunnels. The slusher is a scoop, on a pulleyed rope, that drags the ore on the side tunnel and drops it in front of the mucker. The mucker is a compressed air loader on the rails. It loads the ore by dumping it 'overhead' into the ore carts (also called minecarts) behind it, which are on the same rails as the mucker. Once the ore has been removed and the vein has run out, the empty space is called a stope. The stope is what we hide that 50-80% ore and block it up closed—like we talked about before."

"How many stopes do you have that are full of ore and how large are they."

"By the height, width and length of each four stopes, compared to the cubic size of each ore freight wagon, we have one stope equal to 30 wagons, two equal to 45 wagons each, and one equal to 60 wagons."

Palmer then added, "I have an idea. If we let it be known that there is a stope full of rich ore, using the one with 30 wagons, the Bodine agency could use our protection services to ship the ore to the smelter. This would give us an edge, and hopefully cut the price down for the sale. Of course, we would use the air shaft and compressed air equipment as expensive changes needed."

Mia also had a thought, "other than the stopes full of rich ore, is there something else that would push us to pay more for the mine and not lose the sale?"

"Yes, we found another rich vein of quartz rock full of gold and silver. With an air shaft, we could run two main tunnels, two separate teams, two separate rails, two separate compressed air lines, and double the income. You are the only outsiders that know about this!"

"Wow, that's important to know. Next question, how does an air shaft add safety to the miners?"

"A 3X3 cribbed air shaft provides 9 square feet of space. That would allow us to pass cages up and down, roped to a pulley system called a windlass and attached to a head frame. These cages would hold men, supplies, and buckets of pure gold ore. Can you imagine, that a cave-in in the 400 yard entrance, could kill every man in the mine, if there is no escape route. With an air shaft, we could rescue every man, even before poisonous gasses were released from the cave-in."

Palmer was totally amazed and quickly volunteered, "well, I assure you that if we buy this mine, the first thing going in is a sizable air shaft. And, we'll hire experts for the job, allowing the miners to do what they do best, dig the ore out."

"Then, it's agreed, I will tell my men to let it slip, while drinking in the saloons, that they have been hoarding a stope full of rich ore. Within days, the spies will sell their information to Longley himself."

Mia added, "last question, can you give us an idea how much profit this mine generated in the last 12 months?"

"By my records of the number of shipments we made and the estimated richness of each shipment, minus labor and expenses, I suspect that he cleared $20,000, and never spent one minute in the mine, nor ever inquired how things were going. He didn't want to bring up the subject of digging an air shaft, heh!"

Palmer added, "really, well how much would a 3X3 ft. air shaft cost?"

"You'd be surprised, and I've done some research. By my surveying and my high school geometry, I estimate our air shaft would be a maximum of 200 feet deep, in dirt like the ground over our entrance. A man could dig 3 feet deep in two hours and another man could do the cribbing in another 2 hours. That means that 6 feet per 8-hour shift could be attained by two men, digging in dirt but another two on top to drill, cut lumber, and other chores. So, Let's add it up"

1. 6ft. a day. To reach 200 feet means 34 days of work. Say +-40

2. Hazardous and professional duty pay is $4 a day. So each day of labor costs for four men = $16 a day. 40 days=$640

3. 4X4 inch timbers = $300

4. Connecting threaded J-bolts = $300

5. Miscellaneous +-$400 to include, buckets, shovels, pics, rope, pulleys, windlass, saws, candles, wall anchors, and drill bits.

That comes to $1,700—say another $500 for unplanned expenses."

"Does Longley realize that the cost is so low."

"No, but remember our mine entrance is dirt with walls and ceiling supported by timbers till we hit the rock face. Longley's Mines #1-3 are solid rock from the 'adit (entrance). So, he probably assumes #4 is also rock, but he doesn't come here to check it out. Sooooh, not for me to say. And digging an air shaft in rock is impossible with today's equipment.'"

"Huum, bad for him, possibly good for us, heh? Thank you for your guidance and information, we'll get back to you soon."

***

Riding back to town Mia realized that Palmer had never told her how much money they had in the bank and whether it was enough to buy Mine #4. "You're right, with the kidnapping, love making and planning a wedding, we never came back to the matter. We have $119,000 in our account." "Is it enough?" "Yes, while you were working on invitations to the wedding, I stepped out and went to see the town clerk. Most productive mines with less than 25 miners generally sell for $50,000 to $75,000—depending on the yearly profit margin."

"And we have some idea what that figure might be."

Arriving back in town, arrangements moved quickly. The next day, the Duo bought their wedding attire. The next day, Palmer's parents were arriving. Waiting at the rail yard, Mia was having cold feet, "what if they don't like me, what if I don't like them, what if we don't see eye to eye, what if……….." "Woman, what is there not to like, you're a wonderful person, since when do you not like people, what if, what if, and more what if. I don't care, I like you and love you, so that makes it all Ok, and we'll work it out, heh? Mark my words,

Ralph and Ella will become your best friends and family."

As expected, Mia fell in love with the Bodines' and after a pleasant supper at the Railroad General Hotel, they talked over some coffee and tea for a long time. The major subjects were how Palmer had done with his business since leaving home and Ralph's impending retirement.

Palmer quickly reviewed the past year and finished with mentioning their accumulated bank account. When Mia added the likelihood of an incoming career change. Eyebrows lifted up for the second time, but more info would follow the wedding.

Ralph mentioned that he was letting go the reins to his well-trained deputy. He was ready to retire. Ella added that they saw no attraction to stay in Amarillo. "We only have one son, one daughter-in-law, and possibly some grandchildren, and we're thinking of moving to Silver City if you'd have us so close."

Mia looked at Palmer, after seeing the nod, she exploded with enthusiasm, "my goodness, that would be a dream come true to have both my children's grandparents in town. Oh please come and we'll build you a house next to ours. Will you accept our offer?"

Palmer added, "I agree, sell your house and barn and keep the income for your retirement. Ship your personal items, horse, buggy and household furniture and we'll build you the rest, next to our house, and you know we can afford it." "Sounds good, but at age 57, what does a lawman do at that age?"

"Work for Sheriff Belknap, he needs a second deputy, but he just doesn't have the energy to train a second one. His present deputy is easy going and would make a great partner. The sheriff is a good man."

"That's a possibility. I can commiserate with the sheriff, young men think they know it all, but know nothing and have poor living skills. Us old geezers have plenty of experience and know a lot but don't brag about it. I'll talk to him, at the wedding, about the job."

Waiting for the blessed day, the Duo and the senior Bodines' looked at two building lots across the street from Mia's parents. Since the real estate agent was the vice president of her dad's bank, it was easy to negotiate a price for both lots. The two 3-acre lots sold for $400. The price was paid on the spot. The Duo along with Palmer's parents, went to see Weber's construction company.

Two houses were designed. The senior Bodines' chose a single-story home with one bedroom, a scullery, and a small office, along with a two-stall barn with a drive thru carriage house and a level hay storage area. The Duo chose a two-story home with four bedrooms with a scullery, a large office, and a four-stall barn with a large carriage house and corresponding level hay storage area. The real surprise for everyone was the offer of a well, a windmill pump, indoor plumbing and an indoor water closet. The two homes could share the same well and windmill pump. Along with indoor plumbing came a concrete holding tank and a filtering field.

At the end of the designing, Palmer asked for their tentative prices. Mister Weber said, "the small house and barn will cost $900, and the large house and barn would cost $2,000. Two two-acre corrals would cost $200, and the indoor plumbing, well, windmill and water closets for both houses would add another $800." Palmer gave Mister Weber a bank draft for the entire amount, and asked that the materials be ordered so construction could start asap. With the tentative costs paid up front, any other expenses would be paid at the end of the project.

Leaving Weber's, Palmer mentioned, "It seems the die is cast, you're moving to New Mexico. If things don't work out with Sheriff Belknap, I'm sure I can find some work for you in our new venture."

***

The wedding day had arrived, Palmer was waiting in the church with his dad, as the organist started the classic wedding march. Mia entered looking radiant on her dad's arm. The ceremony was short and sweet and the newlyweds kissed before they led the guests to the RR General Hotel for a reception and dinner. The General's intermediate size room was the perfect size for the wedding party's fifty guests.

During the social hour before the meal, Ralph was seen bending Sheriff Belknap's ear. When

Palmer saw them shake hands, he knew the two had found common ground. The bride and groom personally welcomed every guest in the room. When it came to Mister and Missus Longley, Palmer quickly said, "my wife and I would like to have a business meeting with you after our honeymoon." "Why certainly, come anytime to the office on Water Street. I'm there every weekday from 1 to 4PM.

The social hour came to an end as well as the unlimited whiskey, beer, and wine. The meal included an extravagant menu. It started with an appetizer of a chutney sauce on crackers, followed by a fresh garden salad and a cup of whole yellow pea soup. Before the main meal, the palate was cleansed with a fruit puree served on ice. The coup-de-gras was the main serving of a Chateaubriand au-jus with a twice baked potato covered with sour cream. The secondary vegetable was a fresh string bean casserole. The main course was complemented with sourdough bread rolls and butter. After a waiting period, during which time coffee and tea were served, the dessert appeared. Laughter and guffaws were heard across the hall as an old fashion apple pie with ice cream was served. Mia commented, "well after the flamboyant meal we just had, I expected my dad's tasteless flambé for dessert. The pie and ice cream was a refreshing meal's ending. Now, what's this meat they call Chateaubriand?" Palmer answered, "it's the widest end of the beef tenderloin of a full-size animal. It is the most tender and tasty part of the tenderloin and adding the juice keeps the meat moist and brings out the flavor."

As the meal was finishing, Palmer asked, "who is paying for this reception and meal for over 50 guests?" Mia answered, "my parents are, this was their idea of a simple wedding reception. Besides, they are marrying their only daughter and they can afford it." "Good to know!"

At the closing of ceremonies, the Duo took the train to Deming for their honeymoon away from Silver City. Their destination was the Silver King Hotel. At registration, the newlyweds were told that a week's stay was already paid for by Archibald Longley as their wedding gift.

***

The newlyweds moved into their luxurious room with its own water closet, tub and sink, with cold and hot water. Feeling in the privacy of their apartment, the Duo quickly got comfortable with their surroundings and moved to consummate their public religious and legal marriage. To the Duo, they had consummated their love several times since the kidnapping and now the romantic coupling, as a married couple, felt no different. Yet, the time spent on their honeymoon, was a vilification to the world that their union was now a spiritual and legal union. That allowed everyone involved to call them Mister and Missus Bodine.

The next two days were spent in the suite. Pulling on the central bell for replenishing meals and intermittent liquid refreshments, the Duo spent many hours talking and getting to know the small but significant portions of their lives before their meeting. Intermittently, as the urge came alive, they would couple. Eventually, they lost all inhibitions and could reach intimacy without any holding back. It all came to their being no shame in sharing their bodies for pleasure and love.

On the third day, after baths, the Duo went downstairs to enjoy a replenishing breakfast amongst the living. After breakfast, they went for a walk along Main Street. Several of the stores concentrated on the mining industry. They saw stores specializing in mining canvas or blue-jean clothing, reinforced leather boots, rubber boots, hats with candles/reflectors, face screens, ear protection, durable gloves and more.

The one store that caught their eye was a dynamite store. For $5 the Duo took an hour course on how dynamite explodes, blasting caps, the different burning rates of fuses, when to use half sticks, how to make a controlled explosion to create straight side walls and arched tunnels, how to angle a drilled hole to cause a directed excavation and many more tips.

The last store visited, Wheeler Mining, advertised air compressors to operate small and large tools. The Duo stepped inside to learn more. The air compressor was operated by a steam plant powered by coal. That meant a minimum of an 8 or 10-inch stove pipe—with or without compressed air boosters depending on the length of travel to outside air. The size of the boiler dictated the psi of compressed air. The larger the tools, the higher the psi that was needed. For example a compressed air drill needed 90 psi. Whereas, a mucker needed up to 120 psi to load a full bucket of ore. The floor model that required 120 psi was a mucker.

Moving thru the store they came onto the slushers and muckers. The mucking model was the Finlay costing another $700. The system to operate the slusher was cheaper at $400. The narrow rails with crossties cost another $800 for 1,300 yards. The heavy-duty steel minecarts to fit the narrow gage rail tracks cost $200 each, so for six the bill added up to $1,200. The burrows or donkeys to pull out the loaded ore carts cost $50 each but included the harnesses, or $500 for ten. The compressors, boilers, air lines, and fittings cost another $700.

Mia did some quick cyphering and said, that comes to roughly $4,500." "No, better add a second musher, slusher, and air compressor/plant, and we're looking at closer to $6,500 to run two separate tunnels as Harvey suggested. Remember, it takes money to make money. If we're lucky to get our hands on that mine, the three left over stopes full of ore will pay for a major portion of these expenses or for the bulk cost of the mine itself, or both, heh."

Before leaving this last store, they made arrangements with the owner to start preparing their order for a double system that was tentatively listed for $10,000 and would cover 1200-1400 yards of rails. To activate the order, they gave a $1,000 deposit that would be refundable within 90 days.

The next morning after their usual replenishing breakfast, Mia said, "when we consummated our marriage, I never thought I would ever get enough of you. Now, I can say that I am fully satiated and very very satisfied. I think it's time to return to Silver City, get Weber Construction started, and head out to see A. Longley at his office. After all we still have an apartment to live in, till our house is built, and I'm sure our intimacy will continue uninterrupted."

"I agree, but didn't want to be the one to suggest our return to real life. Start packing and I'll go get us some tickets for the next train."

Palmer took off after changing his clothes into traveling attire. He removed his shoulder holster/pistol, and added Shorty to his side. Walking down the boardwalk, two well healed men with gunfighter rigs told him to stop and challenged him to a gunfight.

"Why are you challenging me, I don't even know you?"

"Because you killed my two brothers in Silver City."

"That's strange, I don't recall being in a gunfight with two men?"

"It wasn't a gunfight, you shot them out of the saddle with a coach-gun."

"Oh, you must mean the Gem Star Freight company attempting to steal our ore wagon-train. They were killed in self-defense since they were shooting at us."

"Don't matter, shut up and draw!"

"I'm not drawing on you, unless you draw first. I can say, if those pistols come out of their holsters, you will never get a chance to pull the hammer back. I will fire, lift you off the boardwalk and push your bodies in the mud and manure. Look around, there are at least a dozen witnesses watching."

"Too much talking! There is no way you can draw that sawed-off shotgun, cock both hammers, and pull both triggers before we plug you dead."

"Listen well, and for all to hear, this is a gunfighting shotgun. It does not have hammers to cock and it has only one trigger."

"Bull ticky, are you ready Bubba? As if on some unrecognizable sign, both men drew their pistols—BANG-BANG.

The bystanders could not believe the outcome. They all swore that they only heard one shotgun blast. Shortly afterwards, the local sheriff arrived and asked what happened. He was flooded with a dozen men who had the same story—clearly self-defense after a series of warnings.

The sheriff asked Palmer who he was. "My name is Palmer Bodine of the Bodine detective agency in Silver City." "Hold on, are you the Shotgun Kid?" "Yes sir, but I prefer you don't spread that information around town." "I was told by Sheriff Belknap that you were coming to Deming on your honeymoon. Well, from a dozen witnesses, who claim you did everything to warn these two of the outcome, even pleading to walk away, I'd say you're free to continue on without any more interruptions. Good luck son."

"Walking back in their hotel room with two tickets, Mia was crying and came into his arms. I didn't see the fight, but recognized the shotgun's double tap and saw the results. I know you're sick of killing, but I assure that with time, your need for the shotgun will fade."

"I think you're right, for now, we have two hours before the train leaves." Walking to the train yard, they spotted a bookstore. As they entered, Palmer asked, "do you have a book on inground mining in New Mexico?" "Yes we do, it's very popular and comprehensive." "Great, we'll take two copies, two notepads to take notes and two pencils."

It took little time for both readers to get involved with the information offered. Notes were taken and issues discussed. Before they knew it, the conductor announced the train's arrival in Silver City.

*****

CHAPTER 6

Mine or Bust

That evening, they discussed their approach in dealing with A. Longley. The basic strategy was to impress on the man that he didn't need this fourth mine and all the headaches, that owning it, would eventually lead to. They made a list of points to cover and the proper sequence to present them.

The next morning, Mia was armed with her Bulldog but Palmer, still leery of outlaw revenge, had his Shorty at his side. Their first stop was Weber's office to confirm that they could start construction. The agreed sequence would be: dig well, install windmill pump/holding tank, install underground pipes to the houses, design and make a filtering field, build Palmer and Mia's house, his parent's house would follow, and the two barns/corrals would be last.

After a full dinner at Grady's Diner, the Duo reviewed their notes over coffee, then left for a walk to Waters Street. Armed with their notes, they walked to his office in town at 2PM, knowing he came to work at 1PM, they gave him time to do some necessary work. Stepping in the waiting area, Palmer spoke to the receptionist. "Mister Longley invited us to a business meeting several days ago." Looking at her scheduling ledger she said, "are you the Bodine's?" "Yes Ma'am." "Please have a seat and I'll check to see if he's available." To the Duo's surprise, Mister Longley came out of his office, ahead of his receptionist, with his hand extended to Mia and Palmer to follow. "Please come in, I've been curious since the wedding why you want to see me."

After the receptionist brought some fresh coffee, Palmer started, "we have a short request and a long explanation. The short request is that we would like to buy Mine #4. Mia jumped in and said, "and the long explanation is why you need to rid yourself of this albatross."

"Most interesting, I wasn't aware that Mine #4 was for sale, nor was I aware that it was an albatross, please continue."

Mia started, "Sir, this is an old mine. The adit is supported by 6- inch timer and 2-inch ceiling boards. The wood is rotting, and several sections will need replacement, if not the entire 1200 feet to the rockface." "I wasn't aware, continue."

Palmer took over, "the air in the tunnels is thin being so far from the adit. Men are weak and barely able to walk out of the mine as it is. If an air shaft is not dug to the rockface, soon you'll have to close the mine for lack of workers." "Again, that's another shocking revelation."

Mia was next. "Digging an air shaft can be a perplexing problem. If we are digging in dirt and we place cribbing every four inches, it is doable. But if we hit rock, and cannot punch thru, the project is done. The air shaft is absolutely necessary for the survival of this mine."

Palmer was next to jump in, "if we are successful in opening an air shaft at the rock face, then we can modernize the mine. To do so, we need to bring in a coal fired steam powered air compressor with the coal fumes up an 8-10-inch stove pipe in the air shaft. With that in place, we buy air hoses, air drills, muckers and slushers." "Wow, that is going to be expensive. Is there any good news about all this?"

Mia added, "the good news was in your three other mines. The rockface was within 100 feet of the adit. Your air compressors are outside, your air hoses are short, and your ore carts don't have to travel 1200 feet to the freight wagons. That's not the case in Mine #4. It requires a large investment of money and considerable risks."

"Sir, be realistic, you don't have to deal with this. This mine's salvage is for young people with an ability to invest money and take chances. So, what price would 'pique' your interest?"

"Before we talk money, let me present the positive side, and see if you can counter my point. Last year I made $20,000 of profit from that mine and never spent a moment working on it, nor did I even go to the mine. Seems hard to beat, heh?"

Palmer said, "that is true, and today that mine is sellable. Next year if workers start dying from lack of oxygen, cave-ins, poor yielding ore, veins running out, ore wagon-train robberies, workers going on strike, liability from cave-ins, re-shoring the 1200 ft adit, and other mayhem, then your mine is worthless. Heck, you won't even be able to give it away. Now, today it is worth some good money for you if the price is right for us. Keep in mind the money we have to put in it to make it a going concern for years to come so we can get out investment back."

"Counterpoint well-presented and deserves serious consideration. Now, my spies tell me that Mine #4 has a blocked-up stope full of rich ore—in the 50-80% range. I figured that the workers and foreman Elliot were holding out on me. If I sell out, this stope is mine."

Mia smiled and added, "certainly, now how are you going to get it to the smelter. Mine #4 is five miles from Silver City over forests and boulders for outlaws to hide. It's not like your other three mines within one mile to the smelter over flat land and dessert? There is still plenty of stolen wagon-trains that appear at the smelter under existing mines and freighting companies. Without any evidence to claim stolen wagons, the smelter cannot refuse ore that appears at their doors. Do you really think your windfall ore will get to the smelter under your name?"

"I will if I hire your agency, like I did for the 90% rich ore."

Palmer had an idea, "sure, we'll guard your wagon-trains for $1,000 per each wagon-train. If your ore runs 50%, each 6 unit wagon-train will yield a profit of $400 after paying for security and labor."

"That's crazy, it's not worth the expense and worry."

"So, give us a selling price, if it's acceptable, we'll guarantee the delivery of all the ore in that blocked up stope—at no charge. If we lose a wagon-train, we'll pay you the value of the wagon-train based on the one with the highest monetary value."

Longley paused and then said, "$60,000."

Palmer came back with, "way too high, how about $45,000?"

Longley said, "no way, $55,000."

Mia frustrated with negotiations and finally put both hands in the air and said, "well, I'm sick of this dickering back and forth. We'll pay you $45,000 as Palmer said, with the wagon-train guarantee, or have a good time dealing with bankruptcy lawyers. And you can kiss the 50-80% ore goodbye, cause we ain't protecting your ore no matter what the fee. That's our offer and we're sticking to it."

Longley pushed back in his chair, looked at Palmer and said, "I think the little lady means it. WELL, LET ME TELL YOU MA'AM, I DON'T NEED YOUR MEASLY $45,000—I'LL ONLY ACCEPT $1, and the mine is yours along with the several stopes worth thousands. Yes, I know about the other blocked-up stopes." Longley stood there with a smile, as the Duo was blown away and, softly said, "but why?"

"The day you got that train to the mint saved all our life's accumulation of gold and silver. There wasn't a half million in the express car, it was one million. You thought you were protecting mostly silver and a few bars of gold. Well you were protecting gold covered with silver paint. My friends who were on this gamble with me wanted to thank you with a $50,000 gift, but I asked them to hold up till I knew what your future would be in town. Now I know and we will welcome you officially to the Mining Association at a dinner in your honor in the near future. Now let's go to the town clerk and transfer the deed."

After the deed was transferred, Longley commented, "now you have to decide what to do with my albatross. I can think of three clear options. Are you going to invest, dig an air shaft and modernize the equipment, or are you going to open up the four stopes and haul all that ore to the smelter and then close the mine?" "That's only two options, what is the third?" "Sell it and let somebody else deal with the albatross. Go home and spend a few days thinking about it, for it is your mine and your decision to make. Good luck, and I'll be watching to see which road you'll take."

***

The Duo walked back to their office in total silence. Sitting down at their desk, Mia finally spoke, "I never in a million years could have predicted what just happened!" "Now I know what it feels like to be hooked like a fish, boy we got the complete hook, line and sinker." As both started to laugh out loud. Mia then added, "did you have any idea that the bars were gold before or after the train robbery attempt?"

"Yes, after the shooting stopped, I noticed that one of the outlaw bullets hit or ricocheted and exposed the gleaming gold. I just push the bar deeper in the pile to hide it. I always wondered if something would be said, but nothing was said, and I forgot about it. Looking back Longley actually played it cool and jumped in both feet when the opportunity came up."

After a good pause, Mia finally spoke, "what's really obfuscating now is how we're going to deal with this situation. Longley was right when he said we had three choices: pull out the ore rich stopes and then close it, or sell it as is to someone else, or invest in it and turn it to our family enterprise and make money. I don't know about you, but I can't make a choice today. What do you say we take a 3-day vacation while we think about it but hold a discussion until the third day?"

"All in favor, we can go deer hunting, go fishing, go riding and check on the construction progress. I know you'll want to spend some time with your folks, and when you do, I'll spend time with Sheriff

Belknap about a related subject—the current status on stealing ore wagon-trains." "Should we discuss the matter with other people such as our parents, Mistah, Elmer Craymore, or foreman Elliot?" "No, this is our decision to make—meaning you and me alone. Actually, let's make this a real vacation and let's not even discuss the matter till three days from now, heh?" "Fine by me, but a real vacation means either plenty of sex or abstinence for three days."

"ABSTINENCE! Have you lost your mind? I'm already in distress and need your soft loving touch. Vacation means sex three times a day like three meals a day." "Well in that case, we're already late for our luncheon treat, so here's my soft loving hand."

The next three days were a real pleasure. They were living the life of the "rich and famous" with several leisurely events. A picnic by a trout pond, an overnight camping/hunting trip, day horse rides and plenty of extracurricular activities as Palmer and Mia both started using the words to announce their needs or wishes. When Mia went to visit her folks, Palmer had lunch with Sheriff Belknap.

"Have a seat sheriff, the steaks are the daily special." "I've never had steak for the noon dinner. What's the occasion Palmer?"

"Mia and I are thinking of becoming mine owners. What is currently happening with attacks on ore wagon-trains may be an important factor in making a career change." "Well hell, Palmer, you didn't have to buy me a steak for that public information, but I'll take it anyways. Since you put Gem Star Freighting out of business, things were quiet for a while."

Now in the past ten days we've had two ore wagon-train attacks where four of the twelve muleskinners were killed. That's a total of twelve ore wagons valued at $3,000 to $4,000. My investigation does not reveal any new freighting company in the area and the receiving department at the smelter claims that all deliveries were made by legitimate registered mines and their own ore wagons."

"Actually, all commercial freighters are not taking any ore deliveries because of the new risks, and that includes McMurphy Freighting. You may recall that this company was the one who hauled that ore you transferred for Longley mining. Actually,

Stan McMurphy told me yesterday that he had laid off Pappy Ruggles, his five drivers, and the six ore wagons were parked in the yard."

"Wow, that's a whole lot of info for just a steak!"

"Well, I want you to understand that gold ore will always attract outlaws. You need to remember that two dozen mines are all 1 to 10 miles from the Silver City smelter and or railhead. That's bait for outlaws, danger for shotgun riders and freighters, and a perfect place to divert an agency like yours to protect our ore wagon-trains."

"Well, that's one way to get involved with the mining industry, but that's not what we have in mind. Although, the information was very useful. Thank you and let's eat, since I see the steaks are coming."

After dinner, Palmer walked over to the construction site, their house was up with walls, windows, doors, porches, and a full roof. The finishing crew was arriving to start their work. The framing crew was heading to start the senior Bodine's house.

Palmer went to pick up Mia at the Myers' home and after a long visit, the Duo went home to their office/apartment to make supper and present their case for their future. Supper consisted of pork sausage, or bangers as commonly called, home fries, scrambled eggs and coffee. During supper, Palmer told Mia about the fine details he had acquired from Sheriff Belknap. After cleaning up the utensils, the Duo sat on the sofa for an intimate discussion.

Palmer started first, "ladies customarily go first, so Mia this is your chance to speak your mind."

"All I want in life is to be with you. I cannot choose which option to take, since it doesn't matter to me. What matters is for you to choose the one you want, and I'll support you 100%."

"By saying that, you're putting our future's choice 100% on my shoulders." "That is true, but I know that I have a wise man for a husband, so speak your mind."

"Alright. First, selling it to someone else is totally absurd. Had that been Longley's goal, they would have given us that $50,000 gift and be done with us. Secondly, emptying the four stopes of rich ore and transferring it to the smelter needs to be done, but closing the mine afterwards is also absurd. True, we could then sell it as an operational mine, but selling it was again not Longley's goal."

"The only answer that makes any sense is what we had originally wanted when we walked into Longley's office and tried to buy the mine. This mine is a challenge and a mission. We need to make this enterprise a long-term family business that will support us, our children, and our grandchildren. The logo 'Bodine Mining' will eventually stand for success."

"That does it, the die is cast. Now that you've got me all fired up, you need to put out my fire, and it may take all night."

***

The next morning, after a replenishing breakfast, the Duo walked over to McMurphy Freighting. Stan came over and asked, "what brings the Bodine Agency to my doors this morning?" "It's no longer the Agency but 'Bodine Mining,' we are now the new owners of the Longley # 4 Mine. We would like to talk to you about freighting our ore."

"Sorry to say, but I'm no longer freighting ore to the smelter. I cannot stand telling the families of my freighters that their loved ones won't be coming home."

"I see, well we saw six heavy duty wagons parked outside. Are they for sale?" "Yes, I'm asking $100 each. I also have seven teams of full-size draft horses, 3 teams of Percherons and 4 teams of Belgians. The draft horses are hard to find, and they include the heavy-duty harnesses. These sell for $500 a team." "Why the extra team?" "To have a spare to relieve a lame horse or the like. It's not to run seven wagons."

Mia said, "so $4,100 will cover it as she hands Stan a bank draft for the exact amount." "Heck, yes. I'll even include two large saddles that fit these beasts in case you ever need to ride one in an emergency for they are all saddle broke."

Palmer then took over, "can we leave the horses in your barn till we have a barn or shelter built at the mine?" "Of course."

"Of interest, what happens to the freighters who were driving these wagons?" "They were all laid off and are likely spending time walking around town looking for work. Actually, Pappy Ruggles is due this morning to come to my office for the laid off drivers last paycheck."

"Do you mind if I try to hire them?" "Heck no, matter of fact, I'd feel better knowing they found work."

Waiting for Pappy, the Duo went to inspect the wagons and the draft horses. When Pappy arrived, he immediately spotted the duo and went to greet them. "Hello Pappy, heard the bad news. Just to let you know, we now own Longley Mine # 4, those six wagons and dozens of draft horses. Now we need some freighters. Are you interested?"

"Now that's a silly question, heck I'd be happy to work for you, and I'm sure the other five freighters will join me."

Mia added, "but you didn't ask what your pay will be or what your schedules and duties will entail!"

'Your right, so let me locate the other drivers and we can meet at Grady's Diner in one hour." "Agree."

During that hour, Palmer made a stop at Weber's to place a quick order and said he'd be back in a couple hours. On time, as the Duo arrived at Grady's, the six men were waiting on the boardwalk. Mia welcomed them and said, "thank you for coming, let's have some coffee and after our meeting we'll buy you dinner."

Palmer started the conversation, "as Pappy likely told you, we are now the new owners of Longley's Mine # 4. We have also purchased your old boss's freight wagons and draft horses. Today, we are looking for full time freighters."

Mia continued, "we know that there is a new gang of robbers that steal ore wagon-trains. What we can promise you is that until these outlaws are killed or arrested, we will provide the same four Navaho Indians that we used to protect Longley's last high-end ore train when the Star Gem Agency was the organized outlaws. Our wagons still have the same protective steel plates, and you'll all have your own new speed shotgun that we use with a single trigger and no hammers to cock."

Palmer took over, "your pay will be $130 a month for five day's work. Each workday, you'll take one wagon-train five miles to the smelter and back. You will be responsible for the care of your draft horses seven days a week, this includes feeding, mucking the stalls, repairing the harnesses and staying over the weekend in the living quarters On the weekends, you will also act as a mine guard and remuda wrangler. The weekend warrior gets an extra $20 in his pay. Like the mine workers we provide medical payments if injured on the job, life insurance of $1,000 if killed on the job, and continuing monthly income till you return to work. And that's what the situation is and what we are offering. Does anyone want to sign on knowing there is bound to be some shooting involved?" Pappy's hand went up as well as the other five men. "Great, the job starts in seven days when the barn is built."

Leaving the diner, the Duo stopped at Weber's and picked up two preordered signs that said "Bodine Mining for the mine office, and one that said "Bodine Mine # 1" for the mine adit. They also arranged to have a barn built at the mine for 24 horses with a loft to hold the necessary feed, a tack room, an overnight room with a heat/cookstove and facilities, and a hand pump well for the horses. Next was White's Hardware where they arranged for a steady delivery of quality hay and oats. Their last stop was the Community Bank where they opened a mining account with a $10,000 transfer. Harvey Elliot was included on the account to make deposits and withdrawals. Thereafter, they picked up their horses at Foster's Livery and rode out to the mine.

***

After an hour, they arrived at the mine. The first thing they did was to exchange the two signs and walked in the office where Harvey was waiting at the door. "Well welcome, I presume you are the new owners, and let me be the first to congratulate you on your purchase. I've got some great news for you. Let's go in the mine so I can show you two great finds."

Arriving at the rockface, Harvey blew the whistle and called for a quick meeting. "Well boys, it is done, say hello to your new mine owners Palmer and Mia Bodine. Applause, whistles and guffaws were all around. Palmer spoke, "there will be many changes made that you will all benefit, the biggest is profit sharing. Until we establish the ratio, we are doubling your monthly pay and to help you pay your past bills, tonight Harvey will hand you $100 as a 'signing on' bonus. Harvey will keep you posted on the new developments."

With the men back to work, Harvey said, "step over here please. What do you feel?" Mia said, "there's an updraft that is moving my hair." Harvey lit a stogie and to everyone's surprise the smoke disappeared upwards. The three looked up and the Duo could see the sun shining thru the rock crawlspace. "What in blazes is that?"

"We had an earthquake and this natural funnel opened up, we enlarged the bottom section and since then, the updraft is sucking fresh air from the adit. The men have new stamina because of the fresh air."

Palmer added, "is the updraft strong enough to handle a coal powered boiler/air compressor?" "Absolutely." "Then telegraph Wheeler Mining in Deming and order one along with drills, air hoses, a Finlay mucker, a slusher and rails. We'll talk more about this later, what is the second find you mentioned?"

Walking down a crosscut, Harvey said, "you may remember that we found a new vein that looked promising. Well here it is, look at that quartz rock, there is a clear yellow deposit that is almost pure gold. The Duo picked up some ore on the ground and said, "this ore will yield a high content of gold, but we don't see much silver."

"Who cares, with the silver crash pending, the US currency will be backed by the gold standard of $20 an ounce while silver is dropping fast to less than a dollar an ounce. "So, gold is worth $320 a pound while silver is worth less than $16 a pound." "Correct." "Ok, let's go to your office, we have much to discuss."

***

Sitting with a fresh cup of coffee, Palmer started, "we've prepared a list of changes, let's go thru them and then you can ask questions or add you requests." "Ok, I'll take notes."

1. "We started a bank account called Bodine Mining and you are on the account. That means you have complete access to the $10,000 balance. Here is your own booklet of bank vouchers.

2. Place that order with Wheeler Mining as we discussed and pay him with a telegraph voucher. Include shipping to the mine via McMurphy.

3. We bought McMurphy's freight wagons and draft horses. We've added five full time freighters who will care for the horses. A barn will be built by Weber and you will have weekend watchmen who care for the horses on weekends and spend the nights in the barn living quarters.

4. You need to start hiring more miners to enable emptying the stopes. See the employment office and ask for Emmett McGivern and miners.

5. We need a bunkhouse to house up to twenty men to start with.

6. We need a cookshack and dining hall. The dining hall will also serve as a meeting room.

7. We need to triple the size of this office, we need a reception counter and a waiting area to deal with employees or business appointments, plus Mia and I need our own offices.

8. Within 10 days, we want to start shipping ore from the four stopes. Have the men unblock stope the entrances. Once we start transferring the ore, we'll do one six-wagon-train every day. Have the men load up the ore minecarts and hold them at the adit. Once the wagons return,

have the men transfer the ore, the same day, to the freight wagons. That way, the wagon-train will be ready to roll by daybreak.

9. Hire an independent team and get a 3X3 ft air shaft built, asap.

10. Hire a dynamite expert to minimize excessive useless rock around the gold while maintaining cleaner crosscuts and tunnels.

11. Hire a receptionist/secretary/accountant for the three of us."

"Now it's your turn"

"Wow, this is a revelation. So, let's quickly go over each one.

1. The bank account. Just a surprise, and thank you to allow me to use it as I see fit.

2. Wheeler Mining------will do.

3. Weekend watchmen, good idea. Will have Weber add a large corral.

4. Hiring miners. Ironically, McGivern's miners have already applied.

5. Bunkhouse. You place order with Weber and I'll take care of the layout, etcetera.

6. Cookshack, you give Weber the order, I'll hire a cook and layout the kitchen with the cook. Dining/meeting room a great idea.

7. Triple office size, give Weber the order and I'll prepare the lay out.

8. The stopes, they'll be open and ready.

9. I've already been working on finding a team to dig a cribbed air shaft. I found one team of four men in Lordsburg and they can be here in a matter of days. I will arrange the delivery of timber and hardware.

10. A dynamite expert is a great idea. I'll notify the headhunters in Deming to start looking for one. Likely, it will be a Swede.

11. A secretary. That is a great one. It will need to be a man who can travel the five miles or a miner's wife. I'll line up candidates for interviews. Would you do the interviews and make your choice?"

Mia answered, "yes, one of us will and it will likely be me."

***

Back in town, the Duo went to the construction office. "Mister Weber, we have more work for you." "Stop right there, it's time you call me Marc, for Mister Weber was my dad." "Fair enough, and we're Palmer and Mia." "Now, what do you need other than that large barn at the mine."

"We need a bunkhouse for twenty men with heating stoves, a cookshack with a handpump well and a large dining/meeting room, and we need to triple the size of the office."

"I see, and of course, you need everything started tomorrow, as I would like. So, here is a proposal. Please allow me to subcontract the three barns you need, starting with the one at the mine. I will use competitor carpenters to work with my men and build your three barns. My regular carpenters will start working on the office expansion to get you into your own office. When that's done, the bunkhouse will be next. By then, the framing team working on your houses will be able to work on the cookshack and dining/meeting room. The finishing team will be done with your house in a week and can do the finishing work in your office and other buildings at the mine. I predict that in a month, you'll be done with construction, including the finish work."

"Will the barn at the mine be ready in ten days?" "With the extra carpenters, it will be ready for horses five days from now. Have White's Hardware deliver hay and oats the sixth day."

With the wheels in motion, the Duo decided to set up a meeting with Mistah, and the three trained Navajo Indians—Red, Whitey and Bluey. Taking a quiet corner in Grady's Diner, Mia and the five men ordered beefsteaks with baked potatoes and beans. After dinner, Mia started by giving the four Indians a synopsis of events since acquiring the mine including Sheriff Belknap's assessment of the recent wagon-train attacks and Pappy Ruggles' team joining Bodine Mining.

Palmer then got down to specifics. "I want to hire you four as permanent guards on the ore wagon-trains. We will make a run each day from dawn to the smelter, and back to the mine by 1PM. One way or another, in a week's time, we will rid the countryside of these ore wagon-train outlaws, including the organizers if any exist. For pay, I will offer you $25 a trip as combat pay. Once the outlaws are dead or in jail, if any have outstanding wanted posters, we'll divide the bounty rewards evenly. Once the danger from outlaws passes, we would like to maintain some degree of security on the ore wagon-trains with at least two armed guards per wagon-train at the same pay rate as the freighters which is $130 a month, plus bounty rewards from failed outlaw attacks."

All four Indians were glad to sign on. The Indians needed the income to support their families which were scattered about between Silver City and Deming. During the next week, the Duo was busy checking on the house's final details. The furniture was arriving by train on a daily basis and by the end of the week, the Duo moved in their house. The first night was a momentous occasion as new homeowners and lovers in their own abode.

Each day, they went to the mine to check on changes. The barn went up quick with eight men on the job. Before moving the remuda to the mine, Gideon Ackerman (wheelwright) had come to McMurphy's and taken the measurements for wheel and axle replacements. Once the barn was ready, the freighters brought the remuda of draft horses harnessed to their wagons along with the miscellaneous tack, leather parts, and hardware for harness repairs.

As soon as the office was ready, the Duo arranged for the delivery of office furniture. The Duo's office had a large double-ended desk with filing cabinets, and a typewriter for Mia. The day came for interviews. Mia had a clear choice; the town clerk was getting married and needed a change to support a wife and family. He offered typing, ledger maintenance, payroll, general accounting and was a vigorous man to run necessary messages deep to the mine's rock face where the worksite foreman was located. That same day, the Duo made it clear to Harvey that he no longer was the working foreman, but the mine's general manager. He was asked to name a new worksite foreman.

With the remainder of the construction well underway, the Duo was ready to start transferring the four stope's ore to the smelter. With Harvey's estimate that one stope had 30 wagon loads, two with 45 wagon loads and one with 60 wagon loads, the total of +- 200 wagon loads presented a big job. At six wagons a day or 30 wagons a week, the freighters were looking at almost seven weeks of work. Fortunately, Harvey had hired eight more miners who had the job of loading the ore minecarts, moving them with donkeys to the outside, and then transferring the ore to freight wagons for morning transport.

The next morning, with the sun creeping over the horizon, Palmer nodded to Pappy as he yelled, "ok boys, keep your loaded shotguns close by and let's take the gold to mama."

*****

CHAPTER 7

Ore Wagon-trains

The draft horses were moving along at a comfortable fast walk of approximately 3 mph. If they kept this pace, they would be at the smelter by 8AM opening time. During the five miles, Palmer was keeping an eye out for signs of attacking outlaws, but was also noting the terrain, background vegetation, forested areas, boulders, ambush sites especially around a bend in the road, open areas and long-range sniper locations. He had asked Mia and Mistah to also be on the lookout for ambush sites and sites ideal for short range attacks on horseback.

With a good road and good horses, they easily made the 5-mile trek in an hour and thirty minutes, without any conflicts. At the smelter's gate, a security guard asked for some identification and provenance for the ore. Palmer spoke, "my name is Palmer Bodine, and I'm the new owner of Longley # 4 mine. Here is my deed signed by Archibald Longley and registered at the town clerk's office. The guard smiled, looked at the papers, and said, "just like I was told by Mister Longley, welcome to the mining industry and to the Silver City smelter. Just pull up to the receiving door in red and the receiving clerk will take care of you."

Pappy whispers to Palmer, his name is Flint Banning, and he's a bossy dickhead. Don't try to make points against him, cause he'll dock our scale and rob us. Just play along, he'll get his due eventually."

Stopping inside the gate, Banning was surprised to see a wagon-train under a new name. Mia was watching and listening from the second wagon in line, without knowing Pappy's warning. "Hey buster, are you going to reread those over and over. We'd like to unload and get back to reload."

"Well little lady, a bit of a rush, aren't you?" "I'm not a little lady, I'm the boss's wife and co-owner of this mine. So, get that stick out of your ass or send us the shop foreman to do your job so we can move along."

"Whatever, each wagon steps on the scale before and after so we can get the total tonnage. That way we can give you the % of precious metal each wagon-train contains. We keep the empty wagon's weight, so you don't have to weigh empty after each load. Just don't remove the wagon's number on the left side wall. Bay 11 is your bay to unload your six wagons." Palmer added, "boy, I don't like that dude's attitude, Mia just slapped him off, so we can expect some crappy payback."

While the freighters and Indians were manually unloading each wagon, the Duo went looking for a tour of the facility. Meeting up with the shop foreman, Ansel Hall, they were directed to Dean Herman, the tour guide. After introductions were done, a new customer to the smelter was due a free tour.

Dean started, "your ore in bay 11 will be given a tag number which will be permanent till the metals are in bricks. The first step is to move the ore to the hammer mill where each rock is hammered, or pulverized, to a powder. Then the powder is transferred to a furnace where it is exposed to low heat to rid the powder of sulfur—this is the roasting stage."

"The roasted ore is then transferred to a bedding floor where it is fluxed with limestone and other reducing agents. These agents allow the release of metals from the ore. The next step is to dump the mixed ore powder with limestone into furnaces. The natural heat is enhanced to higher temperatures by blasting air into the fire—thus calling it a blast furnace."

"As the temperature of the mix increases, tin is first to melt at 450 degrees F. and is then poured off. The next is lead at 650 degrees and so on with Yellow Brass 1660, silver 1761, gold 1945, and copper 1983. Our blast furnace can reach 2000 degrees F. and we don't produce Iron or Steel at 2100 to 2800 degrees F. Four your information most of the precious metals we extract are gold and silver. Yet, the other metals have to be removed by manual ladling from the floating mix to keep the gold and silver bullion as pure as possible. Once the gold, silver and copper are poured off into bricks, whatever is left over is called slag and it basically consists of soft rock, granite, quartz, iron and steel; and has no value in this community."

Mia was curious and asked, "can you give us an idea of what a freight wagon loaded with ore could possibly yield?" "Sure, this is such an example of rich ore in the 50-80% range for one standard size freight wagon:

- Ore=three tons eventually turns to +-three tons of slag.

- Gold=one pound, or $320.

- Silver=three pounds, or $32.

- Copper=one or two pounds, ? value.

- Tin=quarter of a pound, ? value.

- Lead=half a pound, ? value.

- Yellow brass one eighth of a pound, ? value.

Palmer was thinking, "I can see making ingots for gold, silver, and copper. What do you do with tin, lead and yellow brass?"

"We pour these small amounts in a steel mold and keep adding to them from meld to meld. At the end of a month, those miniscule amounts are now worth some good money for you."

Mia then asked, "at the end of the day, what do you do with our precious metals, including the minor ones."

"Today, we'll assign you your own vault with your key. Only you and the floor foreman can open your vault. Today's batch number is placed in your vault. Tomorrow the batch number will also be stored in your vault. When there is a demand from the mint, a train load of gold and silver will be shipped for all our customers. If the buyers announce a need for lead, you'll be able to dispose of your lead. We keep a tally of which metal you have. If you find a private buyer, you are free to withdraw the metal and do a private sale. If you need to convert gold or silver to meet expenses, then your local bank will buy your gold and give you cash."

The Duo's last question, "how does the smelter get paid for its services."

"We charge $50 for a standard freight wagon containing three tons of ore. Anything above three tons is an extra $20 a ton. We expect payment at the end of each week which is why the banks stay open till 8PM on Fridays so we can close the weekly accounts. If you don't settle by Friday evening, then the next time you arrive with ore wagons, you will be delayed to the sideline till you go exchange gold or silver for cash. Because you have ingots in your vault, paying your processing expenses should not be a problem. Finally, the next time you make a delivery we'll give you the receipt for the weight of each precious metal from your previous delivery."

"Well, thank you for your time. It has been enlightening."

> Meanwhile, as the tour was in progress, the first wagon was unloaded and Paddy had left the wagon parked out of sight, while he ran to the privy. During this time, two men walked up to his wagon, applied a saw on the bottom part of an axle and sawed thru half the axle. When Paddy was seen on his way back, the men on the saw disappeared without cleaning up the sawdust. When Paddy arrived, Banning told him to

move his wagon to the outside yard to
wait for the other wagons.

By the time the tour was done, the Duo returned to the receiving area as the last wagon was being weighed. Banning gave them a receipt for their six-wagon delivery. As they walked out, Palmer commented, "I wonder what that smirk on his face meant?" Mia did not say anything because she was trying to figure out why there was fresh sawdust on the concrete floor. Palmer answered, "must be because they use sawdust to flux out impurities in the meld."

The ride back to the mine was uneventful and the wagon-train arrived at 12:30PM. The workers were waiting with loaded minecarts to start the ore transfer to the freight wagons for tomorrow's delivery. The loaded wagons were then parked side by side, wheels were blocked up along with the wheel brake on, and the horses walked to the barn for water and feed before spending the day and night in the corral.

Walking back to the office, Paddy came along. "You know boss, those draft horses did well today and will do well all week, but after that they will weaken and that's not good." "What do you suggest?" "I really feel we need to add another team of draft horses or at least large gelding harness horses, as is used in cultivating land. I think you need to talk to Hector Foster about getting some soon." "Ok, I agree. Along with this, I'll have Weber increase the size of the barn to hold 35 horses."

***

Getting to town, the Duo went to the furniture store to order the furnishings. Elmer had already ordered the appliances to include kitchen sink, cooking stove, manually operated washing machine with clothes ringer, water closet with wash basin, and several coal heating stoves. The furniture store had the balance, parlor sofa and chairs, dining table and chairs, hutch, sidebar, kitchen table and chairs, bedroom sets for at least three rooms, and miscellaneous tables. The office furniture would come from the old office next to Craymore's Mercantile. Since all these items came from Deming, they would arrive in two days.

Their next stop was Foster's Livery. "Hector, we need some horses to help the draft horses, in tandem, haul our ore to the smelter. What do you suggest?" "Boy, that's become a problem. The draft horses have all been sucked up by every mine in the area. The local horse ranches are still putting out some nice work geldings and the harness shop is keeping up with the demand for heavy duty harnesses in tandem. At the present time, I can get you some ready geldings with harnesses for $200 a head by tomorrow evening, since the harnesses were pre-made for each horse. They'll be directly delivered to your mine by the horse ranchers."

"Have you seen these horses?" "Yes sir, and these teams are three-year old top horse flesh, well trained and well matched. Plus they are guaranteed, if they don't work out, the rancher will either replace the horse or the team itself. As an added benefit, they are all saddle broke."

"Fine, we need seven teams. Here is a bank draft for $2,800. How much do we owe you for your services? "Not a dime, the rancher pays me a 5% commission and I'm happy with that. As soon as I close up today, I'll be heading to the ranch to help the owner get these horses ready, and in the morning, I'll help him get the remuda to your mine."

That evening, after a less than adequate sexual encounter, Mia asked Palmer what was preoccupying him. "There is something nagging at me and I can't find the solution." "What is it all about?" "About finding sawdust on the floor of the smelter." "I thought you said they might be using it to flux the metals!" "I know, but if that was the case, it should be near the cauldron, not on the receiving floor. Besides, you can't get close enough to that meld to add sawdust, mix it in, and scrape off the dross it creates, Also besides, fluxing sawdust used in making lead bullets is a fine sawdust, this was very course material as is produced by a bucksaw." "Well, the only thing that could have produced that sawdust is our wagons. So, let's get there by daylight and do a very careful check of all six wagons."

Skipping breakfast and in full darkness, the Duo took the main road to their mine. Arriving at daybreak, they walked to the loaded wagons and found Paddy leaning on a wagon, with a stogie in his mouth and his shotgun on his arm. "What are you doing here this early?"

"Well, I had a meeting with the freighters and suggested we stand guard till this issue with outlaws is settled. Besides, we already are planning to do it on weekends anyways, so we started early, and I was volunteered to take the first night."

The Duo then explained why they arrived so early. Examining the first wagon, which was Paddy's and Palmer's, Mia saw something strange. "Palmer, look how that front left wheel is tipping inwards." "I guess so, OMG, look at the bottom part of the axle, there is a half inch gap in the wood and the tip of the axle is pointing upwards. That gap is a cut made by a saw."

Paddy and Palmer started blocking up the wagon, with the help of a wagon jack, they relieved the pressure on the axle before it broke off and ended up tearing spokes out of the wheel, or worse.

When the freighters arrived, thanks to having spare axles in the barn, they changed the vandalized one for one of Ackerman's original replacements. As they were ready to roll, Palmer warned everyone that an attack would occur today since the vandalized axle would have let go in short order. The altered axle was brought along to show the damage to Sheriff Belknap.

With everyone on high alert, the freighters had the reins under the seat and were holding the reins from the wagon floor protected by the steel plates. Within two miles of the mine, the attack started. Over two dozen riders appeared out of the woods galloping full steam and shooting at the wagons. Surprised to see wagons moving without riders made them lose their concentration. The armed men in the wagons let go the buckshot as outlaws came at them with a fatal frontal attack. Every Indian and freighter's first shot blew an outlaw out of the saddle. The Duo waited for the first volley to end when they stood up and let go two shots a piece. Four more outlaws were down. The remaining half dozen were trying to pick up their wounded buddies, when they were again cut down along with outlaws who came to the rescue. By the time the outlaws got to the protection of the tree-line, only three killer outlaws got away.

Palmer exclaimed, "these outlaws have shit for brains. Whoever heard of a frontal attack, on horseback, against well-armed and trained guards and freighters. In addition, the defense is sitting behind protective plates on a stationary platform. The leader of that gang was dumber than a box of rocks." Mia added, "you can't fix stupid. In this case, their stupidity was to our advantage."

Palmer took advantage of the windfall and instructed the freighters and Indians to check their pockets for ID's and cash. Red, Whitey and Blue gathered the boots, hats and any clean replacement shirts, vests or pants to give to their tribe. The collected pocket cash from 20 dead outlaws came to $800. That was divided between the six freighters and the four Indians along with ammo collected. The pistols, gunbelts, scabbards and rifles were packed in saddlebags or bedrolls for a later sale. At the end, the outlaws were tied to their horses' saddles and brought to Sheriff Belknap for matching to wanted posters.

Mia stayed with the sheriff to help with the identification process and telegraph notices for collecting the bounty rewards. By the time they finished, the wagon-train arrived to pick up Mia. The sheriff finished by identifying 14 of the 20 dead men. He then gave Mia a certificate releasing the brands on the outlaws' horses, so anyone could sell or own the branded horse. Sheriff Belknap gave Mia a special note acknowledging that six of the horses had the brand C—M/F which was registered under Chapman Mining and Freighting Company

As the wagon-train arrived at the smelter, Banning was clearly behaving strange while providing a furtive look. It was clear to Palmer that Banning never expected for the Bodine wagon-train to be arriving at the smelter. To make it worse, the sabotaged axle had been forgotten in one of the ore wagons and had to be put aside to unload the wagon. Banning kept looking in the direction of the axle but kept a straight face.

After the wagons were unloaded and Palmer given a receipt for the tagged wagons, he was directed to the floor foreman, Ansel Hall. This time, with Palmer away from the receiving area, no wagon was left unwatched. "Well Mister Bodine, your first wagon-train was very rich in gold. A 3-ton wagon of your ore yielded one pound of gold worth $320. That is really amazing. Anyways, the value of your first 6-wagons was $1,971. Of which $1,850 was in gold, plus minor amounts of silver, copper, tin, lead, and yellow brass. Here is a receipt of the actual weight of each metal. Do you wish to take your bullion or leave it in our individual vaults? For your security, Lloyds of London insures our vaults up to $25,000." "Well with insurance, it can stay here. I'll just keep my receipts."

Making their way to the sheriff's office, Palmer finally showed him the vandalized axle. Sheriff Belknap volunteered to visit the smelter and plant a seed of suspicion on Flint Banning and Ansel Hall. If either were involved, repercussions would quickly follow—which is what Palmer wanted. When Sheriff Belknap arrived at the smelter, Banning had claimed some illness and left work. Hall was the receiving agent and was not pleased to hear the sheriff ask questions about a sabotaged axle. His only comments, "sheriff, I know nothing about this, but I will confront Banning when he returns to work." "That's assuming he ever returns Mister Hall!"

Meanwhile at Chapman's Mine # 1, Banning was rattling off a series of events that would find him guilty of sabotage. Walter Chapman knew that this babbling idiot would end up implicating himself and his men. Without any warning, in front of several outlaws, he drew his pistol and shot Banning in the face. Chapman finally spoke, "Six of those confiscated horses had my brand on them. The sheriff will soon be here and find the mine boarded up and inactive. The die is now cast. We've made some good money as the old Gem Star Freight and now Chapman Mining. It's time to leave here, head for our cabin deep in the forest, and come out to kill off this entire team of Bodine agents and their freighters. Then we're out of New Mexico and heading to Wyoming where we can restart our trade in their mines." His remaining six men quickly agreed that like the Colorado mines, this type of caper had duration limits, and when the odds of failure were too high, it was time to leave,

restart somewhere else, and fine new
men to add to the gang.

That night, Palmer was feeling at peace and was
able to perform at his best. Mia was stunned and
finally found some energy to finally speak. "My
goodness, in a million years, I would never have
imagined what it would be like to let your husband
run loose. Now I know, I thought my brain was
going to explode."

Getting over the afterglow, Mia asked, "what do
you expect the outlaws will pull tomorrow?" "Since
their numbers are significantly down, I think they
will try to ambush us with rifles at that location
with large boulders." "Do we run for it or do we
fight. The yardage with rifles will be beyond our
shotguns, and other than you or me, the guards are
not very good with rifles." "We do neither, I have a
secret weapon." "I know, go with it for now, heh?"

That morning, each man had a bow, arrows,
a bag of goodies, and cigars to go around lit at
all times. When Mia realized what Palmer had
planned, she commented, "I see you have more
fireworks in mind, like you ravaged me last night,
heh." "Ay-yup, seeing those blue stars was certainly

a lot of fun." "Well, please explain what is going on, since I'm always with you, how did you arrange this without my knowledge?"

"Yesterday, when we arrived back at the mine, you ran to the privy. I went to see Harvey and arranged this caper as prepared by our new dynamite expert from Sweden, Mister Liam Johansson. He would prepare half and full length sticks attachable to arrow shafts with special short fuses that would not extinguish in mid-flight."

"Before we came back to town, Mistah and the three Indians trained the freighters in lobbing their arrows at 40, 60, or 75 yards. This morning, Paddy made sure that all our horses had their ears stuffed with cotton, and here are yours. You and I will keep outlaws pinned down with our rifles while the men attach dynamite to the arrows and light the fuses with their cigars. When the dynamite starts going off, get down behind the steel plates and cover your ears with your hands."

With a nod from Palmer, Paddy slapped the reins on the horses' backs to start the wagon-train moving. One mile from the mine, the area full of large boulders, 60 yards from the road, came into view. The Duo had their rifles up and ready while the four Indians were attaching dynamite to arrows. The freighters knew the ambush was about to start, and jumped in the wagon bed while holding the reins under the top seat. As if on orders to fire, several outlaws popped their heads over the boulders and started firing at the rider-less wagons. The first four full length sticks were airborne and landed in sequence. KABOOM, BOOM, BOOM, KABOOM.

Palmer was amazed, two outlaws were propelled above their boulders and landed in front of the boulders. Other outlaws were laid out flat and obviously unconscious. Several were on hands and knees retching and dry heaving. Hats were thrown every which way, and dirt and rocks were landing on the wagon-train. When some outlaws started getting up and going for their rifles, ten men let go a barrage of half sticks. This last volley brought stillness from the boulders. Eventually the outlaws made their way back to their horses and escaped.

Mia then asked Palmer, "what do we do, do we go after them and take advantage of their debilitated state or do we just let them ride off while we continue to the smelter?"

"Our responsibility is to this wagon-train and our men's security. We'll go after them later today. They won't be in any fighting shape for a few days."

At the smelter, things went smoothly. Ansel Hall introduced the new receiving agent. Elton Brayden was a local man who worked just about every job in the shop. This job had security and tenure for a man with years of loyalty. The Duo was introduced and quickly realized that this man exhibited a natural presence, an amiable personality, and a voice of authority. Before Ansel left, he gave the Duo their receipt for the second wagon-train. According to the weights, the last wagon-train was again worth +- $1,900.

Arriving back at the mine, Hector Foster was standing by the barn's entrance with a new man. "Hello folks, this is Nash Downing of the Bar D Ranch. Your 7 teams of work geldings are in the barn. Each horse has been matched with one that has the same personality and physical ability. Before you unhitch your present draft horses, we want to attach a team of geldings to every draft horse team presently on the wagons. That way, we'll know if the tandem teams can work together." Paddy was hopping happy, "wow, I thought we freighters would have to do that alone. That is great service and the six of us will help you out to do the matching."

The Bodine Trio and the corresponding Navajo Trio went to get their saddle horses and load up the shotguns and rifles. Within a half hour they had eaten a quick snack and were on the trail to where the ambush had been fought. Mistah and his friends quickly found the tracks in and out of the ambush site and were already following the tracks. It took an hour to find the cabin where the outlaws were hiding.

Walking, in their moccasins, to within 50 yards they all had to duck when an outlaw came flying out of the front door, while vomiting all over the porch. The apparent leader was screaming, "throw up in a bucket, the privy, or outside. No more emptying your insides on the floor, this place is beginning to smell like the pit of a privy." As he was giving these orders, he apparently slipped and looking down at the cause yelled out, "which of you animals dropped a turd on the floor." "It couldn't be helped;

I was so dizzy that I fell down and couldn't get up." The leader just grumbled, took off his socks and went back to bed.

The two Trio's heard everything and finally Palmer came down with a plan. Mistah, there is a good amount of smoke coming out of that pipe. If we can hoist you up, would you plug up the stove pipe and when I give you a signal, drop a stick of dynamite down the pipe and get off that roof, in a real hurry." "For sure!" The Navajo Trio added, "we can make a triangle standing on our shoulders and can hoist Mistah right on the roof."

From afar, the Duo saw the Navajo's hoist Mistah up. Withing 30 seconds of plugging up the stove pipe, someone yelled, "Useless #1, get up and open the damper, the damn thing must have closed again, and hurry." "Boss, the damper is open, and the smoke just keeps coming in. What do I do?" "Open the door to the firebox to increase the up draft, it's probably just a bad downdraft. Useless #1 did as told. Opening the door added air to a choking fire as a flame blast burned Useless's face like a tomato pealing in boiling water. Now Useless was screaming to high heaven as the cabin filled with dark suffocating smoke. Outlaws were trying to get up, but slipping in the goop on the floor. Eventually, seven men made it out as Mistah dropped the stick and took off.

The Indians had barely made it to safety as the blast let go. The Duo later recalled how the outlaws on the ground were blown flat in the dirt, the roof lifted up at least three feet before collapsing to the floor, all four side walls were laid flat and on fire. The furniture had been totally torn up and the cabin remnants were all on fire.

Stepping up to the barely conscious outlaws, their hands were tied in the front so they could later hold on to the saddle horn. When Whitey came back from the barn with the outlaw horses, he said, "boss, you'd better go see what is next to the barn, the corral, and the tack room."

Everyone followed Whitey back and to everyone's shock, Whitey said, "surprise, surprise, surprise. That's 10 wagons, 20 draft horses and tack to match. Plus a pile of burnt out wagons, hardware and steel wheel rims." Palmer explained the finding, "the Gem Star freight company has been robbing wagon-trains for years, and the burnt pile was likely the result of their thieving days. What happened to the horses is anyone's guess. Now these intact wagons are current, and those draft horses probably match the wagons and the harnesses. We'll bring a sample to Sheriff Belknap and see what he wants to do about the others."

***

Arriving in town with the seven outlaws secured to their horses' single stirrup, Sheriff looked at all the outlaws' faces when he exclaimed, "Walter Chapman, is that you? So that explains why Foster said six of those 20 horses you brought in had the Chapman Mining brand on them. Something tells me that we're going to have some wanted posters on you boys. Palmer, I'm still getting telegraph vouchers on the 20 outlaws you brought in yesterday, Hector Foster is still trying to ship their horses to other liveries, and now we have 7 more outlaws and 7 more horses. Better plan on a week before we can settle up. But

you didn't include pistols or rifles—what's with them?" "We've decided to keep all firearms to distribute to our freighters, guards, miners and anyone working for us. Now what do we do with the ten wagons and the 20 draft horses we found at the outlaws' cabin?" "For now, leave this wagon and horses on hold at Foster's livery, and I'll speak to Judge Hawkins and get a ruling." "Ok, see you in a week."

That night before supper, the Duo rode over to the new house. The carpenters were finishing the painting, wallpapering and installation of all stoves. The freight office was delivering the furniture and the hardware. Louisa Barkley, the Duo's neighbor and Craymore's employee, appeared to be in charge of where the different pieces were laid out. Louisa said, "you will be able to move in tomorrow night, or you can wait till the barn is built which is scheduled to be done in three days."

After supper, the Duo sat on their sofa and started talking about the future. Mia said, "With the wagon-train thieves out of business, how much longer do we provide security before we let Mistah and his Trio take over?" "Funny I was thinking the same thing, are you sure you can't read my mind?" "Well, I can to a certain extent. I certainly can tell when you want to get intimate." "Heck, that's not mind reading, that's simply looking at my tenting crotch. But besides that, I think we need to see how the new gelding horses work with the draft horses. If everything goes well, I'll authorize Ansel Hall to give the shipment receipts to Mistah, our head of security."

"I agree, so to answer my question, what is our next step?"

"Don't be shocked, but we are both entering the mine with the miners and we're going to work with them. Actually, I'm going to work with them, and you're going to watch and take notes. That's how we are going to know what we need to change in order to make our mine efficient, modern, and profitable for years to come."

The next day, the trip was uneventful, and the horses seemed to work well together. After giving Mister Hall, the written consent for Mistah to receive the bullion receipts, the Duo was ready for their next endeavor—operating a gold and silver mine.

*****

CHAPTER 8

Operating a Drift Mine

The next morning, the Duo was up before daybreak. After a quick cold breakfast, they rode to the mine. In their office, they changed into mining clothes with canvas overalls, reinforced leather boots, denim shirts and gloves. All miners had accessory ear plugs and face screens; for if it wasn't a pic, chisel or sledgehammer hitting stone, then it was dynamite exploding walls of rocks.

Walking the 400 yards from the adit to the rockface, Palmer asked who was loading ore from the hidden stopes. The foreman of that detail was Bruno Hicks. "Bruno, today I'm working with your ten men. I want to know how to do the work you do and maybe I can find an easier way to do it." "For years, this has been pure manual back breaking work—either picking up large pieces by hand or the rest by shovel. Now for the past two days, we have a mucker, a slusher, and tracks up to the mucker. That air compressor you had installed thru that natural vent is a life saver." "Great, can't wait to see it in operation."

The slusher needed two men, one to reset the blade and one to pull the ropes thru the pulley to drag the blade and rake ore from the stope to the tracks where the mucker was parked. Bruno himself was operating the air valves that propelled the mucker at full force into the ore on the tracks. The Finlay mucker was well built to withstand slamming in the pile of ore rocks. With a full bucket, the Finlay mucker backed up to the empty minecarts, lifted its bucket overhead and dumped its load backwards into the empty ore cart. After several buckets, full of ore, the minecart generally held a half ton of ore. It was then moved to the siderail via a Canton switch by the waiting minecart attendant. The last man on the team was harnessing two donkeys to the lead minecart and attaching two more minecarts to make an ore cart-train to the outside. This mine donkey driver would then return the donkeys to the worksite with the harnesses to be reused on another team for the next load to the adit.

Mia was watching intently as she lifted five fingers to Palmer watching eyes. Palmer then realized that five men were leaning on their shovels—a site that drove him bananas. Today would be the last time he would see that waste of manpower. On the next drive to the adit, the Duo followed the three minecart-train to the outside. Once on the rail loading site, the three ore carts were added to the first three.

While preparing to return to the loading site, the Duo saw an ore cart-train arrive from the rock face. These three carts contained worthless tailings. The train stopped; a switch moved the train some 90 degrees to a tailing's drop site. This was a small canyon with a high drop location. The men disconnected the donkeys, tied chains to one minecart, and two men pulled on ropes thru several block and tackle. The result was that the minecart was lifted up and then moved downward, along a gantry arm, where a separate pulley system tipped the cart and emptied it to the canyon's floor. The

Duo was impressed, and Mia was busy making diagrams and taking ample notes.

For the rest of the morning, the system continued till by the noon whistle, every loaded minecart was outside at the loading site, waiting for the wagon-train from the smelter. The cook shack dining room filled up with all the workers, now up to 27 workers plus Harvey. The meal was meatloaf, mashed potatoes and boiled cabbage with plenty of rolls and coffee. Mia was writing notes in her pad, likely regarding the meal's quality and cost.

At 1PM, the return to work whistle was sounded. The 10 stope workers, including Bruno, walked to the freight wagons and started transferring the ore, both by hand and shovels, from the minecarts to the freight wagons. It took four hours to complete the job. By finishing at 5PM, it was an hour before the closing 6PM whistle.

The Duo watched to see how the 10-man team would spend the last hour of the day. Two men went to get several teams of burrows to harness them to several empty minecarts. The result was two wagon-trains of nine minecarts, two men to lead the burrows and one man riding back to the mine.

Once the minecarts disappeared, Palmer asked Bruno, who was that man riding back to the mine?" "That was the mechanic, he needs to maintain the mucker and slusher with oil, grease, and tighten loose bolts and parts." "I see, so that is why you did not resume work. So what happens to the seven men who did not return in the mine till 6PM?" "We get a free hour, I guess!"

"Well Bruno, that is ridiculous, look around. It's not an engineering wonder; let's look at what needs to be done. The horse railing at the office has weeks accumulation of horse manure. Here is a pile of broken tools from wheelbarrows, pick handles and so one. Scattered pieces of ore need to be picked up. The corral needs repairs, the last delivery of hay needs to get to the hayloft. There is junk and trash everywhere that needs to be picked up—need I say more? If that's not enough, we'll find something constructive for idle men to do, we won't pay a day's wages for men to stand around, leaning on their shovels and yawning away our money!"

That evening, the Duo moved into their new home. Arriving with their personal items, their horses were added to the barn along with a new harness horse and a new buggy/buckboard in the lean-to carriage shed. Walking in the house, the Duo went from one room to another in total awe. Mia finally spoke, "Louisa did a perfect job is setting up every room, and the larder is even full of vittles." "Well, I guess we need to experience every room—shall we start with the bedroom?" "Not a good idea, I'm starved and need to eat food. If we start with the bedroom, we'll end up falling asleep in total exhaustion—skipping supper again." "Ok, let's eat first."

During supper Palmer said, "as often as I see you naked, it is always a sight that I may not get used to. Today, as you were changing out of your mining clothes, I thought how the men had no idea how beautiful you are." "Well, it's going to be like that every morning and night, so do we change in different rooms? I'm not blind and could see how distressed you were—heck you could barely button up your fly!"

"Yes, and wasn't that wonderful. The only problem is that it is difficult to ride a horse for five miles while standing in the stirrups to avoid bouncing in the saddle. So from now on, we go to work in the new buggy/buckboard with a padded seat."

"Before we go to bed, should we decide what to do with those idle five workers?" "No, not till we find a place where their help will be needed, which I hope to find today."

The next morning after a replenishing breakfast, the Duo had a pleasant ride in their new buggy. Arriving at 7:30AM, they had plenty of time to change into work clothes, spend a few minutes with Harvey, and head into the mine with the workers. From Harvey, he learned that there were two foremen. One, Fritz Lane, was in charge of the new quartz vein rich in gold more than silver. The other, Boris Harper, had control of the other older vein rich in silver more than gold.

Arriving at the rock face, Palmer introduced himself to Fritz and informed him that he would be tailing him today. When Fritz realized that Palmer and Mia were trying to make his job and his men's jobs easier, he was thrilled to work with them.

Fritz started, "Our job is to blast a 7-foot high 5-foot wide tunnel that parallels this new quartz vein. The day starts with a mess since our last major blast was at closing time last night. It takes all night for the stone dust to settle to the floor and the air to clear. Once the rock ore is cleaned up, our drillers make shallow holes in the quartz vein. The dynamite man, Liam Johansson shows up, places mini sticks and has a low energy blast that simply cracks the quartz. Then three men work with sledgehammers, chisels and pics to release the gold rich ore and load each rock individually in the minecarts. During this time, my two drillers operate the compressed air drills and bore holes according to the map provided by Liam for the next blast. This map shows where to put the holes, how deep they need to be and whether angled or perfectly perpendicular. That man is a genius, look at the tunnel, it is literally perfect like a knife thru butter."

Mia added, "so, as I understood you, nothing new gets started till last night's blast result gets cleaned up." "That is correct, Ma'am."

"So, who is the cleanup crew?" "Me, my two drillers and my three vein carvers." "Oh really, well go ahead and start and I'll get you some help."

Running out of the tunnel to the stope Bruno was working, Bruno saw them coming at a full run, and stopped the mucker, "What brings you here today, you're supposed to be with Fritz?" "Those five men leaning on their shovel, you don't need them till after lunch, is that right?" "Yes." "Well, you'll have them by then. Come with us gentlemen!"

Back to Fritz site, "you have five extra men till noon to help you clean up. If everything goes well, you'll be able to start drilling before dinner, as these extra men bring the minecarts to the tailing pile and then be at the cook shack for dinner. Good all-around for you, for them and for Mia and me, heh?"

'Yes Sir." Fritz said with a smile. "Except, from now on, I'm Palmer and this is Mia—drop the Sir and Ma'am, will you?"

Lunch was another grand success. Miners were happy to get a hot meal and it was clear that everyone enjoyed the fried chicken meal. Realizing the mood these workers were in, Mia grabbed her note pad and line for line, crossed out a half page of notes. Palmer, seeing what Mia was doing, leaned in and said, "I know the meal is expensive, but a happy worker is worth 110% on the job."

At the end of the meal, Palmer got up and spoke, "this afternoon Mia and I are having a business meeting with Harvey. We'll be talking about changes, improvements et cetera. Tomorrow at lunch, we'll report on our decisions. Tomorrow morning, Mia and I will be working with Boris on his old silver vein. Tomorrow afternoon, we'll be spending time with our dynamite man since we have a lot to learn about blowing things up. As the 1PM whistle blew, Palmer saw the ore wagon-train arrive from the smelter.

The Duo walked over to Mistah, Paddy and the Navajo Trio. "Any problems with the horses, with outlaws, or with personnel at the smelter?" With no's and negating head turns, Palmer added, "there will be some loading changes coming in the near future and will explain more later on. Mistah handed Palmer the bullion receipts from yesterday's delivery. The estimated value was still in the $1,900 range.

For a half hour, Mia and Palmer went over her notes. They quickly agreed on the solutions and changes that needed to be made. At that point they invited Harvey to join them in their office.

"Well Harvey, how are things going for you so far" "Very well, our secretary is proving to be a great help, the headhunters found an experienced dynamite expert whom you'll meet tomorrow, and the air shaft is moving along very well with that team of four experts. Today, I just hired a wrangler to handle this remuda and help freighters harness two teams in tandem. Plus, he can handle a forge and can reshod our horses as well as repair harnesses. I've also decided to keep the freighters on night guard duty since we have too much invested to not provide some security. As of tomorrow, two freighters will share the night alternating with sleep and walking guard duty. Plus, the wrangler sleeps in his barn quarters every night."

"Nice work Harvey, so, who is our new wrangler?" He's an old cattle drive cowhand who spent his life taking care of horses. He walks like a horse, older than a horse, looks like a horse, smells like a horse, but loves horses more than man. Our horses are in good hands and he's not bad with a rifle, as I'm told. His name is HOSS Stoddard and his nickname is STUD." Mia added, "oh great, I suppose you're going to add that he's 'hung like a horse.'" "No Ma'am, not in front of a lady."

Palmer, thinking of his new middle initial of B for Bull, and with a smile, said, "now on a more serious note, let's talk about my pet peeve and a case of serious inefficiency. My pet peeve, five men standing and leaning on their shovels with nothing to do for half a day. NEVER AGAIN. We are currently paying them almost triple their wages pending the establishment of a profit-sharing ratio. Today, we corrected this deficiency and I'm sure the word will get around."

"Another example of inefficiency involves 10 men working all afternoon to transfer 18 ore cars into six freight wagons. That is a waste of manpower that could be put to use in the mine to extract more valuable ore. This is what I propose. The tailings have a hoist system where two men can lift a one-ton minecart and then move it downline on a gantry arm, and then tip it to empty it—all done thru block and tackle, pulleys and ropes."

"We want the same system for unloading ore carts full of rich ore. Once unloaded, the minecart can be returned to the mine with the other two empty ones." Harvey interjected, "Yes, but that still requires men to load the freight wagons." "No, the Finlay mucker will load the wagon. With one man on the mucker, and a cleanup man pushing the ore back on the track for the mucker's bucket of catch, the freight wagon can be loaded in ten minutes."

"The freight wagons would be parked perpendicular to the track and the mucker's bucketsful would fill the front of the freight wagon. The freighter would move up a bit and the mucker would fill the center of the freight wagon, then followed by the back end. The full freight wagon would then be parked away for pickup in the morning. The horses would then be put in the corral. Whichever freighter was first today to load, will be last tomorrow—a fair rotation."

Harvey exploded, "ingenuity at its best. Let the machine do the manual work and place the men where they can work using more brain than braun." "Yes, and more money for us!"

Harvey added, I'm on my way to town. White's Hardware can get us another mucker, air compressor, cross ties and rails in three days, we can get Weber Construction to build us an unloading hoist, and we'll get Bruno or Fritz to train two more mucker operators. I really think the mucker operator needs to switch with the cleanup man so both can do either job."

The Duo also headed back to town, but in their comfortable buggy; they were eager to be in their new house. Riding by the porch, a note was left on the front door asking them to come to the sheriff's office. Since it was in midafternoon, they decided to go straight to see Sheriff Belknap.

"It appears you've sent for us, what's up?" "I am done investigating who these 20 outlaws were. Of the last seven you brought in alive, Chapman was the biggest surprise. The people in the Colorado mines were happy to see Chapman leave the state, but were sad they could not administer justice. His robberies killed 4 freighters and the loss of unknown values in ore. He had a $2,000 reward placed by the local mining association. Three of his toadies were with him in Colorado and they each had a $1,000 reward. The other living outlaws each had bounties of $500— all for a total of $6,500. Now for the other 14 dead outlaws. Twelve had bounties totaling $5,500. Here are all the telegraph vouchers that total $12,000."

"Wow, that's a lot of money, and more than we deserve!" "Heck, you'd better sit down. Hector Foster made a deal with a large livery in Lordsburg. He sold all 20 horses with saddle and tack for a clean $2,000 minus his 5% or $100, 5 days of stabling fees for $100, and railroad horse tag transfer fees of $40. And here is Hector's bank draft of $1,760. The last item is my talk with Judge Hawkins. At the judge's insistence, we met with the local mining association and it was a unanimous decision that you should inherit all the ten wagons, harnesses, and the ten teams of draft horses—a thanks for saving the small miners who could not afford to cover their wagon-trains with paid security."

Mia did some quick ciphering and said, "Palmer, that's way too much money. The outlaws were worth $12,000, the horses worth $1,760, and the ten freight wagons/draft horses are worth $5,000."

"Yes, but let's see how much is left over after we pay off the men who helped us terminate these outlaws. Mistah and Paddy each get $1,000. The other Indians and freighters each get $500, and

Sheriff Belknap gets $1,000. That comes to $7,000. We'll deposit $5,000 in our Benefactor Fund to give back to the community. We'll deposit the horse fees of $1,760 into our private account, and we'll build another barn and corral at the mine for the new horses and harnesses."

"So we only get the $1,760 and Bodine Mining gets the wagons and horses. And sheriff, don't object, you earned it and keep building your retirement fund."

With the day finally ending, the Duo was too tired to make supper; so they went to Grady's Diner for a roast beef supper followed by crashing in their bed for some needed sleep without intimate delays.

***

The next morning, awakening in total darkness, the Duo experienced their first "quickey." Not taking the time for a full replenishing breakfast, the Duo had leftover cold roast beef sandwiches and coffee.

Arriving at the mine, Stud Stoddard greeted them and jokingly said, "isn't it ironic, the owners and general manager are the first to arrive on the job. As he walked the harnessed horse to the carriage lean-to, Mia was heading to the privy. Upon her return, she mentioned that using a bucket and transferring its contents to the portable "honeywagon" was not her favorite activity, but admitted that the new corner with a canvas door was a major improvement for her privacy.

Their daily morning meeting with Harvey was short. "Harvey, we inherited the ten freight wagons and 20 draft horses, so ask Marc Weber to build another barn for at least 24 horses with a hayloft like the other barn, but for fire protection, keep them safely separated. For now, don't make any plans with those wagons, we'll talk again about them."

Harvey had only one item, "there is a problem with the #1 crosscut tunnel and the rich vein, but Boris will explain everything once you get on site." Mia was looking at yesterday's bank posted values for precious metals. The silver price drew her eyebrows up.

Walking in, Palmer wondered what the problem might be. Mia mentioned, "I saw the price of silver dropped from $1 an ounce to 60 cents." "Whoa, that's a biggy, especially since vein #1 has more silver than gold. I bet that's part of the problem."

After introductions were made, Boris started, "it's good that you are here today. Two days ago we got our mucker, slusher and air compressor. The problem is that we are too far from the new natural vent to run the coal fired steam compressor. Harvey said we needed to wait for the air shaft to reach the rockface before we can modernize this crosscut tunnel/vein. As it is now, this vein is labor intensive with 10 men being needed to work it. Plus, the price of silver is crashing with the conversion of the US currency now being backed by gold. Guess, it might be time for some changes, what do you think?"

Mia said, "with the loss of silver backing, the government has a major supply of silver that they will dump back in the silver currency market. That means it may take years for the 60-cent silver dollar to be worth a dollar again."

Palmer finally spoke, "Boris, as rich as this crosscut is in silver, it is not worth working it when the labor and other expenses are greater than the income. For now, we need to close this tunnel till silver value goes back up. Do you agree?" "Yes, but it hurts for me and my men to give up the past ten year's work, besides what are we going to do, or do we get laid off?"

Mia jumped right in, "whoa there, no one is getting laid off. We have several projects that need your help."

Palmer then said, "Boris, you and your men gather around me. I'm going to explain where you can be transferred to. There are three choices. First, there are three more stopes totaling an estimated 165 freight wagons of rich ore. We can set up your mucker, slusher and rails to any one of these stopes and the natural vent will still handle the exhaust fumes. This is a five-man team as is now being used."

"The second choice, Fritz's #2 vein appears to be at least two feet wide. Fritz is tunneling to the left and you can start tunneling to the right. That way, we can chip away at the rich vein from two sides. This job can use five men like Fritz's team."

"The third choice is being reserved for any man who needs to get out of the mine because of breathing problems. We'll be starting a second six-wagon freight wagon-train, till we empty out these three leftover stopes. At 12 wagons a day, it will take us half the time to empty the stopes, even if we add all the ore being generated from vein #2. So, this is a temporary job, but if any of you take it, we'll guarantee you work afterwards, we just can't guarantee outside work."

The presentation was clear, and the Duo was observing the 11 men. There was plenty of mussitating and chin-wagging, which quickly changed to guffaws and finally to chortles. At that point, Mia asked for a show of hands. "Who wants to dig the second tunnel on vein #2?"—five hands went up and Boris was named the team foreman. "Who wants to work a stope?"—four more hands went up. "Who is the most mechanically inclined?" Three fingers pointed to Wilbur Cummings. "You will operate the mucker and be the team foreman with an increase in pay." "Who needs and wants to work temporarily as an outside freighter?" The last two hands went up. "You two gentlemen need to move outside and you're on 'full pay leave' till the wagons are ready. Then you'll be driving draft and gelding horses."

"Now let's work together and move all this equipment to vein #2 and stope #3. I'm certain that it will take all day, but you'll all be able to start full time by tomorrow. Wilbur, you are short one man, and we'll get you your fifth man by morning."

Coming out of the mine for dinner, the wagon-train was beginning to get back to the mine on time for the hot meal. Weber's team was arriving for the included hot dinner meal while on the job. Today's menu was chicken casserole and dumplings, with apple crisp for dessert. After dinner, Weber's team started building the hoist over the ore rails while another team was beginning to build the second barn.

After a great meal, Palmer got up to bring the workers up to date. He went over the new wagons and a second wagon-train, the new method of unloading ore wagons and loading freight wagons by using a mucker. He also mentioned, that with the firearm confiscation, he wanted every worker to be armed with either a pistol or a rifle. If any one needed a firearm, everyone was encouraged to see Harvey anytime.

Mia then announced their schedule for tomorrow. "Tomorrow, Palmer and I and the six freighters and guards are going to the outlaw barn. We'll be coming back with the 10 freight wagons and 20 harnessed draft horses. If everything goes well, we'll be back by the noon meal."

When the return whistle sounded, the Duo introduced themselves to Liam Johansson. As they walked by the carpenters building the hoist, Palmer asked if they would join the other carpenters on the barn once the hoist was done. "No Sir, we've been assigned to build the second corral and pasture." "Good, because we're bringing 20 horses tomorrow by noon." "Not a problem, the corral will be done."

Walking to the rockface, Liam took over the subject of dynamite. "For your information, dynamite is manufactured in the US by the Giant Company of San Francisco. It is a mixture of an absorbent soaked in liquid nitroglycerin. The absorbents stabilize the nitroglycerin. Examples of the sorbents are, powdered shells, clay, sawdust and many others. This mixture is then wrapped in several layers of paper board, plus the outermost layer is often coated with wax or lacquer. The ends are capped except one end has a hole to allow the insertion of a fuse into the blasting cap."

"Now the blasting cap is what makes the nitroglycerine explode. It is a copper tube with mercury fulminate inside. The mercury fulminate is the primary explosive, which is highly sensitive to friction, heat, or shock. Actually, the blasting cap acts just like a percussion cap and rimfire cartridges that are both lined with mercury fulminate."

"The third and last component to dynamite is the fuse. The fuse is made up of a core of black powder with several textile overwraps. The outer layers are covered with wax or lacquer for waterproofing. Fuses come in standard diameters but in different lengths. The end inserted in the blasting cap is designed to be crimped into the caps. When the burning fuse reaches the mercury fulminate in the blasting cap, the explosion propagates to the nitroglycerine—just like a rimfire cartridge propagates the explosion to the gunpowder to push the projectile out of the barrel."

Mia, being simply amazed, added, "Sir, I think you gave us all that information in one breath. It was a lot of facts, that finally makes a lot of sense."

"Well thank you Ma'am." "Uh, I'm Mia, and this is Palmer. May we call you Liam?" "Wonderful, wonderful."

"Now, I'm going to show you how to use dynamite to create a perfect tunnel with near straight rock walls and an arched ceiling. Stepping in a tunnel Liam pointed things out. First of all, the wall markings show the last explosion excavated 15 inches in depth of rock. Also notice the back wall is fairly uniform and the quarts rock holding the vein was barely touched."

Palmer was impressed, "how can you make dynamite behave this way?"

"This is the map I made for the last explosion. 6 in. deep holes all around the walls and arch, 10 in. apart and 8 in. from the edge. In each hole I inserted a 1/8 in. stick. Then six 10 in. holes, two at the bottom two at the middle and two at the top of the back wall. In these holes I place half sticks of dynamite. The 1/8 in. sticks had 8 in. fuses, whereas the ½ sticks had 14 in. fuses."

"Why?" "Because, I want the 1/8 in. sticks to blow first, with the short fuses, to cut the edge wall and crack the stone. Then the half sticks give the big bang and literally excavates the next 15 inches. Now all this is possible because the rock we are excavating is relatively soft with a 'Moh's scale' of hardness equal to 4/10 while quartz is 7/10 and polishable granite is 8 or 9/10."

"What is different when you do the so called 'low energy' explosion in the quartz vein?"

"It is hard to drill quartz and it eats up drill bits. We only drill four in. holes in each square foot, and add ¼ sticks to fracture the rock."

"What do you do between each blast?"

"I work all day with the drillers. It's not just a matter of drilling, the angle of the drill is crucial to the proper function of the charge."

"Where did you learn all this?" "From my father and grandfather. Depending on the Moh rating, the rest is experience and passed on knowledge. Actually, I've been doing this for ten years, and I'm still learning."

"Yeah, right. How did we ever find you?"

"The headhunters in Deming introduced me to Mister Elliot, and the rest is history."

"Where are you living?" "In a tent, but I'll be moving in the bunkhouse soon."

"I see you have a wedding band on. Where is your wife and do you have children?"

"I have a loving wife, a new 2-year old son and a very affectionate 4-year old daughter. I had to leave them in our hometown in Sweden till I get settled in, buy a house in town and buy ocean tickets to bring them here. The USA is our future. "

"How much are we paying you?" "Mister Elliot offered me $150 a month, and that is three times what I was making in Sweden."

"What do you owe the headhunters for finding you this job?"

"Two month's pay within 90 days."

"What!!! Well Mia, a man with such a dangerous job needs to be at peace with himself and his loved ones. So, how are you going to deal with this situation? Plus, don't forget, without a dynamite man we are back to the pick and shovel days."

Mia was busy computing and writing. When done, she said, "this bank draft of $300 is to pay off the headhunters. This note is for Harvey, your salary just went up to $250 a month. This bank draft for $1,500 is to bring your family to the US. This note is for my father, Ellsworth Myers,

President of the Community Bank. You can buy any house in town without a down payment. We will guarantee your loan at the low family interest rate. Buy a house fully furnished, with a barn, some acreage for a pasture/corral and a garden." Palmer adds, "Sounds good to me."

"So why are you doing this, no one has ever offered me and my family a helping hand!" "We don't expect more than what you are doing now. We both feel that we should treat our employees with respect and offer a livable wage. In return, we hope you will stay with us for some time."

***

The next day, the Duo rode their horses to the mine since they didn't know how Pappy had arranged the ride to the outlaw barn. On arrival, the guards and freighters were waiting with Pappy pointing to the driver's seat. The Duo got off their horses, gave the reins to Stud Stoddard, and Mia sat in the front seat with Palmer. The men jumped in the freight wagon and off they went to the outlaw barn and corral.

It took two hours to gather all the horses from the pasture. Then each horse had to be matched with his or her partner—fortunately the horse's size, color, breed and sex made that process doable. Then came the harnessing which became a matching process. Each horse needed a harness that would fit. Once that was done, the harness was labeled and reserved for the horse team and individual horse. Once each team was hitched up, the wagon-train was finally ready to roll.

The duo was driving the wagon that had brought the guards and freighters to the job site. The guards and freighters drove the new teams and the inherited wagons. Mia got to talking, "what do you think of our windfall?" "The horses are young, fed well in the pasture, are rested, and simply look great. Four of the wagons look like new, four are obviously used but with many more serviceable years. Two have had better days; yet the wheels, axles, and hitching parts can be rebuilt and used as spare parts. Lumber can always be reused. In short, it's a real nice acquisition."

"I agree, and I guess we have to thank the local mining association and someday, when the need arises, will try to do them a favor. Now, how should we use these eight usable wagons?"

"I've been thinking about this. The most important thing is to increase the size of our present wagon-train from the 6 wagons to 10 instead of 12 wagons. That keeps all the security men on one wagon-train and increases the monetary value from +-$2,000 to +-$3,000 a day. The key is that 10 wagons can be unloaded and reloaded the same day with only two men operating the mucker loader with its 6 cubic foot bucket. At the smelter, once 5 of the wagons are unloaded, they can return to the mine to be reloaded before the second half arrives."

"That's not a bad plan. First, with putting 4 wagons in commission, that means that only 16 of the 20 draft horses will be used any one day. That keeps horses in reserve to replace lame ones or ones that need a rest or are ill. In reality, it also means, we don't have to buy more work geldings. It also means we have 4 good wagons as spares to replace those that need maintenance and repairs. Thus, our Monday to Friday down time is minimized. Now what security should we be maintaining with 10 wagons?"

"Assuming there are no attacks, I would like to maintain a minimum of 5 shotgun guards, or one every other wagon. Let's not forget, it's not to keep from losing the wagons and ore, it's more to protect the freighters who are all family men."

"Great, but we only have four guards, Mistah, Whitey, Red and Bluey. Who is going to be the fifth one?" "I don't know yet, so after lunch I'll offer the job to a man good with a gun." "Oh really, well better look at that woman who is waiting for someone on that Indian pony."

The Duo kept looking till Mistah walked over to the woman, who bent down to plant a prolonged kiss on him. "Ok, woman, what do you know that I don't?"

"Well, it seems that one day a single Navajo maiden, appeared as Mistah's teepee. She was of his tribe and wanted to learn how to be a guide with a shotgun—for she too wanted to help feed and clothe her tribe. Well apparently things went from 'this to that' and a lot more 'that and this,' and well you know, she became a crack shot and they fell in a bit of love and and and........well you know, Mistah is a proud man who doesn't know how to ask for a job for Missi." "Oh, now it's Mistah and Missi, is it?" "Well again, you know the saying, 'next to a happy wife is a contented husband.'"

*****

CHAPTER 9

A Mining Emporium

As the wagons approached the adit, it was clear that the ore carts were being unloaded directly on the tracks. Plus the mucker appeared to be installed and the coal fired steam generator was providing compressed air. Bruno was showing two men how to operate the mucker, and the two men, who had been unloading ore carts full of worthless tailings, were now busy unloading ore rich carts. A sizable mound had already been unloaded.

Palmer went to see Bruno, say Bruno, are you ready to load ten wagons?" "We sure are as I want to watch the new operators. Line up the wagons." Paddy chose the four good wagons and sent the freighters to get the other six. With a 6 cubic foot bucket, the mucker would fill the ore wagons in 6-8 buckets. The total loading time was 10 minutes per ore wagon—with the use of two men in less than two hours to load ten wagons (compared to the old method of 10 men in 4-5 hours to manually load six wagons).

That evening, after a homecooked meal of porkchops, fried potatoes and applesauce. The Duo was relaxing in their parlor with fresh coffee. They commented on how efficient the ore wagon's loading had turned out, when there was a knock at the door. Palmer got up to open door, only to see Elmer and Gwen standing there with a puzzled look on their faces. Mia got up to greet them, "what a pleasant surprise, what brings you here, since you must just have closed up your store?" "Yes we just did, and the store is what we'd like to talk about."

With fresh coffee in their cups, Elmer started. "Gwen and I are at an impasse. The local people want a better choice of clothing, especially the ladies, and more variety in homemaking items and vittles. We cannot and do not want to expand the store's square footage. What we want is to get rid of the miner's section of work clothes, digging tools and safety gear. The suppliers are killing us with small orders with a low profit margin. To get a better discount, we have to order large volumes that we cannot afford. To make it worse, many miners are roughnecks that walk out without paying since they know that two old merchants are not capable of demanding payment. With the walkaways, we are not making any income with that department."

Palmer interrupted them, "whoa, something has to change. If everyone paid, what profit would you make on mining goods?" "10%."

What is your general store profit?" "15-18%."

"If you changed to larger mining orders what would be your profit for all mining goods?" "30%."

Mia eyebrows went up as she added, "wow, that's a nice profit margin." "Yes, it's as good as any retail business in town; and we want YOU, Mia, to own and run it." "WHAT, ME?"

Gwen jumped in, "now you listen to me, this is real girl talk. You have the business background with your working in the bank. This store requires keeping inventories, making large orders with full payment, having school kids restocking the shelves, and putting an end to taking items without payment. Plus, you can become the judge as to whom would benefit from that 'Benefactor fund' you are so intimate with. The bottom line, your experience with the detective agency and the mining operation, makes you the best candidate to handle such a retail enterprise."

Elmer came back into the discussion, "to make it more enticing, Louisa is moving back to Albuquerque with her recently widowed sister. This is another reason we want to keep our mercantile dealing only with garments, vittles and general merchandise—as it was Louisa who dealt with the mining section. Anyways, her apartment is soon to be empty and of course you won't need your apartment either. So this is what we propose; we will 'gut' both apartments, your kitchen will become a kitchenette with the cooking stove and a dinette table for quick noon meals, as well as a back door to the privy. Louisa's kitchen will become your warehouse with large unloading doors. Except for a counter to pack items and hold a cash register, the remainder of the square footage will be wide open for displaying goods."

"How much would you charge for the monthly rent and how much would the renovations cost?"

"The renovations will cost you nothing, it's the landlords responsibility. We'll have an auction to sell all the furniture. Heck we'll even add a large display window over the boardwalk and pay for a new sign—Bodine Mining Emporium. Sounds good doesn't it?

Mia responded, "it does have potential. But how much will the rent be?"

"Both you and Louisa are paying $50 each. So, does $100 a month still sound fair?"

"Of course, but we know that commercial space is a lot more valuable, and commands a higher rent." "I know, but I don't care."

Gwen, then stuck her neck out. "Mia, your husband has a manager, an office secretary, three foremen and a well-established mine that is being modernized. Do you really think you are needed there?" This is a chance for you to start your own enterprise with a product that is needed for the life survival of thousands of people digging out the many precious metals."

Palmer stepped in, "what happens if we don't want to diversify into retailing?" Gwen jumped in and said, "you are our plan A and if you don't take it over, we don't have a plan B. What I do know is that we are abandoning the mining section, because it's just a matter of time that one of them will push Elmer into a gunfight and will kill him."

"If you take that drastic route, what will you do with your present stock of mining goods?" "Sell it at a loss to anyone selling such items."

Mia saw an end to their business meeting and said, "you've given us much to consider. The rent is more than fair, and free renovations are a real fine touch. If we take your offer, we would want to have "first right of refusal" in case you ever want to sell the building—including the three acres behind the apartment building that borders the back street. And, we would pay you for the mining goods at your costs plus the 10%."

Gwen asked, "how much time do you need to arrive to a decision?"

"Well, this is very tempting, and I need to let it grow on me. In a weeks' time, the natural course of events will make me 'chomp' to take the business challenge or be glad to say 'no thank you!'"

***

That night, intimacy was not in the cards, as Mia tossed and turned all night thinking of the Craymore's offer. By morning they made their way to the mine for the early meeting with Harvey. "This morning we get a tour of the men who are digging and building a secure air shaft. Then after lunch, we need to watch the men in operation as two teams are emptying out stopes and two teams are digging tunnels on each side of the new gold vein."

Arriving at the dig site, the four workers were introduced, Victor was the man who cut the 4X4 timbers, Delaney was the man drilling the holes for the J-bars, Amos and Handy were the men digging and building the cribbing. Victor then explained how he had used a transit to measure the angles of the adit tunnel to the rockface over the 1200 feet. After doing the geometric calculations, he had a target point to aim the air shaft. Then he used the same angle to tag the ground for the dig point. According to his track record, he expected to hit the target at the rockface to within a ten-foot circle.

Next, Delany explained how the cribbing was built and why J-bolts were needed. "We are building an air shaft by adding another layer to the walls from the bottom of the existing shaft. The J-bolts hold the new layers to the ones on top."

Palmer added, wouldn't it had been easier and cheaper to build it from the floor of the rockface to the outside—heading up instead of down?" "Yes, that would be true, if there was an adequate amount of air at the rockface. In this case, with a week of building a winze (building up instead of down), the project would have ended from lack of air.

"Oh, I see. Now, I thought we were planning to build a 3X3 foot shaft, this one is 3X4 feet!" Harvey jumped in, "I elected to change the plans. Allegedly, a 3X3 shaft requires the use of short handle shovels, with a lot of bending, and many days off to rest sore backs. A 3X4 shaft allows the use of long handle shovels, with less bending, and no days off. A bit more lumber, but the same number of J-bolts."

Mia asked, "why are the timbers burning over the fire." "The more the timbers are scorched, the more there is natural charcoal and other resins to protect the wood from the dirt's moisture."

"What is the estimated depth of this shaft?" "According to the reliability of current transits, there is 15-foot allowance every 100 feet of depth. We've estimated this shaft to be 110 feet deep and we are at 90 feet today. So, it's possible that we are withing +-20 feet of breaking into the rockface. I know this with certainly, because last night when the dynamite explosion was set at closing time, the four of us clearly heard and felt the shaft shake. Without a doubt, we are close to breaking thru."

"Very good, and thank you for the information." Walking back to the cook shack, Harvey added, "I keep tabs on the timbers coming in, the J-bars, and daily hours; and we are way below budget because we are using professionals instead of our own men." "That is good management, Harvey and thank you for that."

Walking down the mountain, Mia thought, *"Palmer has made some good choices. He had professionals dig the air shaft which resulted in a quick excavation and a financial savings. Plus his idea of using a hoist to empty ore carts onto the tracks, and loading the ore wagons with a mucker was another brilliant idea. I wonder if his other ideas, of having two teams emptying out stopes and two teams blasting out tunnels on each side of the new vein, will also pan out—guess we'll find out this afternoon."*

Lunch was ready, beef stew and biscuits. Harvey looked around and said, "oh boy, the cook will be making an announcement." With everyone sitting down, the cook brought out several pots of beef stew and before the first bowl was filled, the cook said, "my beef stew stands by itself and none of you scoundrels are going to flood my stew with that damn tomato ketchup. The ketchup is locked up in Harvey's office safe and that's my story. Eat it, or get out!"

After a great lunch, the Duo and Harvey lingered a bit after the work whistle sounded, to let the men get back into their routine at the rockface. The Duo wanted to watch the men at work, to see how things were moving along, and see if changes could improve efficiency. As they stepped thru the adit, Harvey mentioned that the newly appointed foreman to take over the second stope was working out well. "Boris chose Wilbur Cummings because of his experience, longevity and a strong work ethic. Come to find out his men like him and, according to Boris, they have become a highly spirited and efficient team."

The talking came to an end when they arrived at the rockface. The observers walked to the two stopes where Bruno and Wilbur were working stope 3 and 4. They were using the same air compressor to operate each team's mucker and slusher. It was clear that the men on Bruno's team were working to keep up with Wilbur's team. Once three ore carts were full, a team of harnessed donkeys was attached to the ore train and hauled to the outside to be emptied onto the pile over the tracks.

Mia asked Palmer, "what do you think dear?" "I think. . . . . .well what do you think dear?" "I think five men are too many since the slusher and mucker are doing most of the work." "For now, I'm thinking the same thing, but time will tell. Let's move on to the other work site."

Fritz's and Boris's teams were working hard to clean up the tailings left from the noon blast. Harvey explained, "during the hour lunch break, the dust had settled enough to allow a cleanup because the natural vent added a suction effect to suck up the dust to the outside while pulling fresh air from the adit. Once the tailings are picked up by the mucker, then drilling will proceed to prepare for the dynamite blast at closing tonight. Liam devised a wick Y connection that allows the low energy blast to the vein to occur just before the big excavating blast to the tunnel, moving deeper in the mine."

As the tunnels were cleaned out, the five-member team divided up to do their own jobs. One man started walking his donkey team to haul the tailings outside, two men started drilling holes with Liam, as two men started chiseling and picking rich ore out of the vein. This rich ore at times looked like pure gold or silver but in actuality it was a mixed ore that had to go thru the cauldron melt for separation and extraction.

Mia was about to say something to Palmer when all of a sudden, a big blob of dirt fell onto her notepad. Harvey and Palmer were stunned, especially when dirt was showering all three of them. Palmer looked up and quickly pushed Mia and Harvey out of the way. As he yelled, "look up!" Mia looked up and said, "my God is that a human boot?" "No dear, it's a boot with a leg following, no, on second thought, it's two legs and two boots."

At that point, dirt was falling at a good clip till a good mound was forming. Then came the unmistakable sound of someone losing a grip and falling, as a man appeared sitting on top of the mound of dirt. "Is that you Amos?" "Yes Sir, I told Victor I could hear you guys talking, but he thought I was hearing voices again from lack of air in that shaft."

Palmer jokingly added, "well Amos, at least now you can finish the shaft from the rock-floor up, heh?"

Walking out of the mine, the Duo agreed that nothing needed changing for the two teams exposing and working the new gold vein. Halfway out, they met up with the remainder of the shaft team. They had commandeered empty ore carts and were moving their operation to include tools, J-bolts, and lumber timbers to the inside of the mine. Victor asked, 'is Amos in a good mood, we know he hates falling out of a hole like a groundhog, but it couldn't be helped." "Well, when we left, he was still sputtering something about putting some of the dirt up someone's body part where the sun don't shine!"

As they approached the adit, Mia was again thinking, *"those miners are efficiently organized thanks to Palmer's suggestions. I just don't see the need, in the foreseeable future, to make any changes. I can see Palmer being a trouble shooter for the immediate problems, and a great planner for future activities. The key to a successful mine is to keep finding a source of the profitable ore. I'm sure that Palmer can be that key person. I don't think that's my destiny. I need something that is natural for me, as mining will be for Palmer. But how do I say this to the man I love—without disappointing him?"*

The ride back home was another silent affair. Palmer knew that Mia was thinking things over, and decided that, after supper, he would force the discussion on the subject. Supper was a chicken pie with all the vegetables and pickled beets on the side. During the meal, Palmer decided to break the ice and take Mia's mind off what was gnawing at her. "Going back to today's events, where do you think my work will take me in the next months?

"I think your job is to keep those 30 men working and making money for us. In a few months, those stopes will be empty, and we'll need another dig to supplement vein #2, and the #1 silver vein is not the answer. You need to find another quartz/gold vein asap, or start laying off miners, freighters and guards."

Mia was on a roll, "now this is my dilemma. I know what needs to be done, but I don't know how to follow thru. For example, where do you start to find another gold vein, isn't it just luck finding one?" "Not really, the rockface has gold veins; eons ago liquid metals flowed into rock cracks which were common with quartz rocks. So, it's a matter of finding new sources of quartz rock." "And how do you do that?" "By sending Liam hunting with a team of drillers and a bag of dynamite. Excavating rock walls is the way the present #2 vein was found and how the next one will be exposed."

"Now, let's change the subject, I know you are being tormented. You have not been yourself since Elmer and Gwen offered us their proposal. Let's talk about it, Ok?"

"I want to talk about it, but I'm afraid to!" "What, why?" "Because, of all material things, you are the only thing that matters to me and I'm afraid I could disappoint you." As Mia started crying.

"Never, never and never. You are a dynamic, brilliant, resourceful and a somewhat beautiful women, that I am deeply in love with. Tell me what you are trying to say. and I'll support you 100%."

Stopping her whimpering, Mia blurted out: I want to take the Craymores' offer, I want to develop a retail business, I like dealing with the public, I want us to buy the apartment building, I want to develop my own line of denim miner's garb, I want to convert the upstairs to a sewing center to make trousers and eventually work shirts. I want it Palmer, way in my heart, I want to take this road. I honestly feel we can help each other with our suggestions and that way, we'll be sharing our family businesses."

Palmer stood there in awe, stepped forward and kissed his wife. Well dear, I'd say you spoke your mind. Shall we take an evening stroll to the Craymores's house and close the deal? Bodine Mining Emporium really rings the bell, don't it?"

Knocking at the Craymores' front door, Gwen opened the door and said, "oh my, please come it. Elmer and I have been dreading this meeting." Stepping in the parlor, Elmer was asleep in his rocker. As Gwen went to get some coffee, Elmer must have smelled the aroma and woke up. "Well, how long have you been watching me, did I snore?" "No, but you passed wind a few times." "Well that's what beans do for you, heh? So what brings you here?"

Mia took over, "we don't want to rent your 1st floor, as some sad faces made their appearance, we want to buy the apartment building as it is." "OH, that's a new twist. We were planning on selling it when we retired as a regular source of monthly income." "Well, when do you plan to retire?" "We're both in our late 50's, and if we stay healthy, we'd like to retire in five years." "What is today's real estate value?" The town assessors have rental property evaluated at $400 per rental for double occupancy." "So a 1,600 rental property today is worth how much in five years?" "Guessing, it may be as much as doubled." "Palmer took over, "we'll offer you $4,000 today to include the three or four acres in the back, all the furnishings and we'll pay for our own remodeling. That gives you a nest egg to collect interest till you retire." Gwen adds, "does that mean that you will be taking over selling mining goods?" "Yes it does Gwen." "Then, we can give you a gift, we are giving you, free, all the mining items we have in our store, lock, stock and barrel."

The two couples talked about the details involved in closing the deal and transferring ownership. The big issue was the two renters upstairs. Elmer said, "in total confidentiality, Leota is dying of cancer and Wilma needs assistance and is planning to move to Katie's Boarding Home that cares for disabled ladies, after Leota passes. So, within a short time, you'll be able to use the upstairs or renovate it to suit your needs." With a scheduled meeting at the town clerk's office for the morning, the couples retired for the evening.

***

After a replenishing breakfast at Bessy's Diner of coffee with eggs, home-fries and link sausage, the Duo walked over to the town clerk's office where Elmer and Gwen were waiting. After the transfer of funds and the signing of a bill of sale, the original deed was pulled out, and rewritten in ink into two copies. After current and next year's taxes were prorated and paid, both copies of the new deed were signed by all parties as well as witnessed by the town clerk. The new owners got one copy and the other copy was filed in the office safe.

The Duo's next stop was the Community Bank where they transferred $5,000 from their private account into this new Emporium account—to separate it from the Mining account and their private account. As they stepped on the boardwalk, Gwen came running down the street. "Leota took a turn for the worse last night and is now in the local hospital for terminal care. Wilma's friends are moving her with her personal belongings to Katie's Boarding house today. We were asked by Leota months ago to move her belongings to the church where the pastor can give them to the needy. In short, the upstairs will be empty of tenants and their personal items by today."

Meeting next with Marc Weber, "we have just purchased the apartment building where we have our office. We are building an emporium for mining supplies. We want the two floors of furniture placed under a tent for a special sale. Then keep one small kitchenette, remove all partition walls, remove the outside stairway to the second floor, build an inside stairway to the upstairs, we'll need a customer counter near the door, several shelves upstairs, a table to handle 4-foot fabric bolts, display cases for clothing with cabinets under the displays, racks for long mining tools and small hand tools, and a manually operated elevator to move a 4-foot fabric bolt and other supplies to the second floor. Keep an area next to the back yard for storage of incoming orders and add a bay window in the storefront. Finally, I want a sign that says, 'Bodine Mining Emporium.'"

Marc was busy filling his notepad as Palmer said, "this is just a list, but either Mia or I will stay with you till all is done. When can you start?" "We'll put up the tent this afternoon on a temporary floor, and move the furniture so we can start demolition tomorrow."

The floor and tent went up behind the building on the four acres that made up the back yard. Furniture was pulled out, including all of Leota's kitchen, any wall shelves or cabinets, and all rugs and window curtains. It was dark by the time the two floors were gutted and ready for demolition.

Palmer looked around and said, "tomorrow the only thing we keep and don't place for sale under the tent are doors with the door frames, everything else goes to the burn pile if it does not sell. After Weber's men left, the Duo went to the tent and placed a price tag on every item. In the morning they would place a sign that said, "daily furniture tag sale till items gone—pay inside."

The next day the Duo went to Craymores' to place an order. Elmer ordered a large fireproof Mosler safe that would fit under a 40-inch high counter. He also ordered a Hough cash register for the store. Then started the work of taking inventory of the goods they were getting from the Claymores. It was a slow tedious process especially in separating sizes. Trousers came with different waists to match different leg Lengths, whereas, shirts came in small, medium, or large. Miners caps and gloves also came in different sizes. On and on, anything that humans wore came in different sizes, down to the size of reinforced leather and rubber boots. The final inventory showed that all mining clothes came as canvas or denim, and in summer or winter grade.

Moving to tools it was double ended pics, pickaxes, short and long handle sledge hammers, stone and claw hammers, crowbars, chisels, short and long handle round or straight shovels, pinch bars, jacks and a slew of strange rock blasting prehistoric tools that Elmer would have to put a name to.

On the miscellaneous display were kerosene lanterns, replacement lamps and wicks, miner's candle lamp and reflectors to fit on the leather cap's brim, the new aluminum head helmets, dynamite, caps and fuses, wrenches to fit the mucker and slusher, ropes, pulleys, block and tackle, waterproof matches, magnesium fire starters and too many small items to mention but all categorized for reorders.

By midafternoon, the Duo was ready to place their first order. They took Elmer's standard order form and matched it with the inventory list. It became very clear, that to place an order, you needed to know what you had and what you were short of. Then it was simply a matter of checking the ones you wanted and adding the number needed.

Before going home, the Duo went back to the shop to see how the demolition was going. The walls were gone to the burn pile. Marc was there himself and said, "the 2nd floor joists are only 2X4's so we have to maintain support posts every 10-12.5 feet of the center studs in order to maintain a solid floor for upstairs activities. The center beam will also be reinforced and also require support posts. The now open area measures 50 feet wide by 55 feet long. Tomorrow we start building an inside stairway to the 2nd floor and we'll tear down that ugly outside stairway. Thereafter we build that manually operated supply elevator. The next day we start building your 1st floor display tables with shelves on top and cabinets underneath the tables for storage of extra products."

Palmer added, "so far great, but why so many supporting posts?" "Now is the time to set supporting posts since we'll build display cases around then. Besides, since no one knows what your 2nd floor will be used for, it's best to have a solid foundation in case of hefty tools, storage boxes, and or workers upstairs." "Of course."

Mia added, "that gives us an extra day, Palmer will go to the mine to take care of issues and I'll be working the tent to try to sell all that furniture. The newspaper ad has been in the daily news for the past two days and if everything goes well, the tent will come down tomorrow night."

That evening, during supper, Palmer was reminiscing, "boy, life has been interesting. I started the Bodine agency, then you exploded in my life, then we buy a mine, and now are building the Emporium. I guess we thrive having to deal with challenges." "Yes, but eventually our challenges may become 'another day on the job." "Yes, I can see that could happen, but if we keep improving, modernizing and following the times, the everyday job can still be challenging." "Well enough philosophizing, I know one challenge that does not need improvement—for if it works well, don't change it, heh." "Yes, like a well-oiled machine!"

It had been a vigorous night, and the Duo overslept. Mia hurriedly dressed and ran to the tent without their replenishing breakfast. Palmer went to Nancy's Diner for egg/ham sandwiches and coffee. After breakfast, he took two more sandwiches and a bottle of coffee to Mia before riding out to the mine. "Wow, just what I need, I'm starved. With a customer milling around, Mia tugged Palmer to the side and whispered, "I didn't have time to bathe this morning, so do I smell of 'sex?'"

Palmer bent over to smell her and said nothing but had uplifted eyebrows. Mia out loud says, "well what?" "Just look, is my distress flag rising? "Great, stay here, I'll be back in a half hour."

With half the morning gone by, Palmer eventually went to the mine and Mia was in a fresh outfit and doing a bustling business. One customer was a homesteading couple who had arrived with a wagon. The lady said, "we badly need a cookstove, our barrel stove is in bad shape, it's falling apart with holes, and cooking for six has been a nightmare." "I have two medium size apartment stoves. One has a water tank with four burners, an oven and warming shelf. The other is simply a wood stove with four burners. Go around and take a look."

The homesteaders returned and the gentlemen said, "sorry, but we can't afford either one. We need food and I'll have to build another stove out of a steel barrel." Mia just looked at them, this was a family having trouble to survive and she was asking $25 and $15 for the stoves. It was clear that they were near starving, needed new clothes and needed a shotgun for defense and to go hunting. Mia had her first epiphany. She turned to the other customers, saw two strong burly men and said, "sirs, would you help loading a cook stove." The burly men grabbed the one with the water tank and walked it over to the homesteader's wagon—with every step the homesteader pleaded with Mia and the burly men to put the stove down for he could not pay for it.

Mia put an end to the man's declarations by handing him a note that said, "Elmer, give this family $200 in food, clothing, a double barrel shotgun/ammo and give him a future credit of $200. Plus, give him a bank voucher to pay for what he needs on the homestead to support his family."

The homesteader was blubbering away and finally said, "what does this paper say, I can't read." "That is not important, just give it to Elmer next door and he'll take care of you. Now git.......I'm busy making money."

An hour later, the homesteader's wife came back as the family wagon was being loaded. "Thank you for your help, your generosity will not go to waste. Remember the name Henry Brubaker, for one day when you least expect it, he will be there to help you and pay you back."

The sales were going well. One customer was walking about looking for something special. She was a real huffy. With her hair in a bun, an outlandish hat of fresh flowers, a bustle that looked like a camel's hump, and a bodice with whale bones, she looked like a shrew ready to argue. Stepping up to Mia she said, "I need those four dressers, how much?" "I can't sell them without the beds, it's a family package of three beds, mattresses, sheets and dressers. Sorry Ma'am." "I don't care about anyone else, I want those dressers, how much?" "Not for sale, I'm going to give the set to a needy family."

"Well that's a waste. The poor can sleep on the floor and even if they had the beds, they certainly wouldn't have anything to put in the dresser drawers." "That's enough, you have a cold heart, a foul mouth, and you're so stuck up that I'm sure you don't pass wind! Get out of here you bag of crap." "How dare you speak to me that way, we'll see what my husband has to say about that," as she huffed away.

By 4PM every item was sold for a total of $300—minus a free cookstove. As the carpenters were tearing down the tent, Mia went to the shop to see the result of today's activities. The outside stairway was gone, the siding replaced, the inside stairway had a fancy railing and decorative spindles, a landing and a large end post. Under the landing was a closet. The elevator was finished, the winding handle was engineered to a mechanical advantage that allowed the lifting of 200 pounds without effort. An operator on each floor could wind, lock and release the elevator. The last touch of the day was the finishing of the posts with a new layer of quality pine boards that had been painted.

That evening, the Duo had a chat about what was new at the mine. Palmer led the discussion. The stopes are down to the last one with an estimated sixty wagons. I've given Liam two teams of drillers to start blasting for a new vein within access to the air shaft; for the compressed air lines to reach the worksite. Nothing yet, otherwise the cage for the air shaft is completed along with the 'winding house' to pull up the cages. The cages are rugged and hold one man or supplies. The cages are two tiered. The bottom level is to load special ore that looks likepure gold. Otherwise, we and the workers are making good money. But to continue this, we need another vein rich in gold. Otherwise, the one surprise is that some of the workers are talking of staying on a monthly wage instead of percentage of the profits. This may avoid the ups and downs of mining income—time will tell. Now how about you, when are you going to need me again?" "In two days when we move Craymores' inventory and unpack our first order." "That's too much work for us, we need help." "I agree, how about if I leave a note at school that we need boys older than 10 to work for us after school—at +-25 cents an hour. Heck, the teacher might let these boys off early, heh?"

The next morning, Mia arrived at the shop at 8AM. The Weber crew had been working since 6AM. One crew was setting up a powered table saw in the back yard, while the other team was installing a front bay window, a new door and the new sign. When Mia arrived, she gave the measurements and designs of the display table with the under-table cabinets, with sliding doors to not obstruct the aisles, plus three shelves.

The foreman made a list of the different boards width's and length's and delivered them to the men outside ready to cut. The boards varied between 6 to 12 inches and were smooth planed pine or fir boards. The day moved along with precision. Once a section was finished, the painters started adding their finishing touch. The choice of a light blue/ grey color added brightness to the store. When the displays were done, Mia went to Elmer's to get a sample of the work tools, so the carpenters could make appropriate racks. The last thing built was a double changing room on both floors as well as specific worktables upstairs—as per pre-designed dimensions. Before the men left, the freight company was at the unloading dock with three large crates. It took four men to bring each crate upstairs. When the crates were torn down, three large commercial Singer sewing machines were revealed.

The next day was unloading and transferring day. At 7:30AM the Duo was looking at the displays and planning on how to make the move when Elmer came up to them and said, "your workers are outside waiting for your orders." The Duo went outside to find fifteen boys with a smile on their faces and dressed for work. Palmer said, "how come you're here so early, it was supposed to be after school." One of the older boys answered, "our teacher, Miss Peacham, said that if we were getting paid for the job, that we had to earn a full day's pay for a full day's work. So she gave us the day off." "Well, let's get to work!"

It took four hours to transfer every item. Palmer was handing each boy an item he could handle, while Mia was at the receiving end and placing the items where they belonged. Mia made an early observation; two boys were very eager to work and demonstrated a pleasant work ethic. An hour before noon, Mia sent Gwen to Grady's Diner and ordered everyone a roast beef/cheese sandwich, three sugar cookies and a bottle of sarsaparilla, plus two coffees.

By three o'clock all crates were opened, the goods brought to the appropriate display and the wood burned outside on the burn pile. When Palmer announced it was pay time, the boys lined up and Mia handed each boy a silver dollar and four bits.

The result was universal, each boy held the money up to their eyes in total awe. When the boys were thanked and started to leave, Mia stopped two boys and held them back.

Mia said, "I watched you two today, you not only did your work, but you kept everyone motivated and working at their capabilities—why? One boy said, "it was a group job," while the other added, "and the poor performance of any member reflected on all of us." Palmer's eyebrows went up, as Mia handed each boy another silver dollar saying, "the extra pay was for managing the men. What are your names, 'I'm Scott Camber and he's Ray Withers." "How would you like to work part time after school or Saturdays?" The two boys almost yelled out, "yes Ma'am, and thank you."

With the display cases packed full, Palmer asked what that bolt of fabric was that was sent upstairs. "Well, we need to go upstairs to show you." Palmer was confused, on a six-foot-wide table were two bolts of blue denim. On the floor were three strange tools. Palmer said, "What are these things?" "These are commercial sewing machines that can sew canvas and denim. At first, I'll have some homemakers up here making alterations to pants' hems for 50 cents per pants, and for shirt sleeves for 75 cents a shirt. According to Gwen, ill-fitting pants' legs and sleeve's lengths is the major reason for failed purchases. And repairs demand changes made on site, since miners don't have the time to return to pick up these items."

"Yes, I see, but what's with the fabric bolt?"

"Ah, that's for later and it will be a surprise, heh."

Resting after supper, Palmer said, "tomorrow is the big day. You've advertised in the paper of the grand opening and since we don't know how that will go, I'll spend the day with you." Palmer turned to look at Mia, only to find her asleep. He carried her to bed and undressed her for a night's restful sleep—while thinking, tomorrow would be a bust or a whopping success.

*****

CHAPTER 10

Present and Future

At daybreak, the Duo was on their way to the store. Walking by Bessie's Diner, Palmer went in to get two coffees in a bottle and four egg/ham sandwiches on a biscuit. At the store, the two homemaker ladies, Alice and Jenny, were waiting. When asked why they were there so early, one said, "we need to find out how to fill the bobbin, thread the machine and how fast to pedal the platform."

Mia was busy making a sign that said, "Opening special, alterations made while you wait—free of charge--today only." Palmer was looking at the pants and shirts as he asked Mia, "what's the difference between canvas and denim and why is denim more expensive?"

"Let's sit down in the kitchenette to eat our sandwiches and I'll explain the difference. "Denim is a 100% cotton two-piece twill. It's made up of inside white thread and outside blue thread died with indigo blue. It is weaved and the result is blue denim outside and white denim inside. The blue is resistant to stains, and the cloth is soft, pliable and durable. I am selling denim as shirts and trousers, not as overalls."

"Now canvas is to make tarps, we sell duck canvas which has a higher thread count and a tighter weave. It is very durable and even water resistant, but the beige/brown color makes it easy to stain. It is stiffer than denim and makes excellent bib overalls. Duck canvas is heavy at 30 ounce a yard compared to denim which is 9 ounce a yard. It will be interesting to see who will pay $3 for denim pants vs. $2.00 for duck canvas. I am selling duck canvas pants and overalls, no shirts."

As they were finishing their coffee, the doorbell rang.....and rang.....and rang again......and again. Palmer said, "what is going on, it must be kids playing tricks." As the Duo arrived at the cash register a dozen people were looking at the overhead signs trying to choose which aisle to walk to. Mia asked, "what are you all looking for?" Blue

Jeans—aisle 4, pickaxe—aisle 1, shirts—aisle 3, kerosene lantern—aisle 7, candles and reflector shields—aisle 6, chewing tobacco—store next door, overalls—aisle 2."

Mia went to help the men who wanted clothes. For pants, "use this measuring tape to measure your waist. The denim comes in waists 28-38, and the leg length from 26-36. Once you found your waist size, if you can't find the leg length, take a pair that looks right and go upstairs where the two seamstresses will help you by altering the pants to fit you. If your waist is larger than 38 inches, you need to buy overalls that go to 54 inches. If you want an item that is not on the shelves, I can place a special order and have it here in three days—such as denim pants size 44 waist/26 pant leg."

The day was busy, with a half dozen men continuously thrashing thru the clothes to find what they needed. Once they found their size, the display looked like a mad wolf had attacked each discarded item. It was then that Mia decided the store needed two attendants on the floor and Mia needed to be on the cash register—the question was how to pay them without cutting the 25% margin she had priced her wares.

Meanwhile, Palmer worked the cash register all day. Every item sold was added to the sales ledger so the Duo could make a tally of the popular items. The seamstresses also kept a ledger of the alterations made to determine which items were missing from the shelves.

By 4:30 the place emptied out. The Duo was starved having skipped dinner and worked all day, so they grabbed their ledgers and headed to Grady's Diner for supper and a business meeting. Over fresh coffee, Palmer said, the most popular four items were denim pants, waist 30 and 32 and leg lengths 28 and 30. We ran out of these and the seamstress had to use the 36-inch pant length to cut them down. The least popular items were duck canvas pants in waist sizes 30,32,34,36."

Mia hesitated, looked at the wall clock and said, "the warehouse in San Antonio is open till 10 PM. On our way home, we'll stop at the telegraph office and add a one-time order of 50 pieces each to replace the popular items. Otherwise, the standard order will continue daily until I make changes."

Palmer added, "well it's a good thing you're getting a delivery tomorrow and each day because you wouldn't make it thru the day without running out of supplies. So who is going to restock the shelves?" "Scott and Ray are coming in after school and they can work independently." "And how do you propose to find two ladies to be clothing attendants?" "Also on the way home, I'll put a help wanted sign in the store's window for two women."

Palmer saw his waitress coming with two steaks and added, "plus we need to stop at the bank and deposit this $972 in my pocket—today's sales. After a fine supper, the Duo took care of their three errands and then arrived home. After starting a fire in the cookstove for more coffee, there was a knock at the front door. Mia went to answer and found two ladies at the door. Mia said, "yes, what can we do for you?" "We are Ava and Arlene Burrows, our husbands are brothers who work for you in your mine, we would like to apply for the job you just posted." "Please come in, have a seat and let's talk."

After Mia explained what the jobs entailed, both ladies were interested, especially since Mia would work with them tomorrow. When asked if they could sew, Arlene said, "we both have teenagers and mining men, we sew all our clothes except the canvas pants they wear in the mine." Mia didn't let this fact escape her. After agreeing on a wage of $2.50 a day, they agreed to meet tomorrow at 7AM for an introduction to the job.

Before going to bed, Mia finally asked Palmer how she could pay these two attendants and the seamstresses doing alterations upstairs. Palmer answered, "did you hear any customer complain about the price of goods and future alterations?" "No, not a one." "So, it's obvious there is money in gold mining. Add another 10% to your cost, keep alterations free, give them two free head gear candles for purchases over $10 and occasionally give a regular customer a discount or a free item. The word will get around that you run a fair store. Rotate your four lady assistants/seamstresses between downstairs assisting customers to upstairs altering items—and pay them all $2.50 a day. Keep advertising in all the town papers and send your ads to outlying newspapers within twenty miles. That way, when you leave the store, the only thing you need to worry about is pleasuring me!" "And what am I, chopped liver?" "Oh no, but fresh meat is more like it, heh?"

***

The next day and the remainder of the week continued operating without complications. The four ladies did well rotating their duties, and Mia got comfortable bagging the purchases, collecting the cash sales, and making good contact with her customers. At the end of the second week, the Duo decided it was time for a business meeting. After an early supper Mia got Palmer to go first by saying, "what's new at the mine?

"Four things. First, all my miners live anywhere between the mine and town. Some walk the five miles twice a day. Others have their own horses. So during the day, the pasture is overgrazed. So I decided to buy a special wagon from the one and only Ebenezer Brinkman that has two long benches that holds twenty men. I pay one man in town to keep the wagon under a lean-to and stable the two horses. Every day, he travels to the mine and back picking up and or delivering the miners at their house or homesteads. The miners love the benefit, and my miners don't arrive exhausted before they start working."

"Second, Liam found a second gold vein in quartz rock. However, it is too far from the air shaft and so to use it we need a second airshaft. Harvey is bringing the pro shaft team and ordering all the modern tools and air compressor. These two veins will keep the mine prosperous for years unless they 'peter-out.'"

"Third, the four stopes are all empty and we cleared a profit of $15,000 in gold. The silver and other minor metals have covered payroll expenses for freighters and shotgun guards. Now, they are starting to haul the rich ore stockpiles from the #2 vein."

"Fourth, I am dividing the ten ore wagons in two. Five will haul our rich ore, and five will hire out to haul ore from the different mines. Pappy is responsible for the hired wagon-train and we charge 20% of the yield. That pays for the labor of ten men per week. When the mine generates a weekly income of $2,000, we still make a profit of $200 over our expenses and labor, and we're helping the small miners."

"Wow, those are major accomplishments for ten days of work, considering you worked with me at least four of those days." "Now, about me?"

"I also have four issues that are really revelations or eye openers compared to accomplishments. The first is that if we kept a better inventory of different pant sizes, we wouldn't need to make alterations. This would free up my workers for another project."

"The second, I didn't increase my prices. Instead, I now save 7% if I only make triple size orders twice a week."

"Third, my ladies want me to start making our own denim pants. All four have checked out the denim blue jeans from the factory, and they feel it is a standard sewing production item that requires two yards to make a pair of pants. Now, denim fabric sells retail for 68 cents a yard. If I buy ten 40-yard bolts, I can make 200 pair of pants and the cost per yard is down to 35 cents a yard. Elmer tells me that a good deal is the one that spreads out the cost—1/3 for materials, 1/3 for labor, and 1/3 profit. The key to a profit depends on the production of finished products against labor costs. To establish this 'cost basis,' my gals want to train themselves in sewing several pairs before embarking on a weeklong trial, uninterrupted, to see how many pairs of pants they can put out in five working days."

"I see, this could mean a higher profit, but what is the advantage?"

"According to miner's suggestions, we would add four new features—at no extra cost. Sown-on knee patches of denim, where most miners wear out kneeling on rock. Replacement patches would be available for a fee. A denim loop on the right thigh seam to hold the miner's rock hammer. Wider 2 ¼ in. belt loops to hold 2 in. belts for comfort, and add some extra material to the thigh areas for bending comfort since most working men have bigger thighs than cowboys on horseback. The pants with the extra thigh room would be labeled with a bold X."

"The fourth and last item is the need for more accessories. Laundering tools for drift miners who live in a bunkhouse and placer miners who live in a tent. They need a washer board with coarse and fine ridges, a square tub, and an attached manual ringer. Another frequent request is for pans and sluice boxes. Apparently, along rivers and streams, are many placer miners that extract gold from the bottom gravel of both rivers and streams. Hand panning is the old standby, but using a sluice box is much faster. The popular size is a 3-foot long box, 12-inch wide with 6-inch high sides, that is attachable to make longer sluices. The bottom of the sluice has wooden ridges called 'rifles' that block the flow of materials causing a low-pressure area where gold collects away from the faster flow of water. In areas where water is scant and streams are nothing but rivulets, the sluice box in converted to a rocker box, to slosh the water/gravel back and forth."

"Sounds like we need to add sluices, but where to get them?"

"From Weber Construction, Marc has agreed to manufacture them and to stick to the 1/3 rule. He will deliver them to the back lean-to, and we can sell them for $5 apiece and $6 for the rocker sluices. He even includes a 5- and 7-degree wedge to help set the proper sluice angle depending on the speed of flowing water."

"I like all the changes you've done and propose." "Well, I've already implemented the first two items, and Weber Construction have already started building sluices. The only one that I'm still undecided is making our own mining pants and putting a Bodine label on it." "Why, are you afraid you're infringing on the original patent by Levi jeans?" "No, because the denim pants we are presently selling are produced by the wholesale factory that sells us the denim fabric. Elmer calls these 'generic mark-offs.'" "Then what is holding you back?"

"I was waiting to see what you thought of the idea." "Well, you have nothing to lose, if there is no money in it, you can always go back to buying them and modify them for a fee." "Ok, I will hire a new floor attendant and let the four gals develop their own system. I'll be watching their progress and add suggestions if needed."

***

The next day, Palmer was working the cash register and Mia was training another miner's wife, another friend of Ava and Arlene, who also lived in town. Miranda Fellows was a quick learner and also a seamstress. By the noon dinner, she was working independently. Mia took over the cash register as Palmer installed a rope, from the cash register, thru the ceiling to the second-floor ceiling and a brass school bell was attached to each ends of the rope. This warning system would allow people from each floor to summons someone from another floor.

It was three days later that Mia was upstairs watching how the gals had dismantled all the seams of a denim trouser, tacked the resultant fabric to a paperboard, and had marked the fabric's edge on the paper with an ink pen. Two of the gals were cutting the paperboard on the ink's outline when the bell rang very loud and clear. Mia took off at a full run, going down two steps at a time. When she got to the display tables, three men were throwing piles of pants in the air to see how many they could catch at a time.

Mia exploded, "STOP, what do you fools think you're doing. Pick up this mess, NOW. Put everything back in the batch they belong." "Ah, heck, Ma'am. We're only having a little fun!" "FUN? You don't have enough commonsense to know the difference between insult and stupidity." When the pants were properly rearranged, she added, "now step to the cash register, pay up, and get out of my store."

"That's four pairs of canvas pants for $10, and two pairs of denim pants for $6, or a total of $16." "Well, little lady, put it on my tab."

"Whoa, stop right there. First of all, this is a cash business, cash on the barrel or the equivalent in gold dust. I don't sell on credit. Besides, you peckerheads don't even live in town, I don't know your names, and I'll probably never see your ugly faces again." "Like I said, you bitch, put it on my tab," as they picked up their pants to leave.

Mia was furious, she slipped her hand under her vest, pulled out her Webley Bulldog, swiped it across the face of the apparent leader and smashed his nose to a bloody pulp. The front sight must have scraped an eye since the arrogant pinhead was screaming and dancing up a storm as he held his eye and nose.

"The terms of the sale are the same, pay up or drop the goods and get out. Either way, I don't ever want to see you in my store again, and I don't forget ugly faces." "This is not the end, here is your money but the payback will be another day!"

Miranda was a bit disturbed, but Mia explained that such an occurrence may never happen again. "Remember, if there is a problem and I'm upstairs, walk away, pull the bell and step outside if necessary. If I'm not in the store, the gals upstairs will come down to help you."

The remainder of the day was uneventful except for the 1PM delivery of her triple order. Scott and Ray arrived on time and went to work. Miranda followed their lead to refill the displays.

At closing time, Mia had a mission. With the five gals, they walked in Elmer's store. "Ladies, go to the reticule display and get your own reticule, just don't get two alike." Then as they walked home, Mia stopped at the nearby gun shop. She bought five Webley Bulldogs, and 15 boxes of 44 shells. Now each lady had a Bulldog and three boxes of shells in their reticule. Stepping out of the gun shop, Mia said, "Sunday afternoon we all meet at the town gun range to practice shooting. From now on, you don't leave the store without your reticule/Bulldog. Is that agreed?" In unison, Mia only her two words, "Yes, boss" and several soft 'thank you.'"

That Sunday afternoon invitation turned into a party. All the husbands came to see their wives shoot. Of course, the men all managed to find an excuse to try the pistols. Fortunately, Palmer had anticipated the attendance from rumors at the mine, and he showed up with another 20 boxes of shells. Everyone shot to their delight, but the ladies were the important ones, and the Duo left satisfied that each lady could easily defend themselves with their double action pistol.

That night, the Duo got a telegram from Palmer's parents:

Furniture arriving by train Monday noon STOP

Could you arrange pickup and delivery STOP

Distribute furniture and crates by rooms STOP

Will arrive by noon---have a change in plans STOP

I want to work with some mine activity STOP

Mom wants to work in Mia's Emporium STOP

The Duo was mystified. It was Mia that said, "your folks are like any retired elderly person. They need to keep busy either with a hobby or with a low energy job. I know exactly where Mom can work, she'll become the customer attendant at the displays, and Miranda will get booted upstairs with the other seamstresses. Now they can set up an assembly line with five workers. Assembly lines is the proven method for getting the most efficient production. Now what have you got for your dad?"

"The worker who drives the worker's wagon is going into the hospital for surgery, and may never return to work. Dad can take the morning and evening run. He has a good size barn for the two horses and a carriage house for the wagon. During the day, the wrangler is asking for a part-time helper to do odd jobs. He can occasionally be a relief shotgun guard on the ore wagon-trains. Plus, we now need a regular messenger to deliver notes from Harvey to the underground foremen. Oh heck, I'm sure Harvey will keep him busy, and by bringing the men back home, he'll be home every night to have supper with mom. I'm glad of their decision and dad certainly didn't need to be a deputy sheriff—he's been on the firing line all his life and now is the time for normal living."

Palmer added, "tomorrow, I'll take the day off to get his furniture delivered, pickup his horses and buggy at the railroad yard, get some firewood delivered, get some hay and oats in the barn, and pick up all the vittles to load up the larder. If I have time, I'll unload the crates of tools that go in the barn or unload the kitchen crates of cooking and eating utensils. As a house-warming present, I'll pickup a single trigger self cocking coach shotgun. What do you want to give mom?" "Get a clothes washing machine with a ringer and get it installed in the scullery."

The next week went smooth and the Bodines moved into their new home and their new jobs. Ralph was trucking the men and working with the wrangler repairing harnesses. Ella took over the floor displays and being a neat freak, kept all the clothing piles in perfect order. Melinda had happily moved upstairs to be on the ground floor of making the Bodine brand of denim mining pants.

Mia decided to close the week and the store at noon on Saturday. The miners, "weekenders," who had come to town for weekend drinking and carousing were done shopping by noon, and the afternoon a was dedicated to serious drinking. What Mia and the gals didn't know was that there were three "weekenders" with nefarious and carnal ideas who had been watching the Emporium for hours.

Three of the gals took off to pick up some groceries at Elmer's store. Mia headed home with Alice, Jenny and mom. They were busy talking and walking when near an alley, three men jumped out of the alley while holding knives on them. "Hey Little Lady, I told you we'd be back for payback. So step in the alley and we'll do all of you like you've never had a real man."

Like cows pushing young calves behind them so they could face predators; the gals squeezed mom behind them and stood side by side to face their attackers. Mia spoke, "we have and know real men—our husbands. We don't need you pipsqueaks with your pea brains. Why I could put your three brains in a pill box and rattle it like the tail of a rattle snake. Afterall, what idiots comes to a gunfight with knives?"

"That's enough Little Lady, we'll tie you all up and the three of us will do you first." "Take one step towards us, and you'll feel our wrath!" As the three ladies placed their hands in their reticule, the apparent leader said, "hah, hah. What are you going to do, hit us with your hair- brushes?" As the attackers stepped forward, all three ladies pointed their reticule and fired—BANG....BANG/ BANG. The result was dramatic and drastic. All three reticules had the bottom blown out, the knives were dropped, two of the would-be rapists were caterwauling and jumping up and down with apparent holes in the top of their boots. The leader, moaning out loud, had collapsed to the boardwalk with a shot that had missed the foot but was a direct hit to the ankle bones.

The incident being only a block from Sheriff Belknap's office, the sheriff came running with his pistol drawn. "What in hell is going on here?" Mia answered, "these three wiseasses threatened to rape us at knife point. We defended ourselves and shot them in the feet thru our reticules. We should have aimed for their oysters and sausages— for that's what they deserved."

Sheriff Belknap said, "I see, if you four ladies are willing to write a complaint and file charges, I'll arrest them and bring them to the hospital for medical care while manacled. There may be a trial if they don't plead guilty, but prison term is guaranteed for attempted rape." "Will do, plus we want $15 to replace our three reticules."

As the three men were carried away, manacled and secured to a wagon, Mia turned around to make sure Ella had not been too frightened. What she saw was the elderly lady holding a pocket pistol in her hand as she said, "well, I was aiming for the leader's crotch. It was too bad he had collapsed to the boardwalk, heh?" None of the ladies had known that Ella was a crack shot with her pocket pistol.

The next week was a normal pace for the first-floor activities. The second floor was still in the organizational stages for setting up an assembly line. Alice pointed out that the assembly line could not stop to make belt/hammer loops, inside/outside pockets, and knee patches. Mia decided to hire a young mother with seamstress abilities on a sewing machine, but one that would work at home since she had three young children. Mia hired her and provided her with a commercial sewing machine, commercial heavy-duty thread, and all the remnant pieces of denim cut out of the patterns. Her pay was based on "piece work" and she was well paid to sew all these accessories.

To help the five seamstresses set up an assembly line, Mia got Palmer to take over the cash register while she spent the week upstairs helping out with her observatory ideas.

Mia knew that the gals had taken apart several denim pants to learn how the pants were made. Then, using actual finished pants, they had made a cardboard pattern of the front left side that would flip to form the right front side. This pattern included the fly and the two cutouts for the front pockets. The rear of the pants had a similar pattern on the left that also flipped over to make the right pattern, but this side was without a fly or pocket cutouts. The result was four separate pieces to be sewn together, and all four pieces had the trademark widened thighs.

When Mia realized that they had two cardboard cutouts (fronts and backs) for every waist size from

28 to 38 inch and a standard leg length of 34 inch, she took all twelve cardboard cutouts to Weber Construction to convert the cardboard shapes to a more durable and reusable pattern made out of wood. The shop foreman explained that they had a new 3/8-inch sheathing, made up of three 1/8-inch thick wood glued together. With the use of their powered jig saws, they would cut out all twelve patterns in a matter of hours and would deliver them to the shop by noon.

With a precut supply of denim ready to sew, they set up their assembly line:

STATION 1. Miranda would sew the two front pieces together from below the fly to the crotch, then turn around and add the two back pieces and sew them from the beltline to the crotch.

STATION 2. Jenny would then sew the front left leg to the back leg—both inside and outside. Then repeat the same on the right leg.

STATION 3. Ava would start the finishing process by forming and sewing a double layered belt backing and attaching the preformed belt loops. Then finishing the fly with three buttonholes.

STATION 4. Arlene would then finish the edges of the two front pockets and sew the preformed pockets inside the pants. She would then attach the two outside preformed rear pockets.

STATION 5. Alice took the tail job and had to attach the hammer loop, the two knee patches, the belt band button, the fly buttons and the suspender buttons. She had the sewing attachment for the four-hole standard button. Last of all she would attach the Bodine logo on a preprinted leather piece. **B 30W 32LX** (X for wider thigh fit).

After watching them for hours, Marc Weber arrived with the finished wood patterns. It was then, that everyone realized, who was going to mark the denim and cut if off the roll?

Mia looked at the gals and said, "either we hire another person, or we all get together and cut out the denim ourselves. It was Alice who said, "along the same line, we also have to decide if we are going to do the same station every day, or occasionally rotate to another station?"

Mia said, "maximum production goes along with doing the same job repeatedly to be the most efficient in developing tricks to get the job done faster. But boredom or fatigue is quick to set in. So, what do you think of this schedule: 8 to 10AM everyone mans its designated station. 10AM to 10:30AM everyone grabs scissors and cuts out denim patterns, 10:30AM to noon everyone is back on their stations. Dinner break. 1PM to 3PM back to your stations. 3PM to 3:30 everyone cuts out patterns. And finally 3:30 to 5PM your all back on your machines. If we get to surplus cut patterns, we can skip cutting times as is needed."

There was silence in the room as Mia broke in, "if you're willing to give this a try, I will promise you that if it's a failure, we will try rotating the stations and or hire a sixth worker, or both." Alice answered, "let's try it, we have nothing to lose."

Mia went to see Elmer and picked up ten pairs of heavy-duty-high grade steel scissors—five to use and five in the sharpening shop. After a week of following this assembly line with two daily fabric cutting periods, the workers were comfortable and wanted to continue. It was at the end of the week that Mia was watching the entire production and finally realized that every 20 minutes (3 per hour), Alice was putting the finishing touches to a finished product. Mia did the mental math: the gals were on their stations 7 hours a day and could generate 21 pairs of pants per day. That meant a total of 105 miner's trousers each week. The labor costs computed to: $2.50 per day per worker, or $12.50 per day, or $62.50 per five day week.

The final ledger entries for the week were as follows.

Sale value. 105 trousers at $3 each is $315

Cost of materials—105 trousers required 210 yards of material at 35 cents a yard, or $73.50

Labor costs--$62.50.

Profit--$315 minus $73.50 and $62.50 equals $179."

That evening, Mia presented these figures to Palmer. "What do you think of such a high profit margin per week?" Palmer looked at the figures as well as other expenses. "Wow, $179 is a 57% profit margin compared to the +-25% profit you make from buying the finished product. But realistically, you have to figure the building's and the sewing machine's depreciation, the carpenter fees, commercial thread, replacement needles, buttons, scissors, sharpening fees, heating stoves to be installed, cost of coal, shipping charges for those fabric bolts, and even the cost of that leather logo. So this is my recommendation:

1. Those gals are really working hard, and I think you should increase their pay to $3 a day.
2. We need to add up expenses at the end of one year and make adjustments as needed, but for now stay the course.
3. If you need more than 105 denim miner's trousers per week, hire a sixth worker, or more. Remember, these gals are making money for you."

"Ok, right now 105 of our product sounds about right since there are customers who are not miners and who want the slimmer factory- made products without the hammer loop, the knee patches or the wider belt loops."

***

Over the next two weeks, it became clear that the store could sell more than 105 Bodine miner's pants per week. Mia was going to put an ad in the local paper, but the gals had friends in town that were looking for work. Mia quickly filled the two positions. With a sixth sewing machine and within a week, the upstairs was putting out 160 pairs of miner's trousers a week. Finally, a small surplus started accumulating, and the extras were kept in the cabinets below the displays. Soon the surplus got bigger and the warehouse receiving room was used for storage.

Weeks later, a well-dressed drummer, showed up at the shop. Ella was aware that the man was snooping around. His interests finally peaked at the denim trouser display. He looked inside, at all the seams, the hammer loop, the patches on the knees and the wide belt band and loops. Finally, he asked Ella where the Bodine label came from. "Why sir, didn't you see the sign on the storefront? These are Bodine miner's pants made right here." "Where is your factory?" "Upstairs." "May I speak to the owner?"

Mia was introduced. "My name is Waldo Steiner. I am a statewide distributor of new clothing lines. I'm completely enthralled by the quality of these trade specific trousers you are manufacturing.

May I see your manufacturing set up?" "Certainly, follow me upstairs."

Waldo could not believe his eyes; the ladies were working independently without being told what to do. He then asked, "how many pairs of pants can these seven ladies make each five-day week." "Right now, they are all experienced and they are producing 170 trousers a week."

"Well Ma'am, you have a gold mine. Now, could it be possible for me to purchase some, say 200 trousers, at your full price of $3 each. "Why yes, I have accumulated a surplus, and for a cash sale of $600 you can have a full set of every waist size and leg lengths we make." "Fine, here is my bank draft and I'll make arrangements for a freight pick up to the train depot some time tomorrow."

"Now, can we talk about the future. Have you considered expanding your production area and going commercial. I could distribute these trousers throughout the mining communities of New Mexico and Colorado. I know that they would sell like hot cakes. Miners are sick of canvas and duck canvas pants and overalls. You could expand your denim product into overalls, which is another group of customers, the farming homesteaders."

"Are we getting ahead of ourselves. Don't you think you need to spread these pants around Colorado to see what the response will be before any expansion is considered. We know they sell in New Mexico, but what about in other states? In addition, were we to expand, I would need my husband's total support. So, for now, let's put a hold on things till you have news from retailers." "Ok, but I'll be back in a week and you need to realize that I could easily take 300 units a week."

That night, after supper, the Duo had a long talk. "Today a man came to the store who claimed he was a clothing distributor of new items. He bought my surplus of Bodine trousers, 200 pairs for the full price of $600. But that wasn't the end of him. He planted the seed of expanding production and distributing thru all of New Mexico and Colorado. He was talking about 300 units a week."

"Wow, you're talking about a financial investment for a separate factory, and many more employees. Is this what you want?" "I'm not sure what I want. It's all about the small or the big picture isn't it. The small picture is to stay the way we are, and the big picture is to expand and build a major manufacturing enterprise with the marketing headaches and the big money."

"Yes, but there is also a compromise that doesn't put all your eggs in one basket. That is to expand within reason. Let me give you an alternative avenue to consider. We own 4 acres in the back of the shop. Our building is 50X60 feet, or 3,000 sq. feet per floor. We can actually double the building's square footage, or increase it to our choosing.

Now let's just say we increase it by 30 feet. The first-floor store would not change since it's already the perfect size for the items we sell. So the first-floor addition could be used for manufacturing. That way, the 30-foot extension upstairs could easily handle six more stitchers. One person would work downstairs to receive fabric and supplies, transfer them upstairs as needed, store the balance and then spend the days cutting out fabric before sending the cutouts upstairs. This person could be a man. The result upstairs would be that the weekly production would go from 170 units to 340 units. This would supply distributors like this Waldo

Steiner. Besides, city water and sewage is coming to town soon, and being on Main Street, we'll be first to get the services. Construction time is the ideal time to put a water closet on each floor, heh?"

Mia thought a bit and finally said, "huum, and I wonder who you have in mind for the man downstairs?" "Yes, it's dad. He is not doing well working for the wrangler at the mine since he has lived all his life in Amarillo where the altitude is +-3,000 feet compared to the mine area where the altitude is +-6,000 feet. Plus an old man won't last long being exposed to rain, cold and even winter snow. I really think it's time to give him an easy inside job."

"This sounds great. One could say this expansion could be thought of as a transition to a commercial factory, or it can be considered an expansion to last for our generation."

"As food for thought, have you ever considered adding a second shift instead of an expansion to maintain a day shift?" "Yes I have. The problem with that is that my gals are all housewives and being home when kids come home from school or husbands come home for the night, is very important. Now if I was building a factory, a second shift might be a necessity, but with this modified expansion, I'd rather stick with a day shift."

"So, let's wait for Waldo to come back from his investigative trip and we'll go from there. That gives us plenty of time to think about this."

During the week, Mia spent time away from the cash register whenever there was a lull in sales. She watched Ella who was working too hard and should be at the cash register for an easier job. She watched the gals upstairs and envisioned more space, cutouts arriving from downstairs, a water closet and six more commercial machines. She was standing at the back of the retail store in the small warehouse room and could envision a large receiving area for fabric bolts and other supplies. Storage for finished products waiting for freight service to the train depot, and Palmer's dad happily cutting out denim fabric.

Getting realistic, Mia realized that Ralph could not put out 70 cutouts per day with all the other duties he had, so it would be up to the upstairs foreperson to help out when things were copacetic with the production assembly line. So, who would be the ideal foreperson?

Waldo finally arrived. The Duo met him at the train depot and took him to Grady's Diner for a business meeting. "Folks, it's been a rewarding trip, and I am so enthused that I am willing to build you a factory if I can have all your products. I made two major stops, Albuquerque NM and Denver CO. I could have sold ten times the products that I had. I have five retail locations in each city that want a regular supply of your trousers. Many want denim overalls as well. The offer is still the same, $3 per trouser and $3.50 for overalls, and no shipping costs to you to my warehouse in Deming. So, what say you?"

Mia looked and saw Palmer's nod, "we will expand our present location and can guarantee you at least 170 units per five-day week. Any surplus we have, you get them as well, and if we add a Saturday shift, you'll get those as well. If things are profitable, we'll consider expanding to a self-standing factory and go commercial." "And if that comes to pass, I'll do all your marketing free of charge as long as I get all the products I want. To facilitate things, here is a deposit of $5,000, for goodwill, and to establish my line of credit." "Deal," and all shook hands followed by a celebratory meal of Texas Crossbred steaks.

The next week went flying by. Marc Weber and crew were on the scene the next morning. Mia doubled her denim fabric bolts and her supplies, she ordered six new commercial sewing machine and one especially geared to sewing buttons. When she announced the changes to her gals, she asked for a vote of who they wanted for a floor person. Alice won unanimously. The advertisements were placed for new employees and both Mia and Alice interviewed the applicants. Ralph came to see the changes as they occurred, while Alice and Mia prepared him for his job.

The construction went well. An additional feature was a roof over the loading and unloading area. A spiral staircase was added to save room and ease Ralph's access to the second floor to unload the elevator. Ralph's room included shelves for finished products, railroad crates for shipping, shelves for fabric bolts, a large cutting table, and plenty of shelves for supplies. The old storage room on the first floor was kept for receiving and storing extra store items—to keep it separate from the production department.

By the third day, six new gals with sewing experience were hired, and Alice spent the rest of the next 10 days training them. The original gals seized the time to ask for an optional rotation system. Some gals didn't want to stay on the same station from day to day. Mia spent some time and finally announced: "Every 2nd and 4th Monday is rotation day."

"During the two weeks, if you want to change stations, then check the 'job board.' If you see a posting you like of say Station 3A (A stands for the original team and B stands for the new team), then you take it off the board and add your own spot, say Station 2B. Then Station 2B becomes available for someone else. If no one posts a station as available, then you stay where you are till the next rotation postings. That way, those who want to rotate can, and those who like to stay in place can as well."

Production started and after eight days of operations, Waldo got his first order of 300 units which included all of the shop's surplus and eight days of production. At the same time, Mia hired a new attendant and Ella took the cash register. Mia became a gopher and organizer.

Mia's day was spent helter-skelter. She trained the new attendant, and helped her when needed, she helped Scott and Ray restock the shelves, when Ella had a problem or wanted to use the Benefactor Fund, Mia was there. Although, Mia spent more time upstairs. There were many chores to be done: restocking thread, buttons, labels and preformed patches and hammer loops, helping to move finished products to the elevator, going downstairs and help Ralph cutout some denim, running to the bank for deposits, going to the telegraph to send messages for orders and Waldo notifications. At times, she was needed at all three locations at once. If someone was out sick Alice would take their station, but that meant more work for Mia. Mia didn't get a bit flustered; she went from one crisis or job to another with a smile on her face.

***

After a year of operating a mine, a retail mining Emporium, a clothing manufacturing shop, and commercial wholesaling, the Duo decided to have a meeting to review the financial ledgers and their goals for next year. Mia went first. "My biggest expense was labor and construction. My 17 employees made $900 each for a total of +-$15,000. Construction cost was $5,000. Wholesale purchase of denim and supplies came to +-$30,000 for a total cost to do business at $50,000. Income from wholesaling to Waldo and store retailing came to $70,000 for an absolute profit of $20,000 these past twelve months." "That is great, so what are your plans for next year?"

"I've grown content and happy with the way things are. I know it's really the small picture, but I'd like to leave things as they are for now. If Waldo starts pushing more, who knows what we'll do then, heh?" "If you're happy, then by all means, let's leave things as they are for the year to come."

Palmer was next. "My major expense was labor. I have 15 men making $4 a day to total $1,100 a year. Ten men making $1,400, four making $1,700 and one making $2,500. That totals $35,000. Other supplies, two air shafts, several air compressors and tools, two barns, one bunkhouse and one cook shack came to +-$20,000. Our total payments for precious major and minor metals came to $105,000 and hiring out freight wagons produced another $10,000. Bottom line we made a profit of $60,000."

"Palmer Bodine, that is embarrassing. In 1896, no one makes that kind of money or should be able to make that kind of money legally. What are we going to do with all that?"

"Well, we gave out $10,000 out of the Benefactor Fund, but that is no longer as needed as it was a year ago, so don't expect as many donations next year. Actually, I've made a list of where we can share some of our outlandish profits next year.

1. Start a retirement fund for workers vested with 20 years of service. A fund that will guarantee at least 40% of their last income level.
2. Short- and long-term disability for sick and injured personnel.
3. 100% free medical expenses, including the vested retirees.
4. All employees go on profit sharing. With the guarantee that next year's income will not be any lower than this last year's base income. This base income will maintain the

guaranteed income for the next five years, then we need to negotiate the base income minimum again.

5. Silver has become a minor metal with its lowered value. Copper has now become the #2 metal because of indoor plumbing copper pipes. Fortunately, Liam has delved deeper in the mine, away from the adit's rockface, and has found a promising vein of copper. Being far from the other two air shafts, we'll need a third air shaft to mine the copper.

6. It will cost $7,500 to add a rail spur from Silver City to our mine adit. We'll be able to unload minecarts directly in the rail cars. This will also free five ore wagons and this wagon-train can be rented out like the other five-car wagon-train. With a rail switch at our mine, we can have two rails that allows us to split the ore cars and put gold ore in one, and copper ore in the other."

"Well, those are some well laid plans, but I suspect they will still leave us with too much money." "Well, you know, you never have too much money. Besides, money leaves the doors open to potential new endeavors. Who knows what we'll be doing in the next years. I can't see in the crystal ball, but we haven't been bored yet, heh?"

*****

The End

Author's Note

The end of any fiction allows the author to either close the possibility of a sequel or guarantee the story will continue. This ending is a modified cliffhanger that allows either.

Some readers may not see the potential of continuing the saga since the major events have already been explored. Others see that there are four potential areas of growth and change. The obvious is the building of a manufacturing factory to go commercial with their own line of mining denim. Another is to change the principal mineral from gold to copper and provide all of the trade secrets that go with mining this metal. Also, entering the 1900's, Palmer and Mia could go into a new entrepreneurship complementing the next century, or could even rejuvenate the Bodine Agency into a real detective agency of the times.

Irrelevant of the outcome, if a sequel is written, I will write a prologue that outlines the previous events that led to the end of the primary book— which allows you to move along without confusion.

Richard M Beloin MD

Printed in the United States
By Bookmasters